Roses Take Practice

Roses Take Practice

Connie Biewald

For Doug —
I hope you
enjoy this book.
Practice. Practice
Practice.

Connie Biewald

iUniverse, Inc.
New York Lincoln Shanghai

May 2006

Roses Take Practice

iUniverse books may be ordered through booksellers or by contacting:

iUniverse
2021 Pine Lake Road, Suite 100
Lincoln, NE 68512
www.iuniverse.com
1-800-Authors (1-800-288-4677)

ISBN-13: 978-0-595-38501-0 (pbk)
ISBN-13: 978-0-595-67622-4 (cloth)
ISBN-13: 978-0-595-82882-1 (ebk)
ISBN-10: 0-595-38501-X (pbk)
ISBN-10: 0-595-67622-7 (cloth)
ISBN-10: 0-595-82882-5 (ebk)

Printed in the United States of America

For my family—
those who went before,
those who will come after,
and, most of all,
those who are here now
keeping me company
during this precious time
on the planet…

Acknowledgements

Many thanks, yet again, to:

Maxie Chambliss and Susan Fehlinger who make the covers by which my books are judged;

my companions and teachers in the writing life: Samantha Schoech, Laura Brown, Brooks Whitney, Mark Ford, Marjorie Saunders, Eileen O'Toole, Anne Walsh, Judith Felsenfeld, Candace Perry, Bessie Blum, Nathan Long, Joanie Grisham, Patty Smith, Judith Hert, Nancy Tancredi, Tracy Winn, Donna Tramontozzi, Carolyn Heller, Pat Rathbone, Maggie Bucholt, Hallie Touger, Allan Gurganus, Marie Howe, Tom Jenks, Michael Cunningham, Dick Bausch, Anne Bernays, and Grace Paley;

colleagues and families at the Fayerweather Street School;

the Fine Arts Work Center, Vermont Studio Center, Millay Colony, Massachusetts Cultural Council, and the Wesleyan Writers Conference;

my family and friends, especially the people who lived with me during the writing of this book: Jeannie Ramey, Bruce, Lukas, Mollie, Georgia, Izaak, Emmett, and Roza Biewald, and Jeff, Jake, and Owen Thomas.

CHAPTER 1

▼

WYLIE

The paper plate with 'help wanted' scribbled on it in the window of Ida's bakery stopped me smack in the middle of my usual rush home from school. I needed a job. I needed money. I needed more than that if I could be honest with myself, but I couldn't. Who can? If we were honest with ourselves we'd all be walking around with 'help wanted' signs taped to our backs.

I knew even then that money doesn't solve all problems. But when you hear someone say, "Money can't buy happiness," you can bet that person's never eaten two weeks of ketchup and mayonnaise sandwiches because her mother sold the food stamps to buy booze. You can bet that person's never seen her little brother squeezing without fuss into shoes that don't fit because as young as he is he knows enough not to ask for anything new. You can bet that person's been on a vacation to Maine or Cape Cod or New York City.

You can bet that person goes to the dentist. Check her teeth. Rich kids might whine about their mouths full of metal, but for the rest of their lives they'll travel the world smiling perfect smiles while kids like me grow up to smile with lips closed in photographs taken at the mall when a special deal and coupons in the paper coincide with an occasion.

Dust frosted the plaster wedding cakes in the bakery window. Three tattered bells of honeycombed tissue paper hung clumped together in a corner. Another had fallen onto a cake and lay where it landed, like a passed-out drunk. Most everyone in the valley bought birthday cakes at Ida's. The only other bakery in

Rivertown, Connecticut, in 1975 was the thrift store out on Route 8 where the cakes came in cellophane packages stamped with last week's dates, where they accepted food stamps, where my family shopped. I wondered if Ida gave employee discounts.

I'd skipped lunch to meet up with Danny under the bleachers so I was hungry and craved a donut, chocolate frosted or glazed, any kind really. I tried to think about selling donuts instead of eating them, to look like a professional who knew the bakery business, someone who would be friendly to customers. Licking my lips and the gap between my front teeth, I adjusted my patched denim bag so the strap fell neatly between my breasts instead of squashing one of them, straightened my shoulders and went in.

Sunlight striped the glass cases to my left. Behind them stood shelves of bread and rolls, a slicing machine, and a cash register. In the back stretched a breakfast counter and a row of green, vinyl covered stools patched with duct tape.

"Can I help you?" a tiny old woman asked from behind the counter. Her tone suggested she thought she couldn't. She set down a stack of saucers with a clatter.

"The job?" I crossed the floor of gleaming green and white linoleum squares and dropped onto a stool. "I saw the sign."

"You want a job?"

The woman glared at me through her glasses, her eyes steely—like the reservoir on a cloudy day. She said want with a Dracula accent, vant.

"I do."

She wiped the clean counter with a damp rag. "Have you any experience?"

I laughed.

"What's funny?"

"What kind of experience do you mean?"

"Bakery experience? Sales?"

"No. But I'm good at math, for making change." Maybe I didn't always finish my homework, but I was quick at adding and subtracting in my head. "And I do all the cleaning at home. Cleaning up must be part of the job, isn't it?"

The old woman narrowed her eyes, her face as creased as a crumpled paper bag. "What's your name?"

"Wylie Steele," I admitted. My family was notorious. My younger brother, Robbie, had been caught more than once setting fires and breaking into cars. My father left when I was little. Until he died four years ago he'd come around once in awhile to sweet talk my mother into taking him back. She would, for a few days, then they'd both get drunk and fight so loud, about money, about sex, about which channel to watch or who drank the last beer, that the neighbors ended up calling the police. He'd still be coming around if he could. She'd still be letting him stay, then throwing him out. When they heard he was dead, Mom, Robbie, and Kevin cried. I didn't.

"Wylie?" the old woman said. Vylie. Dracula speaking again. "What kind of a name is that?" I let out the breath I'd been holding.

"My father named me after his favorite cartoon character, Wile E. Coyote." I smiled without showing my teeth. He'd misspelled it on the birth certificate.

"I am Sofie Schmidt." The old woman held out her hand, index finger bent like a claw. The nail scratched my palm and kept our hands from fitting together. "For twenty years I work here. In 1955 I started."

That was three years longer than I had been alive.

"To this job there are many parts. Cleaning, yes. Also waiting on customers, putting up orders, filling donuts, decorating cakes." She paused.

"Decorating cakes?" I said. "You mean writing happy birthday and anniversary and all that?" I wasn't sure how to spell anniversary. I knew I couldn't spell congratulations.

"Writing." Sofie gave a quick nod. "Making borders, flowers, everything. Come." She motioned me close to a case full of cakes covered with names, flowers, good luck and best wishes.

"I would have to do that?"

"I would teach you," she said, voice flat. She didn't sound like she was looking forward to the lessons. "Roses take practice. But see those drop flowers." She pointed at some small, yellow flowers on a sheet cake. "Those, you could learn in twenty minutes, maybe fifteen."

I thought of the time Ms. McLellan, the art teacher, trusted me to put the finish on the huge, papier-maché football the freshman class had made for a Memorial Day float. I brushed on paint thinner by mistake, dissolving hours of everyone else's work.

Sofie led the way back to our stools.

"I thought you were Ida," I said.

"Ach, *nein!*" She cackled. "Ida, no one knows anymore. A good German name, but I hear this Ida, she is coming from one of those places where all the time they have hurricanes, where sugar is growing. A *schwartze*, colored woman. Started the bakery, too busy working to marry, have babies. All tired out, alone, she dies. They say she was saving money to go retire to the island where she was born." She shook her head. "Eye-talians take over her business. The Martinos. Tony Martino, for fifteen years, has owned this bakery, since his father died. His father owned it since before I came here. That's fifty-one years now since I came from the old country."

"What old country?" I asked.

"Germany." That explained the accent.

Fifty-one years. She would've been young then, crossing an ocean. Ida, then Tony's father, then Sofie, traveled all those miles, from all over the world, to end up in a bakery on Main Street in Rivertown, Connecticut. I wondered if they'd had any picture of where they were headed. Rivertown had never been the subject of a *National Geographic* article, I was sure of that.

Until high school, when I began spending my free time with Danny, all I thought about was going away. I'd sit at the library for hours, paging through those magazines, studying maps, memorizing routes and distances between Rivertown and San Francisco, Paris, Honolulu. I ran across the Golden Gate Bridge, wrote poetry in smoky cafes, and picked golden fruit from strange trees. You never imagine people in the places you dream of wiping hairs from their sinks, running out of milk, or having to work for a living.

Sofie continued. "Tony's father kept the name Ida's. It's a good name; people know it, why change? Tony is the boss." She leaned close to my ear and lowered her voice. "But I run the place." Her warm breath made my beaded earring dance.

"His kids, they work here, sometimes, after school." Her voice dropped to a whisper again. "They're all lazy. And his wife, Teresa, she's worse than the kids. You see that window?" Sofie waved her arm toward the front of the store. "A disgrace, an embarrassment. I'm offering to fix it up and Teresa says…" Sofie stuck her nose in the air, shook her finger at me, and mimicked, "I will take care of that, Sofie. Window design requires an artistic eye.

"Artistic eye." She scowled. "Ach! All that window is needing is someone to clean it. She won't hear so I close my mouth and do my job. If washing and mopping were up to her, the health inspector would every week be shutting the place down." She wiped the bottom of a metal cream pitcher, set it on the counter so hard the lid jumped. "Tony, he works hard, all night baking, making deliveries, keeping the books." Sofie paused, tilting her head as though I was supposed to say something. I needed a cue. I hadn't had a job interview before, but I thought they usually involved some questions.

"You'll have to start work at five o'clock on weekends."

"Five o'clock in the morning?" No wonder the job hadn't been filled.

"You'll leave at one on Saturdays. On Sundays, we close at one, so you'll have to stay later to clean up. We could use you sometimes after school if we have a big order."

"Wait a minute," I said. "You're talking like I have this job. Do I?"

Sofie studied me as if I were a bug in a jar.

"You'll have to tie that hair back." I tried to flatten the tangle of hair Robbie said looked like the fur of an electrocuted poodle, gave up, and rested my hands in my lap.

"You're the first to come in." Sofie picked up the cream pitcher, examining it from several angles. "For a year I've been saying we should hire someone. Those kids, the four of them together don't do the work of half a person. I told Tony, 'I'm seventy years old. I can't be the only decent salesgirl in the place.' Finally he is telling me 'go ahead, put up a sign.'"

She came from behind the counter, settled on the stool next to me, and frowned at my worn jeans and ripped sneakers before squinting into my face. I waited for her to comment on my mismatched eyes, one green, one blue. Most people said something about them. Sofie didn't.

"Tony said I should make this decision. But how do I know whether to hire somebody? Are you a hard worker?"

I cooked the meals at home, cleaned the house, dragged the dirty clothes to the Laundromat, and did the shopping. I took care of my brothers. The month before I'd even fixed the toilet when Kevin dropped a metal car down it.

"Yes."

"Are you honest?"

I thought about the makeup and underwear I picked up at the mall, right from under the noses of the salesclerks. I thought of the nights I spent at Danny's when I said I was sleeping at Maureen's.

"Yes," I said.

"Will you be on time?"

"Yes."

Sofie sat up straight and slapped the counter. "Be here tomorrow, right after school. On the weekend it's too busy for showing you what you have to know. You come tomorrow, Thursday, and Friday. By the weekend, you'll know enough to be some use."

"Thanks."

I had a job.

"I'll be here. I get out of school at two." I would have to be careful not to end up in detention. No skipping classes, no matter how boring.

"You'll be paid $2.10 an hour. Minimum wage." Sofie's eyebrows arched over her glasses, as if daring me to say that wasn't enough. When I nodded she went on, "More, once you begin decorating cakes."

We shook hands. Sofie's palm felt rough and warm like towels dried on a line.

I eyed the tray with a lone glazed donut stuck in the corner. "Would it be alright if I had a donut?"

Sofie followed my gaze. "You have to pay for it."

"I didn't think you'd give it to me," I said, though I'd hoped she would. I told myself the familiar ache in my stomach was just hunger. Sofie walked behind the bakery counter and rang up the purchase. I let her go ahead and put it in a bag even though I planned to eat it right away.

She stood in the doorway, arms folded across her chest, watching as I waited for a car to pass before racing across Main Street. I didn't want her to think I wasn't careful.

We lived just up the hill from downtown, behind Saint Mary's Church on a street of two family houses occupied mostly by families who had lived in them for at least three generations. Grandparents, cousins, in-laws. Unrelated renters were suspect. Our landlord, Mr. Clark, had no family as far as anyone knew and had rented to my family since before I was born. My mother, Lucy, had charmed the old man back in the days when she and Joe still laughed once in awhile without being drunk. Over the years, Mr. Clark had less and less to do with us even though he lived upstairs.

The TV blasted in the dim living room. Lucky for everyone Mr. Clark was almost deaf. The TV always blared. Kevin watched cartoons cross-legged on the linoleum floor curled over a plate of fish sticks and ketchup. He didn't look up as I passed through to the kitchen.

Robbie leaned against the wall, holding the phone with his shoulder, scheming with one of his delinquent friends. Lucy, her old pink bathrobe spotted with cigarette burns, played solitaire in her usual place at the table. She had a few favorite spots—that particular kitchen chair, the end of the living room sofa closest to the TV, and her bed, all of which held the shape of her body. No one ever saw her anywhere else except when she was on her way to one of these nesting spots or standing to pull the vodka from the freezer and a glass from where I'd washed and dried and stacked them. She never even got up to answer the door or the phone.

"Where've you been?" she asked, eyes on her cards. "Dinner's in the oven. Robbie made it. Help yourself." She took a swallow from her half empty glass and set it back on the Formica table with a sharp crack.

Robbie covered the mouthpiece of the phone. "Come on, Ma. I'm trying to talk here." He made a big show of turning his back.

I helped myself to a handful of shriveled french fries and a dried out fish stick, glad I'd eaten that donut. "Did you eat yet, Mom? I'll make you a plate."

Lucy slapped a red queen down on a black king, freed up another pile of cards, and laughed. "Ah hah! That does it. Maybe I'll win this time. Did you say something?"

When caught early enough in the day, Robbie or I could get her to swallow a few mouthfuls of scrambled egg or cereal, but the wobbly tilt of her head and her droopy eyelids said she was beyond eating.

"Forget it."

Robbie hung up the phone and pulled his coat from the back of a chair.

"Where are you going?" I asked.

"None of your business." He punched me on the arm and snatched a fry from my plate.

"I thought you were sick. Remember?" Just that morning he'd faked a fever, leaving me to walk Kevin to school. Lucy had been too hung over to get out of bed.

"I'm better now. Besides, it's none of your business."

"Leave your brother alone." Lucy pushed her cards into a messy pile. "Damn. I thought I had it for sure that time."

"Yeah, leave me alone," Robbie said.

"Leave you alone so you can go hang out with Jimmy Daley and those guys? Break into cars? Mom, tell him to stay home."

She tilted her glass back and forth, watching the ice melt.

I wanted to slap her. "You don't care. You don't care what he does."

"And what are you? An angel?" Her attempt to throw me a haughty look failed. She couldn't keep her eyebrows raised.

"I made dinner." Robbie defended himself.

"Big deal. Any idiot can put frozen french fries in the oven. Some idiots can even cook food without burning it."

"You don't like it, don't eat it." Robbie slipped a few crumpled bills out of our mother's purse. "You don't mind, Ma. Do ya?"

"Put that money back!" I yelled as he disappeared out the back door.

"Don't pick on your brother." Lucy sorted through the cards, stacking them face up. "He's not a bad kid."

"He's thirteen years old!" I shouted. My mother couldn't see farther than the games of solitaire she laid out in the same patterns over and over again on the sticky table top.

"He just took five dollars." I clenched my fists to keep from sweeping the cards onto the floor. "We need that money. For food. Rent. Little things like that."

"You pick on him too much."

I threw my plate into the sink. The plastic rattled against the forks and glasses. Robbie could do the dishes when he got home. The kitchen still smelled of burned french fries.

"I got a job today. At Ida's bakery. Making real money. In case you're interested."

"Congratulations." Lucy shifted a row of cards. "I had a job once too. Bet you didn't know that. Down at the River Restaurant. I could carry a tray of six full dinner plates. Customers tipped me so well I had to empty my apron pockets, ten, fifteen times a shift. We wore those little black aprons over cute red dresses. Some girls complained about having to wear such short skirts. They said the tops were cut too low. Not me. Good for tips and I looked great. No one ever dared touch. And there's no harm in a little looking."

I couldn't remember the last time Lucy had strung so many words together. "Why did you stop working, if you liked it so much?"

"I married your father. He didn't like people looking at me in that outfit I guess. And he made enough money roofing; I didn't really have to work. Then I got pregnant with you." Her voice trailed off.

"Well, I won't get pregnant. Or married either," I said. "Not for a long time."

"The right guy comes along, you'll change your mind." Lucy smirked at her cards. "Danny's a nice boy."

Kevin raced into the room, swinging his empty plate, clutching his fork in front of him like a dagger. "Robbie said he bought me a popsicle."

"In the freezer." Lucy put a two of diamonds on the ace.

I fled to my room, the pantry, really. I'd turned it into a bedroom the year before. Until then I'd shared what would have been a dining room with Robbie. With no doors to shut, people were always stomping through. Robbie moved in with Kevin, and I ended up in the pantry. We never had any extra food on the shelves anyway except for the things no one would eat, like instant potatoes and canned yams.

I slid my lock into place, the lock I'd installed with no help from anyone. I'd covered the worst crack in the wall with a Janis Joplin poster, the one where she's singing her heart out in the sun, her long, ragged hair blowing. Next to her I'd taped an old magazine cover of three smiling hippies on a sidewalk in Haight-Ashbury. I'd stare at it and pretend I knew them, my friends. I stood behind the camera, taking the picture, or I would have been right in there, between the beautiful black boy with the giant Afro and the pale, stringy haired blonde girl with a tie-dyed headband. I had wild hair and a suede vest with fringe and no shirt under it and jeans with colored patches and a feathered hat. The whole time I pretended, a voice muttered deep inside, "Dream on, sweetheart. You have too little money and too many people needing you to go anywhere." That's when I put Janis on the tape deck I'd bought for five dollars at the Saint Mary's white elephant sale, full blast, to drown out that mean, little voice and the TV and my family.

I fast forwarded to "Summertime," let Janis wail, and thought about Ida's. My new job. I could make cakes for Danny or my brothers. My mother's thirty-eighth birthday was in December, two days before Christmas. She always complained we ignored it.

I'd learn to make flowers and leaves. Roses.

When I was little and could barely see over the windowsill, Dad would come home from work, grinning, a six pack under his arm, lunch box in one hand and a big bouquet of yellow roses, my mother's favorite flower, in the other. Lucy would be in the kitchen fixing dinner, singing along to Oklahoma or South Pacific or one of the other musical matinees she'd take me to see at the Capitol over and over again. I'd race to tell her, "Daddy's coming. With flowers." Lucy danced to meet him at the door. Joe would pop open a beer and hold it to her lips so she'd catch the foam before it spilled over. She'd put the flowers in a plastic pitcher or empty juice bottle. Robbie wasn't even born then. Mom, Dad, and I would sit around the table for dinner with the roses in the middle, every petal still attached.

Saturday at Ida's was busy. Sofie said Sunday would be worse. When my alarm buzzed at four thirty a.m. I knew in every part of my body, from sticky eyelids to burning calf muscles, that staying out late with Danny, proving to him work wouldn't interfere with our Saturday nights together, had been a mistake. Splashing water on my face and pulling on my wrinkled, grease splotched, yellow and white uniform, I wondered how I would stumble through the day.

The boys slept with their door open a crack. I sneaked in, stepping over Robbie who lay on the floor wrapped tightly in a sheet like a well rolled joint. Even his face was hidden. Kevin breathed through his mouth, covers thrown off, arms flung wide. The kid never stopped moving. I dug in dresser drawers for Kevin's clean clothes, arranged a shirt and pair of pants at the foot of his bed. In the quiet kitchen I put out some bowls, spoons, and the box of Cheerios. Lucy snored on the couch. Nothing woke her until she was ready. I clomped right by, my feet loud on the bare floor, and let the screen door bang.

As hard as it was to get up, I liked the deserted feeling of Rivertown at five a.m. The shadowy streets were mine, and not because I was hanging out late after the good girls had gone home to their ruffly, pink bedrooms and worried parents. I was going to work.

Two stray dogs sniffed at an overturned garbage can. Soft gold and blue neon glowed in the windows of the empty bars. A car approached, fast, from behind me, a long way off. I turned to see who it was. I knew lots of people who broke the speed limit racing down Main Street, but early Sunday morning they'd be passed out in bed or on a friend's floor.

The car, a red Volkswagen beetle, screeched to the side of the road like a giant insect in the shadow of the foundry, and stopped, engine buzzing. Main Street stretched in front of me all the way down to the mall. No other cars, no other people. I thought I could see the lights and tattered awning of Ida's. Rivertown's one traffic light blinked on and off, on and off, like a warning. The foundry walls loomed beside me. Nowhere to hide. I felt in my pack for a weapon. My fingers closed around a pencil. I could poke the guy's eyes out. Hoping the crazy driver didn't have a gun or a knife, I gripped the pencil and slunk along, close to the wall. The car door opened. I froze.

"Wylie?" Sofie's voice, faint beneath the sound of the idling engine—Vylie. I leaned against the brick wall, breathing hard, still clutching the pencil.

"Wylie? Is that you?"

"Yes," I hollered, heart thumping. I couldn't believe it, the old lady driving like a teenaged maniac.

"Come, I'll give you a ride."

I sprinted to the car. Even in the thinning dark, the wax gleamed, hard and shiny like a billiard ball.

"Go easy with the door," Sofie said, as I pulled hard on the handle. It slammed.

"Sorry." I was used to the large interior of Danny's Bonneville. In Sofie's car, the steering wheel, seats, windshield, everything, had been tucked into place, fit together, no space wasted.

Sofie shook her head and stepped on the gas, ripping down Main Street. I put a hand on the dashboard to brace myself. As we tore around a corner, I held onto the door to keep from falling against Sofie—not that the old woman would have noticed. She sat perfectly straight, as if someone were giving her a haircut, and stared at the road. Danny was a lean-back, one-finger-on-the-wheel, elbow-out-the-window, kind of guy. I was a huncher, maybe because I was still taking Driver's Ed. When I got my license, I'd relax.

Sofie jerked the car into the parking lot and squealed to a stop, switched off the engine, and sat back. "My favorite time of the day. On the drive home, there's too much traffic. Takes two times as long to go the same distance."

She stroked the dashboard. The inside of the car was as clean as the outside, as immaculate and well cared for as Danny's. "I don't go far. For sixteen years I've had this car, and it has only twenty thousand miles. Martin, my son, can't believe it. But I only drive to work. This car looks as good as the day Martin drove it off the lot. He bought it for me. A Christmas present. For a Volkswagen the wait then was six months, they were so popular." Sofie rubbed the polished steering wheel as if it were the silky ear of a pet.

"Worth waiting for, a good car like this. From a German you will not be finding sloppy work." She stared out at the sky turning pearly gray at the edges, behind Saint Anthony's steeple and over the flat roof of the mall.

"Does your son live around here?" I asked.

"San Francisco."

San Francisco! Questions poured out. I couldn't help it. "Have you ever visited him? Does he live near Haight-Ashbury? Is he a…hhh…" Something in her face told me not to say hippie. Sofie was old, her son probably too old to be a hippie anyway. "What does he do?"

"He is a very important electrical engineer." She pressed her lips together, then surprised me by continuing. "No, I've never visited. When I have money for traveling, I visit my sisters in the old country. They are all the time inviting me." Sofie pronounced each word, with big spaces between, as if she was angry. I regretted being so nosy so soon. "Haight—I don't know."

"Do you have any other kids?" I asked, trying to move the conversation from the son I seemed to have asked too much about.

Sofie turned and looked at me. The air in the car thickened. She stared without speaking, until I had to look down. I considered rolling down the window, but fidgeted with the zipper of my knapsack instead.

"No," Sofie said. The word sounded like a lie. Sofie tucked her keys into the outside pocket of her purse, took out a tissue, swiped at her nose. "We need to get to work."

Sundays at Ida's were even worse than Sofie had described, a crush of people after each church service or Mass, in for their donuts, pastries and rolls. They'd trample their own grandmothers to get the biggest coffee cake. You'd never guess that just ten minutes earlier they'd been praying and singing together.

At about eleven o'clock a pinched-faced woman in a black, straw hat with a fake bunch of grapes stuck to it, pulled a jelly stained jacket from a bag and shook it at Sofie. "I bit into a donut and raspberry jelly squirted, positively e-rupted, all over the collar of my new wool suit." The crowd muttered and shifted behind her. "And I'm not the only one. Everyone at coffee hour had jelly dripping from their fingers and splattering their church clothes."

"Next?" I said. I thought the jelly was the best part so I'd given each donut two pumps of raspberry instead of one.

"Where's the boss?" the woman yelled. The grapes on her hat jiggled. "He should see what his donuts have done so he'll know what's going on when I send him the cleaning bill."

I gave the next customer his raisin bread.

"I can't imagine how this happened," Sofie said to the woman. Her sidelong glance collided with mine. "Here, give it to me. I'll show the boss myself."

Tony was home sleeping. Sofie disappeared through the swinging door, to the back of the bakery.

"Come on," someone shouted.

"Next?" I waited on a string of customers, while the woman stood tapping her fingers on the counter, frowning and twitching.

"Here's your suit." Everyone turned as Sofie sang out across the store. "A cleaning bill won't be necessary. Soap and water worked just fine." People snickered. The woman pressed her lips together for a long, silent moment. Sofie hurried back behind the counter.

"Here." She held out the jacket to the woman, pointing to the damp, jelly free spot, smiling like someone on a detergent commercial. Somebody laughed. The woman snatched her jacket, stuffed it into the plastic bag, and elbowed her way out.

"Next?" Sofie said, still smiling.

She slid a loaf of rye from the shelf and carried it, like a baby, to the slicer where she waited for me to finish cutting through a loaf of pumpernickel. "So why did the jelly donuts squirt when people bit them?" she asked, her tone more harsh than the clattering slicer.

I pretended I couldn't hear. "What?"

"The jelly donuts." Her triumphant smile had disappeared. "We'll talk later."

I was hiding in the back, at the sink, attacking a stack of trays when Sofie marched over and turned off the water. She jabbed the air in front of my chest with an accusing finger. "I told you to give each of those donuts one pump of jelly!"

"I'm sorry." I scrubbed at a spot of burnt sugar.

"I've been working here twenty years." Sofie put her hands on her hips.

"Well, what do you want me to say?" I flung the brush. Water splashed. "I'm sorry. Now I know. There is a right amount of jelly to put in a donut. Now I know. Okay?"

The swinging doors slapped shut behind Sofie. Plunging my hands into the hot water, I groped for the brush. Every tray had its place. Every counter, every inch of glass had to sparkle. The second a smudge appeared on my apron Sofie made me change. I wondered again why she'd hired me so quickly. I wondered if she'd fire me before I quit. I put up with enough hassles at home. My feet hurt.

Sofie headed for the back door, carrying the slicer tray. "Come here," she ordered. She began to toss handfuls of crumbs outside, into the air.

"Ignore her," I told myself as I rinsed the last tray and pulled the plug. I had enough of Ida's, enough of Sofie.

"Come here, please." Sofie's voice was kinder. I dried my hands on my dirty apron.

The parking lot had turned into a rolling gray ocean of birds, countless pigeons in one place. They must have come from miles around. They couldn't all live in Rivertown.

Suddenly they rose like spray from a fountain. Some landed on the roof of the bank. Some settled on the big letters that spelled McIvers Chevrolet. Most just disappeared leaving the asphalt as still and smooth as black ice.

I remembered hours of sitting on splintery porch steps, clutching the shaker of salt my mother told me would tame a bird if I could only get close enough to sprinkle it on the tail feathers. By the time I was three or four, I'd already learned that chasing them wouldn't work, so I waited, unnaturally, achingly still. When a bird did hop into sprinkling range, no matter how I made my move, the shadow of the salt shaker always sent it flying, far out of reach.

Sofie tucked the empty tray under her arm. "Did you see the colors on their necks shine? People think pigeons are dirty, ugly. But if in the world there were just twenty, folks would be paying all of a sudden big money for a pigeon feather. Does that make any sense? Why because something is not common, is it more beautiful, more desired? A beautiful thing is a beautiful thing. A good thing is a good thing. The more, the better." Sunlight flashed off the metal tray. I wondered what I was doing spending my Sunday staring at an empty parking lot with an old woman full of secrets who had done nothing but boss me around the last few days, whose idea of fun was ripping down Main Street like a teenager at five in the morning and feeding a bunch of birds.

"I used to think you could tame a bird by shaking salt on its tail," I heard myself saying. "My mother told me I wouldn't even need a cage. It would never fly away."

"Ha! Better you should use bread crumbs. Birds, they are made to fly away. But with the bread crumbs, they will be coming back." Sofie pushed past me.

I struggled against the urge to cry, to grab Sofie's arm and squeeze it until it hurt, to tell her I was quitting.

"We have much cleaning still to do before Tony comes for the money and we can go home. Come on. I'll teach you how to mop a floor." She stopped and glared. "On Friday, you made puddles. I was here after you left. For an hour. On my knees with a sponge."

I wanted to hit her with the broom or give it to her so she could straddle it and take off for the sky. Witch.

"I will teach you about cleaning. Even as a child, my son knew to pour water from two feet in the air onto berry stains, and when it was better to use a sponge than a rag. He knew how to clean a bathroom too. He would make a good husband."

I hefted the wheeled bucket into the sink. I wondered, as I strained to lift it full of soapy water, how Sofie had managed it alone.

"Make sure you squeeze the water out with the press." Sofie demonstrated. "I ask myself many times if Martin will ever get married. Already he's fifty." She gave the mop a few even, energetic pushes across the floor and handed it to me.

I ducked my head to hide my smirk. Pathetic. He was fifty and his mother still hoped he'd get married. She probably wanted a granddaughter she could dress in white tights and patent leather shoes that shone like mirrors. She'd take her to the park, sit her on a bench, and tell her not to get her clothes dirty. Or teach her how to mop properly.

"He has a good job. Still…" Sofie untied her apron.

I sweated pushing that stringy, old mop, heaving it into the press, wringing out the scummy water. I wished Sofie would shut up, stop watching me, stop talking about a man I didn't know or care about. If Sofie had visited San Francisco, even once, then I might be interested.

"Hey girls!" Tony burst in and strode across the wet floor to the cash register. "How's business?"

"Business is booming," said Sofie. I wheeled the bucket of dirty water to the back.

Danny's face appeared in the window of the door to the parking lot. I signaled I'd be there in a minute. As I started for the front to tell Sofie I was leaving, I heard Tony ask, "How's she working out, the new girl?"

"She's young. But a hard worker."

I cracked the swinging door so I could hear better and spied on them.

"That's all that matters." Tony took the money from the cash register and tucked it in a zippered green canvas bag. There must have been at least a thousand dollars. "Young, old, fat, thin, black, white. Makes no difference as long as she works hard."

"She should learn decorating. We've had lately so many cake orders. I have a feeling about her, she is smart, a tough one, learns fast. But always a scowl on her face."

"Reminds me of someone." Tony laughed. "Yeah, especially the tough part. And the scowling." He put his arm around Sofie. "You want her to learn decorating, go ahead, teach her. You're the boss."

I decided to give the job another week. Give my aching feet a chance to get used to it.

"If I was boss," Sofie said, "we'd use butter in the icing instead of shortening." She stepped away and shook her crooked finger at him.

"Sofie, we've talked about this at least a thousand times. All bakeries use shortening. It's cheaper, holds its shape, and keeps better."

"That's why I never buy a cake from a bakery and I never will."

Tony laughed. "I'm glad everyone doesn't think like you. We'd be out of business."

They were done talking about me. I pushed the door open. "My ride's here."

"Wait a minute," said Tony. "I want to talk to you."

I walked to the front and leaned against the refrigerator case. Sofie frowned. I straightened up, waiting. I had smeared the glass.

"Next week," said Tony. "You think you could come in after school for some decorating lessons?"

"Sure." It sounded better than washing trays or waiting on unhappy customers.

"My kids can work the front. They complain, but tough luck, I say, it's this bakery that puts clothes on their backs and a roof over their heads. Sofie, can you stay late for, maybe, three weeks?"

"That's enough to start," Sofie said. "I don't have to teach her all I know."

I moved toward the door. "I really have to go." Danny could get sulky if he waited too long. I was too tired to coax him out of it.

"Go on," said Tony. "Have a good time. Don't get into any trouble."

"See you tomorrow here," said Sofie, without a trace of a smile. "Be on time."

I grabbed my jacket and bag and ran to where Danny stood by the powder blue Bonneville. He greeted me with a long, close hug.

"I feel like a glazed donut," I said into the shoulder of his leather jacket. "Smell the grease in my hair. I think it's even sunk into my skin."

"Mmmm." He licked my face and neck. "I love greasy food."

"Can't you wait until we're in the car?" All I needed was Sofie and Tony watching me and Danny necking in the driveway. I caught his arm and with my free hand opened the passenger door. "Get in." I pushed him onto the seat, and he pulled me down on top of him.

I dropped my bag onto the floor and spread my hands flat on his chest, lifting myself up so I could look at him. I loved his sharp cheekbones, his eyes the color of bitter chocolate, his wide grin full of teeth. I felt his hips move under mine and traced his lips with my finger. "I need a shower," I said.

"Okay. Okay." He slid his legs out from under me and moved to the driver's seat. "Your house or mine?"

"Yours." If we went to mine, Lucy would want something from the store. Kevin would leap on Danny. It would be hours before we got out of there. I kept extra clothes and a toothbrush in my bag to avoid going home when I could.

"Okay, my house." Danny gunned the motor down Main Street, the five and ten, city hall, ice cream parlor, cigar store, and foundry all blurring together on either side of us. He wasn't afraid of cops. He said he wasn't afraid of anything. That was almost true. He hated the pictures of Janis and my hippie "friends." Maybe they didn't scare him, but they reminded him I wanted to leave, and I knew he was afraid of that. Sometimes, knowing the fact of that fear he worked hard to keep secret even from himself, I felt strong and safe. Other times it frightened me.

Danny's house was full of quiet so thick you could feel it as you walked from room to room. The walls were smooth and bare. His father spent most of his time off work around the corner at Casey's bar and moved through the house like an ultra considerate guest when he was home. Danny didn't have brothers or sisters or a mother. She'd left them when he was three. His silent, uncluttered house was a large part of the reason I loved him. The other part was his sadness. We both knew what it was like to lose parents. We both knew what it was like not to want to talk about it. A housekeeper came in once a week to clean, and with Danny and his Dad as neat as they were, things stayed where they were put.

He had big, thick towels, clean and folded in a special closet. At my house towels lay flung under the table wet with spilled milk, in damp heaps on the beds, or in corners where they sat for days growing mold. "Hurry up," Danny said, kissing me hard, wrapping a fluffy pink towel around my shoulders like an expensive fur.

I stood in the shower, the stream of water beating against my lower back, looking forward to an afternoon in Danny's bed. The bathroom filled with steam. Since we'd figured out how to use a rubber and stopped worrying about impressing each other, we had sex every chance we got. We could forget everything, with arms tight around each other, in a house so still our breath and heartbeats and the creaking of the bed were the only sounds. His sheets were as clean and sweet smelling as his towels.

When the shower had melted away all traces of Ida's I turned off the water and left the bathroom in a steamy cloud, one pink towel wrapped around my body, another around my hair. "Danny?"

"In here." He sat at his desk, straddling the chair. He always turned chairs around before sitting on them. It drove teachers crazy. He put down his needle-nosed pliers and the wires he was connecting on an old radio and stood up. His jeans hung below where his hips would be if he had hips. His shirt was unbuttoned. He was my height, but thinner. Even after all our time together, two and a half years, since we were freshmen, the sharp, perfect outlines of his ribs startled me. He held out his arms. Anyone else would have thought he was about to shrug, but I knew that between those arms he was making a space for me. I stepped into it and felt his fingers lock together behind my back.

I raced down Main Street, stuffing a bunch of my hair through an elastic band, an hour late for my first decorating lesson. Remembering I'd have to tie my hair back for work, I'd searched out an elastic band at the end of art class, arriving five minutes late for math. Another detention. I was sure Sofie had started without me.

"Sorry!" I shouted my apology, letting it enter Ida's before I did, hoping it would smooth my way. The three small, sheet cakes ordered for the next morning sat unfrosted on the table. The bowl of icing in Sofie's hands glowed an even pink. I stood frozen, Sofie's disapproval a giant vacuum sucking away all explanations. But she'd waited for me. A whole hour.

"I'm so sorry," I tried again.

Sofie frowned, muttering in German. "*Der Apfel fällt nicht weit vom Stamm.*" Then, in English, in case I didn't understand, "The apple doesn't fall far from the tree. Like mother, like daughter." Sofie's friends from the German Hall must have told her about Lucy's drinking, Joe's disappearing acts.

I set my shoulders, preparing to take whatever came next without flinching, but Sofie just dipped the largest spatula into the pink icing, spread it around the sides of the first cake, then covered the top with long, smooth strokes.

She began to beat a bowl of white. "A seventy-year-old woman, even in good health, should not be standing on her feet from four in the morning until so late in the afternoon." The words splattered against me and stuck, like the flecks of icing that dotted Sofie's glasses.

"No one should," I said with a nervous laugh. "I'm sorry I kept you waiting."

Sofie struggled to open a jar of yellow coloring, her bent index finger and thumb clamped around the stubborn lid. I still hadn't asked her about her claw.

"Blood poisoning," she said, wiggling the finger. "My crooked hook, Martin called it. Bent for about sixty years now. In the old country we have no money for doctors." The fingernail curved, sharp and dangerous. "Are you planning the whole afternoon to stand there? Or are you helping?" She thrust the jar at me.

I ran hot water over the lid, then loosened it, relieved when it twisted easily. I placed it in the exact center of Sofie's outstretched hand. "Does it hurt?" I asked, peering at the finger.

Sofie's frown softened. "Ach! *Nein.*" With a toothpick pressed between her thick fingernail and thumb, she speared a tiny dollop of paste, drew it through the mound of clean white icing. She mixed, the pinprick of color marbling the white. Seconds later she held a bowl full of yellow, as bright as the sun in a kindergartner's drawing. She handed me the green and the blue.

When we'd mixed all the colors, Sofie picked up a pastry bag, folded the top down over her fist, and with a spatula, pushed icing down deep inside. "For what are you waiting?" she asked, scowling again. "We don't have much time."

Careful to imitate Sofie's motions, I filled a bag with blue. Icing stuck to my knuckles. I reminded myself not to lick it off. Sofie eyed me, ready to pounce on any mistakes. I fumbled with the pastry bag, but managed to pull the spatula out clean, determined not to let Sofie unnerve me.

She slapped a tray covered with wax paper in front of me. "Practice board." She jabbed the tray with her hook, nicking the wax paper. "Before you work on the cakes, you try everything I teach you on here." The pastry bag snug in her gnarled hands, she demonstrated stars, elongated shells, reverse shells, and zig-zags, all carefully and perfectly formed. I hesitated. I'd never tried to make any-thing before. My mother never sewed. My father never built things. I never had a grandmother to teach me how to knit or put together gingerbread houses at Christmas time. I had no reason to think I was good with my hands.

"Come on," Sofie urged, choosing another pastry bag. She pushed out a yel-low drop flower. "Try these first, if you want. Nothing to it. Just remember to stop squeezing before you lift up." She forced the bag on me.

After several false starts, rows of blobs, and ragged squiggles, flowers began to bloom across my practice board. I filled it with the designs Sofie showed me, scraped it, filled it again. Blue stars shone, shells promised the sound of the sea, my zigzags made me grin.

Sofie watched, icing bag dangling from her hand, as I created my own pat-terns, tumbling waves, shooting stars, dancing breezes. When every place on the board was full, I looked up and found Sofie staring at me, gray eyes silvery.

"I've never done anything like this before." I felt breathless.

"You are reminding me of my son," Sofie said. "Martin. On the last day of third grade, after he gave to the bully who all year teased him for his German accent a bloody nose."

I pointed to the cakes, empty pastry bag flopping in my hand. "Can I do it for real now?"

Sofie pushed one close to me. "*Bitte.*"

I was writing on the last cake and Sofie was beginning to wash the spatulas when Antonia, Tony's oldest daughter, pushed through the swinging doors.

"I just found an order for tomorrow." She waved a slip of paper. "I took it a week ago, put it in my pocket, and forgot about it." She winced. "For Angela Per-rone's shower, four doll cakes. My father will kill me!"

"Four doll cakes?" Sofie repeated. "For tomorrow? Ordered last week?" She wiped her hands on her apron, tightened them into fists, and flexed her arms as though she might hit Antonia.

Antonia cringed near the door and bit her lip, leaving teeth marks in her lip-stick. The order dangled from her fingernails like a used tissue.

Sofie rearranged her apron, taking a long time to retie the strings. If Angela Perrone needed cakes for her shower, she would have them. Sofie wouldn't let Tony down. One mix-up could start a bad reputation. She had the same decided look in her eye she'd had when the pinch-faced lady tried to stick Ida's with a cleaning bill. Sofie would do the cakes, but she'd make Antonia sweat a little first.

"Sofie, please," Antonia wailed.

"I don't know." Sofie looked at the clock and shook her head.

"Please. You can do it. Here." Antonia broke her longest nail pulling out a tray of cakes shaped like overturned bowls. "Use these."

"Those are for Lisa Pulaski's Cinderella birthday party," Sofie told her. "Tomorrow I do them."

"Dad can bake new ones tonight." Antonia checked the order slip, so intent on convincing Sofie, the ragged fingernail went unnoticed. "Two chocolate. Two yellow. See? Just what we have here."

"Isn't that lucky?" Sofie said. "And what if the order was for all yellow or all chocolate? Or marble?"

Antonia looked at the floor.

"Oh, come on," I said, tired of the game. "You know you're going to do those cakes."

Sofie's frown said I had a lot of nerve predicting what she would or wouldn't do. Antonia smoothed the crumpled order slip. We waited for Sofie's next move.

"You're right." The edges of Sofie's mouth twitched. She raised her eyebrows in my direction. "And you're going to help me." I sucked in my cheeks to keep from smiling.

Antonia handed me the slip, keeping a safe distance from Sofie. "You won't tell my father, will you?" She wiped at the streaks of mascara on her cheeks.

"What if you hadn't found that order and the Perrones came tomorrow, right before the shower, and there were no cakes?" Sofie scolded. "Do you know what that could do to your father's business? Of course I'll be telling him."

"I'll never put an order in my pocket again." Antonia edged toward the door.

"You bet on your life you won't," Sofie told her. "Wylie, give me that slip. Antonia, clean up front. Never mind about the slicer tray. I'll empty it later." While Sofie rummaged in a deep cardboard box full of cellophane wrapped plastic dolls, Antonia made her escape.

"Here we go." Sofie's hand emerged with a fan of dolls. "One blonde. Three with dark hair."

"They tell you what color hair they want?" I couldn't believe it. I read the order slip again.

"It has to match the hair color of the people in the wedding party."

"What about eyes? Do we match those too?"

"No. The blondes and red heads come with blue eyes. The dark haired ones have brown. We just match hair and skin."

"Crazy." I shook my head. "Like Barbie except below the waist, she's got this spike." I touched the blonde's point through the cellophane. You could hurt someone with it.

Sofie glued the cakes to round cake boards with icing. She put one on a turn-table in front of herself and one in front of me. "The point is for poking them into the cakes, their skirts."

"What if someone wanted a doll in pants?"

"Couldn't do it. If people want that women's liberation stuff they can go somewhere else."

"What about kids who order these things? They probably expect a whole doll and when their cake is gone, all they have is a doll shaped weapon." I imagined myself as a kid, running around with a doll like that, after I'd licked the icing off, trying to stab Robbie.

"You'll learn ruffling now. For the skirts. Right away we start so we can go home."

We ruffled all four skirts. "Do we stick the dolls in now?" I hoped Sofie noticed how fast I worked. "How do we make the tops of the dresses? I doubt they want a topless wedding party."

"No," Sofie said. "Switch to a star tip and I'll show you. We cover her skin with little stars, close together so no plastic is showing through. Outline it first."

I poked my bridesmaid into the cake, a blonde with startled blue eyes, naked from the waist up, in a green cake skirt. "Half woman/half cake, like a mermaid who can't swim. She can only stand there and be eaten."

"For heaven sakes it's a cake, that's what it's for. Bend the arms out," Sofie said. "Otherwise the part underneath will be impossible to decorate."

She worked on the bride. I gave my bridesmaid a star on the tip of each breast, then filled in the rest quickly without looking up to see if Sofie had noticed.

"Wylie." Sofie spun her doll on the turntable. She'd filled in the bodice, except for the breasts. Two plastic cones poked through the icing like mountain peaks through clouds.

I laughed, hitting myself in the cheek with the bag of icing. Sofie worked to keep a serious expression, but she started laughing too, in helpless snorts. Gasp-ing, she took off her glasses to wipe her eyes. Antonia poked her head in, wondering what the noise was. The sudden appearance and disappearance of her face in the door started us laughing again, even louder.

"We've been working too long, too hard. This is what happens." Sofie wiped her forehead with a clean towel. I knew laughing like that had never happened before, no matter how long or hard Sofie or I or anyone had worked. It couldn't have.

"We should finish." I rubbed icing from my cheek with the hem of my apron.

Sofie stuck another doll into the yellow skirt. She gave her the top of a bikini bathing suit. "Here." She handed me the last doll. "Your turn."

Sofie nudged me, a gleam in her eye. "Go on."

I jabbed the doll into the green bridesmaid's skirt and stood back, considering her from all possible angles.

"Use both yellow and green in the top," reminded Sofie. "And they want yellow flowers on the skirts."

I squeezed a green star onto the doll's right shoulder. Sofie watched me switch back and forth between yellow and green icing, connect a line of stars, twist it around a shoulder, between the breasts, down one side, and end on the lower back with a shape like a snake's head. The doll looked like an ancient goddess. I'd transformed the mound of cake from a skirt to a mountain, a volcano. We stared at the cake, avoiding each other's eyes.

Something stirred inside me, something that escaped through my hands, found its shape through a pastry bag. I sensed its power, feared it might be dangerous, longed to release it again.

The snake woman held our gazes like she'd never let go.

Finally, Sofie shook her head. "A shame we have to turn her into a bridesmaid."

"Can you do it?" I asked.

"Alright." She sounded resigned, sad. "Do the flowers on the other skirt. Fill in the maid of honor's bikini. Be careful not to get icing in the hair."

I dressed the maid of honor while Sofie worked on the snake woman. The clock ticked. Trays rattled far away in the front of the bakery.

"Look." Sofie rotated the doll slowly on the turntable. The bridesmaid still wore the snake. If you knew it was there, you could see it, camouflaged in the surrounding yellow and green. Sofie smiled like she'd just handed me the perfect gift.

I took it all in, the hidden snake, the smile, the gift. "Do you think they'll notice anything unusual?"

"If they do," Sofie said. "They won't be able to put their fingers on what it is."

I tackled the sink full of dishes. Sofie wiped the scarred wooden table until it gleamed. The bridal party stood in boxes on the shelf. If I stared at the box with the snake goddess long enough, I thought I could see the cover move.

The blast of the Bonneville's horn, as familiar as the foundry whistle at noon, split the quiet we shared as we finished cleaning. I didn't have to look out the window to know that Danny was sitting, tapping his fingers on the steering wheel, the door on the passenger side perfectly aligned with the back steps of Ida's. I sunk my hand into the lukewarm, soapy water to open the drain. On the surface, yellow and green icing floated like slugs. I had to clean the sink. Danny could wait.

As I splashed dishwater, I turned to look for a sponge and saw Sofie glaring at the door. Framed in the glass, Danny slowed himself to a slouching walk and winked. Usually, the backs of my knees tingled and my heart bounced at the sight of him. The door opened. I wished he'd waited for me in the car. My face ached as if my skin was too small.

He leaned against the door frame, jangling his keys in his pockets. "Hey."

"Danny." I rubbed the space between my two front teeth with my tongue, trying to imagine his lips on mine.

"You ready?" He jerked his head toward the car.

"Almost. I have to wipe out the sink."

When Danny looked at me, I felt beautiful. When he listened to me, I heard my own voice hum like a finely tuned engine. When he touched me, my skin sang. But he didn't belong in the back of Ida's with Sofie watching him watch my uniform tighten and inch up my legs as I leaned over to rub the farthest corners of the deep sink with cleanser. I rinsed the sponge and hung the dishrag over the faucet to dry just as Sofie had shown me.

Radiating disapproval Sofie hadn't moved since Danny walked in. "You've met Danny?" I asked, sure she hadn't. Sofie's arm began to swipe the rag back and forth across the table like a windshield wiper, as if my voice had activated a switch. She tightened her lips.

"My boyfriend?" I added, wincing at the odd question mark I heard in my voice, fighting the urge to tell Sofie how clean he kept his car, how hard he worked, how he wasn't as tough and bad as he tried to appear. I wanted to yell at him to straighten up, shake hands, ask politely and sincerely 'How are you?'

"Hi," he muttered.

Sofie tipped her head a fraction of an inch in his direction. She bunched the rag in her fist.

I looked from one to other, a rope in their tug of war, wondering why they disliked other at first sight and why I cared so much.

Danny eyeballed me. "We better get going."

Sofie frowned.

I had done my work. I was free to leave. "See you tomorrow." I hesitated a moment before grabbing my jacket.

"No you won't." Sofie's voice was like steel wool. She hung her rag over the edge of the sink and took pains to adjust mine, so that both sides hung evenly.

"Why not?" I stopped, coat sleeve hanging.

"My day off and heaven knows, I am needing it. We have tomorrow no lessons."

Danny twirled his key ring. "Come on."

"The crumbs!" I said. "I'll make sure Antonia saved them."

"Don't be bothering." Sofie tried to push past me as she moved toward the swinging doors. "I'll do it."

I stuffed my hands in my pockets. "Okay, but…"

Sofie waited.

"I wish one of us was going to be here when the Perrones pick up those cakes." We glanced at the shelf where the cakes waited like prizes on a game show where contestants pick the right box and are set for life, or the wrong one and end up with a case of Rice-a-Roni.

Sofie stepped around me without saying a word. The swinging doors slapped shut behind her. My bag weighed heavy on my arm. I felt a wanting I couldn't name.

Danny shoved me with his voice. "Let's get out of here."

Suddenly wanting to be anywhere but Ida's bakery, I moved to the door. Danny squeezed my shoulder and walked me out. He shut me into the Bonneville before sliding in himself on the other side. He hummed along with the engine he took such care to maintain, ignoring me.

The streetlights burned white. People spilled into and out of the bars, after work crowds and after dinner crowds overlapping. We crawled along Main Street.

"What's that old lady's problem?" he asked.

"Nothing." I had been wondering the same thing, but when he asked, I felt a surge of anger. "I don't know. Maybe she thinks you're not good enough for me." I forced a laugh.

"She doesn't even know me!" He punched the dashboard.

"I know," I said, wishing I hadn't provoked him. "I'll tell her about you…Come on, Danny, you know how old people are—they judge you by how you look. You should've seen her glaring at me when I applied for the job. But when she gets to know you—"

"You're always at the bakery," he blurted.

"I'm not. I'm here now, aren't I?" The air around me grew warm. Minutes away from bed with the guy I loved, I decided to feel happy.

Uneven light from the street lamps slashed across our faces. In the side view mirror my green eye glittered, my blue eye filled with tears. I turned toward Danny.

"What?" he shouted. I jumped.

"What's wrong with you?" I asked. He leaned back against the seat, gripping the steering wheel, elbows locked.

"I don't know." His voice dropped. "I miss you. When we're not at school, you're working."

"I haven't even worked a full week," I protested. It did seem longer. Danny and I were used to spending every afternoon or evening together, cruising the town, kissing in the car until we couldn't keep our hands off each other and had to go back to his house. I shivered just remembering it.

"When we're together, which is, when? Between classes, at lunch, and for an hour late at night, and then all you do is homework, all you talk about is Sofie."

"Yeah, right. To complain about her. She's picky. She cares about the pigeons more than she cares about me or anyone else as far as I can tell—"

"Sofie. Sofie. Sofie," he mimicked. He thunked the steering wheel with the flat of his hand. "What do I care about her? Miserable old bitch."

"Don't say that." I tensed as he pushed the accelerator to the floor. I shouldn't have defended Sofie. "Danny?" He swerved the car onto the River Road, heading out of town toward the Rock, where everyone parked and leaned against their cars with bottles they'd picked up at Roy's, where the clerks would sell to anyone tall enough to see over the counter.

"Danny, wait. Where are we going?"

He smiled, the confusion in my voice soothed his rage, gave him permission to be generous. "I thought we'd go see who's hanging out." Back in charge, he reached for my hand.

I slipped my fingers from his grasp. "I wanted to take a shower before we went anywhere."

"You're alright," he said. "If we waited for you to take a shower, it'd be too late. Even hard-core partiers wouldn't be out that late on week nights."

"Maybe I don't want to stand around talking to people. I'm tired. And besides, I'm wearing my uniform."

"Sit in the car then." His voice was tight as a rubber band stretched to the limit.

I folded my arms, jerked my leg away from his touch, and turned toward the window. Outside, the dark woods rushed past.

"You have extra clothes in your bag," he said.

"Yeah, so what?" I yelled. "How do you know what I have in my bag?"

"You always have extra clothes." The gentleness in his voice sounded false.

"How do you know I have extra clothes? How do you know so much about me?"

"Come on, Wylie. We've been together forever. We know each other."

"You don't know me!"

He flinched.

"You don't know anything about me! No one knows anything about me. And don't think you do, Danny DiBona. Don't think for one, tiny, infinitesimal moment that you know a damn thing about me!" I slapped at the tears running down my cheeks.

Danny pulled the car off the road, into a dirt and gravel parking lot overlooking the river. The headlights shone on scattered trash and a few wrecked picnic tables. "I know you," he whispered. He wouldn't have said anything if he'd known it would lead to a scene. He turned off the engine. I found the door handle and stumbled out of the car, following the trampled path to the river's edge, hunched against the wind that tangled my hair and plastered my uniform to my legs.

The river noise roared in my ears. Water rushed past, dark movement and rotten smells. By daylight you could see its bright and changing colors, sometimes yellow, sometimes turquoise, sometimes fuchsia, depending on which factory had dumped which chemical into it. I noticed a flat rock, just outside the beam of the Bonneville's headlights, a still and solid shape about two feet from shore. I jumped onto it and sat, arms wrapped around my knees.

Danny had never yelled at me before. He acted like I was the one who was different since I'd started working. I thought he was the one who'd changed.

The car door slammed, then Danny was beside me on the rock. "Whew!" he said. "Smell that water."

"Yeah." Across the river a small red light blinked on top of the radio tower.

He cleared his throat. "I was thinking we'd get married. Sometime after graduation." His words seemed as much a surprise to him as they were to me. He added more matter of factly, "I figured we would, you know? I mean, we've been together so long…"

My toes curled inside my sneakers, an attempt to hold tight to the surface of the rock. "Why are you talking about this now?"

"I figured you were planning on getting married too," he whispered.

The smelly water rushed past. I could throw myself in; let it carry me to the ocean. If I drowned, so what?

"Hold me," I said.

He pulled me close, burying his face in my hair, breathing hard. A car pulled into the lot, its headlights soaking us, two kids, huddled on a rock, clinging to each other, surrounded by contaminated water.

If we'd been cakes, baking together in an oven, his marriage proposal had just turned the temperature up too high. My brain told me I had to get out or burn, but he kept me in the circle of his arms. I breathed the smell of his jacket. Beneath my closed eyelids the crazy patterns stopped jerking around and froze. If I pretended he hadn't said the words, pride might keep him from repeating them.

The car backed up and drove away. Dark wrapped around us. After a long time, Danny said, "Do you want to drive back?" He was trying hard to give me something, trying to make me happy. He didn't like being a passenger.

"Back home? Not to the Rock?"

"Yeah."

"You sure?"

"We've done enough practicing in parking lots. If you don't have some road time, you'll never pass your driving test."

I picked at a patch of frosting stuck to my uniform.

"Just don't smash it up. Without it I'd be another loser on a bus."

"I'll be careful." He looked hard at me until I had to turn away. "I promise," I said.

Together we jumped for the bank and walked to the waiting Bonneville. Danny handed me the keys.

*   *   *   *

Beyond Ida's locked front door, wet snow fell, thick and slow. I watched it through the steamed up glass. Sofie banged cream pitchers around, pretending to empty them, but I knew the moment I turned around Sofie would be staring, the way she had for the last few weeks, waiting for me to say why I was miserable, everything she already knew and pretended she didn't. The whole town knew.

The wall I'd been building since the afternoon of Robbie's arrest, since he'd opened our door to a parade of parole officers and social workers, threatened to crumble under the weight of Sofie's silent pity.

That bright October day, Robbie and Jimmy Daley had made their usual after school stop at Ida's to pick up a snack of squashed éclairs, broken brownies, or cookie crumbs. They headed out across Barton's field toward the woods with a lighter and matches in their pockets and the bag of day-old jelly donuts I'd given them.

I heard the wail of the fire alarm and the sirens as I emptied the slicer and swept the floor, never thinking the sounds had anything to do with me until Lucy called. "Your brother's down at the pleece station. Arrested. They say I hafta pick'm up and my show isn't even half done."

I called Danny to pick her up and meet me at City Hall where we dragged her up the steps. Robbie huddled at the end of a long beat up bench, his baseball cap in his lap instead of backwards on his head. His hair stuck out all over in knotty twists he rolled between fingers. He saw me and smiled. The urge to smash him, growing inside me since Lucy's call, crashed flat as a wave hitting a beach.

Officer Belinsky tried talking to Lucy, saw it was pointless, and turned his bulging blue eyes to me.

"Your brother doesn't seem to realize the seriousness of his offense. When we found him in the woods he was laughing like he thought it was all one big joke." I pictured tongues of flame licking ferns, bushes, every stick the fire consumed adding to its size and power, Robbie in the woods, stepping back to give his fire more room.

Belinsky went on. "He can plead youthful offender and end up with a sealed record, but that only works once." Robbie chewed his lip and bent the visor of his baseball cap up and down. When I nudged his dirty sneaker with mine, he looked up, satisfying Belinsky with a nod.

One big joke. I imagined the moment Belinsky twisted Robbie's skinny arm, confiscated the matches, snapped on the handcuffs, and seated him in the squad car. Robbie Steele, the star of his own show, best actor, best director, best soundtrack, best cinematography, best picture. I bet he smiled for his mug shots.

Lucy signed the forms. Her signature started big and ended small so she could fit it on the line. Kevin could write his name more clearly, and he was barely seven.

"You all take it easy." Belinsky made an ordinary good-bye sound like a cross between an order and a warning. We guided Lucy out the door.

On the way down the steps to where Danny waited in the Bonneville, Robbie looked at me over Lucy's head. Belinsky should save his sloppy concern for himself. What right did some fat, small-town cop have to feel sorry for us? The guy's idea of fun was free coffee and donuts at Ida's and driving around busting kids.

"Wylie?" Sofie's voice jerked me back to the snow, the bakery key hot in my hand, the floors waiting to be washed. "Did you see Mrs. Parker today? How she made me pick up every cream puff on the tray so she could make an inspection." If she thought our old game of sharing worst customer stories would take my mind off my problems, she was wrong. In front of the bakery, a car fishtailed as it approached a red light.

Belinsky didn't have to be a detective to see that Lucy was plastered. Thanks to him we were being threatened with foster homes. Or thanks to Robbie. I supposed it was really Lucy's fault. Maybe. Someone was to blame. Maybe God, the old practical joker in the sky. Practical jokes are cruel if you stop to think about it. You never see the victim laughing, do you, except to cover humiliation?

I brushed past Sofie and picked up the broom.

"Coffee?" Sofie said.

"No." I bent down behind the refrigerator case to sweep crumbs into the dustpan. The broom crashed against the shelves, leaning at a crazy tilt. I sunk to the floor.

Sofie shuffled over. I reached for the broom handle and pulled myself up. I could be a regular person with a normal life. No one could tell otherwise.

Sofie peered over the counter, her glasses slipping on her nose.

"I'm fine," I said. "Fine." My voice loud and clear. "Nothing's wrong." I raised my chin, daring Sofie to contradict me.

Sofie pressed my arm with her hook the way she might test a cake to see if it was done. My breath spilled out in a choking rush. Sofie wrapped her fingers around my wrist and pulled me up until we stood face to face, the counter between us.

"What kind of fool are you taking me for?" Sofie asked softly. "For so many days, you are miserable. I'm here waiting for you to talk. To smile—maybe not, but at least to say something. I think to myself, I can wait. I can still be waiting. But don't you tell to me, there's nothing wrong."

I jerked my arm to free it, but Sofie's fingers held on like a handcuff of muscle and bone. "A *Dummkopf* keeps quiet with her troubles when there is someone wanting to listen."

"Don't feel sorry for me." I narrowed my green eye, trying to flash sparks. Sofie loosened her fingers. I slipped from her grasp and stepped back. "I don't need anyone feeling sorry for me." I turned away, trying to hide my tears. They trickled down my face and neck, under the collar of my uniform.

"Why should I feel sorry?" Sofie pressed a hand to her chest, sounding more like her usual self. "You are not the only one with problems in this world. You are young, healthy. I feel sorry for only one thing," she said. "All that feeling trapped inside is like poison. It will kill you. It will kill the part that matters unless you tell someone."

"I'm alright, I told you." I held the broom in front of me like a lance and moved from behind the counter. "Let's get the floor mopped so we can get out of here."

"Don't you be snarling at me." Sofie grabbed the end of the broom handle. "Wait."

My body and eyes ordered her out of the way. I'd scare Sofie into leaving me alone. The technique always worked with Lucy, teachers, even Danny.

"I'm not the foolish old woman you think I am."

"How do you know what I'm thinking?"

Sofie snatched the broom from my hands and shook it at me. "Listen. After Martin, I had a girl, born dead. A perfect baby. Fingernails like tiny shells. Dark hair, all over her head. So much hair on such a tiny baby. Ten toes—so small. All of them there. Perfect. She didn't breathe. I didn't speak good enough English to understand why. It doesn't matter why, with something like breathing. You do it and you live. You don't and—"

"Why are you telling me this?" When I swept I'd smeared a glob of chocolate icing across two squares of linoleum. Sofie hadn't even noticed. "Why are you telling me this?"

Sofie arranged the broom and dustpan against the wall. "My husband, Oskar, he said we should never talk about her again. For a long time I didn't. Never to him. Never to Martin, because Oskar said not to. A secret hurting that poisoned my heart. He did not want even our relatives in the old country to know. Only my sisters had known I was pregnant. I told them in a letter the baby did not live. That's all. Until after Oskar died, and I made my trip back there. I told my sisters everything. About the small fingers and toes. About her skin, warm then cold. Sadness I still have, but sadness is better than the thing I couldn't name that squeezes and tears inside."

Sofie clutched my arm again so tight the skin turned white. "Oskar, he would never talk. He felt guilty, I see now. He insisted we go to a hospital like rich Americans. Then he thought the hospital killed her. He tells me this now, now that he is dead. If he told me when he was alive, I would have said, it was not his fault, over and over until he believed. And we would have had a better life. He thought not talking was best, that it would help us to forget. Instead we together made a terrible silence full of remembering." She dropped my arm, removed her glasses, wiped her eyes, then the foggy lenses, with a shredded tissue.

"I don't see how telling your sisters helped. The baby was still dead."

Sofie didn't flinch. "*Geteiltes Leid ist halbes Leid*. Trouble shared is trouble halved. Even the telling is sharing." She waited. And waited.

"Alright." I said—to crack the hard silence, to break Sofie's penetrating stare. I'd start with a small problem, the smallest one on my list. I'd work up to the bigger ones. "I have a project due in art class tomorrow. My little brother scribbled with black pen all over the collage I made and left me with nothing to hand in. I'll fail art, which may not seem like a big deal, but without the credit, I can't graduate. Unless I make it up. My schedule for next term is packed with requirements. So, I need to put together a new project this afternoon. I'd better finish here so I can get home and think of something."

Sofie raised her eyebrows and waited. She knew the tears, the silences, were not because of an art project. She slid the tray of crumbs from the slicer, giving me time to squirm, and finally asked, "What kind of project? What is a collage?"

"Oh, a picture I made, gluing lots of other pictures together. The assignment is to make an autobiographical statement. A work of art that shows your inner self. It doesn't have to be a collage." I finished putting leftover donuts together on a tray and brought them to the freezer.

Sofie shook her head and followed me to the back. "Martin never had to do anything like that. What happened to lessons in grammar and mathematics?" She opened the door and scattered the crumbs.

"Ms. McLellan is the progressive type."

Sofie snorted.

Several inches of smooth, white snow covered the parking lot. Not a bird in sight. "They appreciate the crumbs even more in winter," Sofie said. She threw one handful, then another. The pigeons appeared, gray shadows among the snowflakes. They scuffled in the snow for the bread and flew away, leaving behind a lacy pattern of tracks.

I lifted the empty wash bucket into the sink.

"What about a cake?"

"What?" I yelled, over the sound of running water. "You want to feed the birds cake now? Maybe a stale one, but I don't think—"

"No, your art project. Make a cake. Remember the snake woman?"

"You're saying I'm a snake woman?"

"No, I'm saying the snake woman could be art maybe."

Sofie left to return the slicer tray to the front. I had made a lot of fancy cakes during the past two and a half months, but I didn't think of them as art. Still, when Sofie and I worked up a batch of Halloween cakes together, mine sold first. My jack o' lanterns glowed and grinned. My black cats looked ready to jump out of their cake boxes. My haunted houses terrified kids under twelve. Maybe I could make a cake that revealed my inner self.

I wrestled the bucket of water to the ground, rolled it out of the way. The floors could wait. I set out a cake board, pastry bags, and coloring. Sofie took the mop from the closet.

"It's not so easy," I frowned into a handful of spatulas. "What would you make if you had to do this assignment?"

Sofie rolled the bucket toward the swinging doors.

"I can do that," I said.

"No. No." Sofie stopped. Water sloshed onto the floor. "You do your project."

"But what would you be?"

"Don't laugh." She shook her hook at me. "I'll tell you if you won't be laughing."

"I won't."

"I would make a bird. A bird with feathers of every color, red, purple, gold." She stared at the ceiling as if she could see it perched up on the light fixture. Then she looked back at the water bucket. "Or maybe not, I don't know."

"A one of a kind bird. Valuable feathers. Hmm." I paused. "I look inside and all I see is a hole, a swamp, a pit, a worm."

"Ach!" Sofie scolded. "I told you before. You are young and healthy. A worm?" She caught my hand and dragged me over to the unfrosted cakes. "Come on, choose. A worm? Ach! *Eine Raupe*, maybe. A worm that will be a butterfly."

"A caterpillar you mean?" We'd had a caterpillar in elementary school, the chrysalis a pale green, with a circle of jewels around the top. One of the loaf cakes could look like a chrysalis if I rounded the corners, stood it on end. Maybe. I chose one reluctantly and brought it to the table. Sofie wheeled the wash bucket through the swinging doors.

I mixed an inspiring purple-blue icing, the color of the top of the sky, soon after sunset, on a summer night at the reservoir. I covered the loaf with ruffling, then added curlicues and stars of pinky-orange, the paisley patterns in my hippie friends' clothes. I began to feel the familiar sensation of working on a cake, moving like a river, sometimes smooth, sometimes rushing, flowing toward an invisible end. I could imagine lying inside the purple chrysalis, waiting, looking through the gauzy purple ceiling to glittering fireworks outside.

I pushed a dark haired doll into the top end of the cake, at an angle, like the figurehead on a ship. I redid the icing where the doll's body had mashed it down. I cut wings from an unfolded pie box, covered them with foil, and hitched them to the doll's torso with a delicate harness of string and gave her a bikini top of apricot stars.

When I glanced up, finished and out of breath, Sofie was nodding. "Your inside self. I like that."

"I don't know if she's really my inner self." I scraped icing from the pastry bags, glancing at the cake every couple of minutes out of the corner of my eye.

"She looks like she could break loose and fly," Sofie said.

"I wish."

"Here." Sofie folded a cake box. "Put her up on that shelf. She'll be safe there until tomorrow."

"Yeah, I'll pick her up on the way to school."

Only I would have a cake. Ms. McLellan would be impressed. I pictured my classmates, mouths hanging open in astonishment when I lifted the butterfly girl from her box. I could hear them breaking into spontaneous applause.

"Hey girls!" Tony burst through the door in a swirl of snow. "You'd better get home while you can. This is a blizzard."

"We're not done cleaning up." I tossed the pastry bags and bowls into the sink.

"Leave it," he said.

"That bad?" Sofie craned her neck to see out the window.

"It's slick. I'm going to empty the register and clear out."

Sofie turned to me. "I'll give you a ride home."

I hadn't been in the VW since the morning Sofie had scared me. "Thanks."

Sofie unfolded an accordion-like sheet of plastic, her rain bonnet, set it over her white curls, and tied it under her chin. She stooped to slip on her plastic boots, the kind that folded in front and fastened with an elastic loop over a button. She gathered her purse and bundles. I pulled on my pea coat and buttoned it, wishing I had a hat.

"Be careful driving," Tony warned.

"Oh, I never worry about that."

Sofie refused my arm as we started across the parking lot, heads down, watching our feet. I was glad I had high-tops.

An icy spot surprised us, and Sofie slipped. I caught her elbow and kept her standing, but her loaf of rye dropped to the ground, the wax bag split open, and the slices of bread spread out across the snow in a crusty fan.

"Let me get that." I started to bend over.

"No!" Sofie clung to my arm. She swallowed, smoothing out the terror in her voice. "The birds will come."

"You and those birds!" I kept my voice confident and cheerful as I opened the car door and helped Sofie in. "You warm it up. I'll clean it off." I found the scraper on the floor.

Sofie sunk into her seat, eyes closed. Through the windshield, she looked tiny and frail, the Volkswagen's little steering wheel large in front of her. I lifted the windshield wiper to brush away a ridge of snow, reaching easily over the rounded hood to clear the whole window.

I slid in beside Sofie, shaking snow from my hair. "I'll tell you one thing," I said to make conversation. "I am sick to death of pies."

"We'll see many more next week with Thanksgiving coming." Sofie concentrated on the road.

"I wouldn't even let a pie appear at my Thanksgiving dinner, would you?"

"No."

We inched along Main Street. There was no other traffic.

"Unless perhaps I heat a pie of frozen turkey. No sense in cooking more."

"Your son isn't coming?"

"No, too busy."

"You're going to be alone on Thanksgiving?" If she could pry into my business, I felt free to poke into hers.

"What is so terrible? It's another day to me." Sofie pressed her lips tight.

I surprised myself by wanting to invite Sofie to dinner. I planned to cook a real Thanksgiving dinner that year. But what would Sofie think of Lucy? Our house? The boys' manners? We couldn't impersonate a normal family no matter how hard we tried. Forget it. I had the sense to keep my mouth shut.

"If you would like to come over…" Sofie began. "I know you'll be busy with your family but maybe for dessert, in the late afternoon? No pie." She stared unblinking at the road, her face blank. I knew that trick; it meant she really wanted me to come.

"I'd like that," I said. If Sofie tried to get me talking about myself I could always change the subject.

My mind was so busy trying to imagine Sofie's house, I almost missed my corner. "You can drop me off right up there, on the corner of Fourth. The side streets are probably worse than this."

"Well, good." Sofie stopped the car. "I'll see you in the morning, when you pick up your butterfly girl."

"Yeah, thanks. Not just for the ride."

Words belonging to someone else, an orphaned five year old in a sappy, old-fashioned story, certainly not to me, tumbled through my mind. 'I love you.' 'I can be good.' 'Take me home.'

"Thanks," I said again. "Sofie?"

"*Ja?*"

"What was your baby's name, your little girl?"

"Hanna." Sofie answered so quickly she seemed to know the question before it hit the heated air. "Hanna Amalia Dora Schmidt. Amalia and Dora for my sisters. Hanna for my mother." She stared straight ahead.

I nodded and closed the door gently without slamming it. The VW crawled away slow and steady until swallowed by the snow. I walked the two blocks to my house, imagining Sofie at home, making a cup of coffee, soaking her feet, miles of ocean between her and her sisters, miles of land between her and her son, talking to her dead husband who told her things he couldn't say when he was alive.

Snow fell through the night. I woke long enough to hear the school cancellations, clicked the radio off, and sank back into bed to sleep until noon if Kevin let me.

Robbie pounded on my door. "Wake up!" he yelled. "Phone."

"You don't have to break the door down. Who is it? I'll call them later." I wrapped my pillow around my face.

"It's your boss. Says he has to talk to you now." Robbie ended his sentence with a blow of his fist against the wood. I threw my pillow at the door. My breath formed clouds in front of my face. We'd run out of oil. I tried to think where I could borrow the money to fill the tank. The landlord sometimes lent it to us. He didn't care whether we froze, but he did care about his pipes.

Wishing I had a real bed so I could swing my legs over the side and slide my feet right into a pair of fuzzy slippers, I wrapped my blanket around me and slogged across my lumpy mattress, really waking when my bare feet hit the icy linoleum. The sound of cartoons jangled through the house.

Tony hadn't wasted any time trying to get me in to work. Maybe I'd say no. I had to track down oil money somewhere. If I started using the roll of bills tucked between my mattress and the wall—that was it. I'd never see it again. Lucy was more likely to pay the landlord back than her daughter. Robbie had left the telephone receiver dangling on its springy cord.

"Hope the snow keeps up," I said in a variation on Tony's standard joke about rain—if it keeps up, it won't come down.

"I need you to come in," he said.

"I could really use a day off." I wound the phone cord around my finger. "It can't be busy down there."

"It's not busy," he said. "My kids'll come in later, but I need someone to put up orders, someone who knows what she's doing. Sofie's in the hospital."

Preoccupied with planning my next wise ass retort, I wasn't sure I'd heard right. "What?"

"Sofie fell yesterday and broke her hip."

"But I was with her yesterday. She was fine." I stood first on one foot, then the other to warm my feet against my calves. I pulled the blanket tighter at my neck.

"It was in the afternoon. She fell walking from her car to her house. A neighbor's dog found her. You know, her neighbor, John, comes in here sometimes? The guy with the harmonica? She'd been there awhile. Maybe a half an hour."

My ear hurt. I was mashing it with the phone. I saw Sofie sprawled in the snow, a dog sniffing around her, a huge drooling rescue dog with a barrel around its neck, but I didn't know any dogs like that in Rivertown. "How is she?"

"Not too good. I called her son in California. He'll be here when he can, but with this weather who knows when that'll be? I thought I'd head over to the hospital this morning after deliveries—say hello. When can you get here?"

"Soon," I whispered. "Right away. I'll get dressed and leave now."

"Great!" Tony sounded cheerful then, like the Tony I was used to. "I'll time you. See how fast you can make it. Wear your boots. Snow's deep out there. Fourteen inches and still falling."

I hung up the phone and stood, switching off feet to keep them from freezing, clutching a fistful of blanket, elbows tight against my stomach. I should've helped Sofie to her door. When she slipped in the parking lot, I should've known not to let her walk alone. I'd heard of old people breaking hips and never recovering. I could've helped her to her house, but I hadn't.

Robbie walked in wearing his coat. His tough-guy walk had become a natural part of him, so natural that he'd walk that way in his sleep. Before he was arrested, he only used it in public.

He rummaged around in the mess on the counter. "Where's the bread?"

I didn't answer. What did bread have to do with anything?

He turned. "Come on, Wylie. I want some toast. Are we out of bread or what? What's the matter? Your boss fire you?"

Robbie had seen Sofie at the bakery, but didn't know anything about her. I had hardly mentioned her at home. I lived in a house full of people I couldn't talk to about anything important. The Haight-Ashbury hippies, they knew about expressing themselves and love and making art together. They'd spot the snake hidden in the bridesmaid's dress. They'd understand the butterfly girl with her colors and shining wings.

"Hey?" He stepped closer to me, his forehead wrinkling. In his dark eyes glimmered the faintest suggestion of a crack in his attitude.

"I'm not fired," I said. "He wanted me to come into work. The woman I work with fell yesterday in the snow. She's in the hospital."

"You don't want to work, tell him no." He turned away. "You think there's any bread left around here, or should I stop wasting my time looking for it?" He tossed an empty cereal box and a rotten banana into the trash can. "Two three pointers!" He picked up one of Lucy's glasses and turned it upside down. "Look, her ice melted and froze again during the night. I think we're out of oil."

"No kidding." We shared the same family, the same cold house, the same dead town, but we might as well have been born and raised in different galaxies. He found the end of a loaf of bread and dropped it into the toaster.

"I have to go to work." If he didn't pop the toaster up by hand, the bread would burn. "Do you think you could call the oil company?"

"Sure, but what will I do when they ask for money?"

"You figure it out." I shut myself in the bathroom and leaned my head against the door. Don't, don't, don't, don't cry, I thought. Wash your face. Brush your teeth. Get dressed. Get out of the house. Everything will be okay.

"Damn," Robbie yelled.

I passed through the smoke-filled kitchen, the ruined toast a slice of charcoal in Robbie's hand. I didn't stop until I was out on the porch, not even to pull on my coat. The houses across the street looked like shadows behind the thick veil of falling snow.

"Robbie," I yelled back before pulling the door shut. "Make sure Kevin has his coat on. And mittens if you can find any. Borrow the oil money from Mr. Clark." I didn't wait for an answer.

My fingers, toes, and cheeks stung. I thought of Sofie, on the frozen ground for half an hour. She could've been covered with snow, left until neighbor kids came to earn money shoveling her walk.

Main Street, blanketed by packed snow, lay deserted, as far as I could see, except for a lone police car parked in front of Ida's. Officer Belinsky. Sofie told me he came in every weekday morning, drank two cups of coffee, ate six donuts, all on the house, and never left a tip. Officer Belinsky. The last person I wanted to see. A plow growled past.

Light from inside Ida's spilled warm and buttery onto the snowy sidewalk. Tony stood behind the counter, pouring coffee. He belonged in back. Sofie should have been holding that coffee pot.

"Glad you could make it!" he boomed, the moment I opened the door. "Take off your coat. Stay awhile."

The yeasty air filled my nose and throat. The fluorescent lighting hurt my eyes and gave everyone's skin a bluish tinge.

"She's still asleep." Belinsky lifted his cup in my direction. "Give the girl a break. Give her some coffee."

"I don't need a break." I hoped he wouldn't try to start a conversation about Robbie or my mother. "I just got here."

"Then let's see you move," said Tony. "Bread, rolls, donuts—everything has to be brought up front. Orders have to be put up." He looked at his watch. "We're late, hours late."

"Give her a break," Belinsky said again. "Everyone will be late for everything today. I don't see the crowds beating down the door here."

I looked from Tony, smiling behind the counter, red bandanna around his head, to Belinsky, wiping donut grease from a thick lipped grin with a wad of paper napkins. I couldn't remember why I'd wanted to be there.

"Bring me another glazed donut, honey, will you?" said Belinsky, adjusting his belt buckle.

"Get him a donut," said Tony. "And he's right, about the crowds he doesn't see. Put up the orders before you bring stuff to the front."

Belinsky pretended not to notice that I slammed his donut down in front of him so hard the plate should've cracked. "Thanks sweetie." He winked. "I hope you're keeping an eye on that brother of yours. Or maybe it's your mother who needs watching."

I bit my tongue until the doors swung shut behind me. Alone in the back, I packed dozens of hotdog and hamburger rolls for the Townline Diner and boxes of assorted donuts for the seven corner stores in town. I turned putting up orders into a matter of life and death by telling myself that if I lined up a row of chocolate covered donuts without any of them falling over, Sofie would get better. If I cut a tray of brownies and all the lines were straight, Sofie wouldn't die.

"I'll start loading these into the van," Tony said. "Are you almost done?" His sudden entrance almost toppled a row of donuts. I steadied them with a finger and sighed. "Are you alright?" Tony asked.

I nodded. He had no idea how close he'd come to causing a disaster. "These bags and boxes are ready. I'll have this one full by the time you load the others." I quickly filled the last box and met Tony at the door where I set it in his gloved hands.

"Wait." I caught his arm. His eyes were level with mine. "Can you tell Sofie..." Tell Sofie what? I'm thinking of her? Hope she gets better? I didn't want to sound like a get well card.

Tony waited. The van's engine ran, spewing clouds of exhaust into the cold air. "Tell her to let me know if she needs anything. Anything."

"Will do." Snow covered his boots. "Hold the fort," he yelled over his shoulder. "At least one of my kids should show up soon."

After he left, the bakery was still as a graveyard, rolls, bread, and cream puffs all waiting to be moved. The radio played in front, the easy listening music Tony thought customers liked. Sofie and I always switched it to rock and roll. It helped us work faster.

No customers came in during my trips back and forth to fill the cases so I didn't have to smile at anyone.

Antonia arrived just as I brought out the last tray of dinner rolls. "I can't believe he opened the bakery. In this weather. I could've gotten killed driving here. He's crazy."

"Everything's out of the back," I said. "You can stay here and wait on customers. I'll do the cleaning up."

"I doubt we'll have any customers." Antonia shook the snow off her coat onto the floor where it melted into a puddle. She could wipe it up. I wasn't about to add her to the long list of people I cleaned up after.

A hunched, dark shape pushed against the door, bringing with it a torrent of snow. "Hey, ladies." When the man took off his snow-covered, black knit cap, I recognized John MacKenzie, Sofie's neighbor, the one who had been to Vietnam, the one who worked now and then with Danny at Swan's Auto Body, the one who came in to Ida's to gulp coffee before heading over to Rivertown Billiards where he switched to beer. "Coffee and beer," he always said as he paid his bill with shaking hands, "poor man's cocaine." He'd found Sofie, maybe saved her life. I hurried to set him up with a cup and saucer.

"Ooooh baby, it's cold outside." He took off his gloves, rubbed his hands together, and seated himself at the counter; Antonia scurried to grab the pot and slosh coffee into the empty cup.

"Go on." She glared at me. "You said I should wait on the customers."

I tried to think of something scathing to say about how efficient Antonia was when it came to waiting on handsome men. I wanted to ask John about Sofie, whether she was even conscious when he found her. How close had she been to freezing to death? Did she blame me?

My tongue felt too big in my mouth. I couldn't form words. He spun on his stool, leaning his back against the counter, his legs sticking out halfway across the sand and salt splashed floor. Sofie would be mopping it if she wasn't in the hospital.

"Wylie Steele, right?"

He knew who I was.

"How long you been working here?"

"Since September."

I had to ask about Sofie. Had she said anything? How long had she been lying there?

He took a long swallow, emptying his cup, and reached around to rap it against his saucer, signaling for more. Antonia poured again.

"I was talking to your boyfriend the other day while we were pounding out a fender. On a Plymouth Duster. A real wreck. Thought you should know—he's feeling a little neglected. His woman working all the time."

His woman? Danny had no business talking about us. He wasn't even friends with this guy. John had graduated the year before we started high school. His woman. Danny wouldn't say that. Those had to be John's words.

"Your neighbor," I began. "Sofie…"

John didn't hear. "I told him, if he doesn't want you working, he's got to work harder himself. To provide for you. Buy you nice things. Take you places. Why do think I'm out this early on a day like this?"

"Why?" Antonia asked, leaning over the counter. "Ready for more coffee?"

"Thanks, sweetheart. My truck is right outside. With a plow on the front. I've been waiting for this snow. Driveways, parking lots, I've got a whole day of work. If it keeps snowing like this, I'll work all night. I could keep a harem of women happy on what I'll make. Tell your boyfriend to plan ahead. Buy a truck." He grinned, pulled his harmonica from his back pocket and slapped it against his thigh.

"We don't tell each other what to do," I said. "I'll be in back, Antonia." I bet Sofie's husband hadn't told Sofie what to do. I couldn't imagine anyone telling Sofie what to do.

Safe behind the swinging doors, I fell into the rhythm of washing trays, the small splashes of warm, soapy water, the scratch of the scrub brush against the worn metal. Lucy's drunken face appeared among the bubbles, brightening as she talked about wearing a short red dress and holding heavy trays high, until she got married, until she got pregnant, until she became a drunk in a pink bathrobe who lived for solitaire and soap operas. I scrubbed it away. Strains of music came from the front. Antonia applauded. John played some more. I switched on the radio, full blast, to our station, Sofie's and mine. I thought about Danny, how he scratched my back just right, not just where it itched but the whole thing. I pictured him in bed on his day off. I'd call him later. His woman. He'd never call me that.

It wasn't until I'd dried and stacked all the trays that I noticed the box with my butterfly cake. It seemed like months since I'd made it, not just a day. I couldn't look at it.

Sofie in the snow saved by a neighbor's dog. No one told Sofie what to do. When she slipped no one was there to steady her. Sofie. Questions knotted together in a tangle so tight my head ached. If I could only find the beginning phrase, the first word, of any one of them, maybe I could ask John MacKenzie for the information I needed. What if I asked and he didn't have the answers? What if no one did?

I stopped thinking. It hurt too much. I assembled tips, bags, spatulas, and mixing bowls. The air took on weight and a greenish tint. My movements were slow and deliberate. Nothing clattered. A muted underwater roaring sounded in my head.

I chose a small sheet cake from the rack and carved into it from the edges, leaving a solid chunk of cake in the middle with twisted spokes sticking out from it on all sides, like tentacles. I forgot Ida's, forgot Antonia and John MacKenzie and my mother. I forgot Sofie. I forgot Danny. The icing, cake, and spatulas were all I knew. I stacked the cut away pieces of cake onto the middle chunk to build it high and covered the mound with icing the color of a day-old bruise. I used a ruffling tip. Instead of ruffling in careful rows, one on top of the other, the way Sofie had shown me, I switched directions again and again, vertical, horizontal, and diagonal rows crisscrossing, overlapping, six layers thick in some places, barely hiding the cake in others.

When the whole thing was covered, I reached into the box of doll picks and, without counting, grabbed seven of them, one for each tentacle. I tore off the plastic and jabbed them into the cake, blonde, brunette, black, white, upright, face down, belly up. Each was in the clutches of a tentacle, helpless, panicked, stiff plastic arms raised. A bit more icing around where I'd shoved the bodies and I was finished. Emptied, I collapsed onto a stool and closed my eyes.

"Wylie." Antonia pushed open the door. "I don't need to be here. Nobody else is coming in today. When my father gets back..." She stopped. "What is that?"

"I don't know."

"Well, it didn't just magically appear. You made it, didn't you?"

I studied the backs of my hands, spread out in front of me and slowly turned them palms up. I curled my fingers into fists, then unclenched them. The pattern of lines on my palms almost matched the cracks in the ceiling over my bed. I'd never noticed that before.

Antonia stood in the doorway, behind me. "It's terrible," she said. "Why would anyone make anything like that? What is it?"

"It's an art project."

"What kind of an art project is that? It's hideous. My father isn't going to like it—you wasting all that icing and cake and all those dolls."

"Shut up, Antonia," I said. "Shut your mouth. Go up front and check your makeup."

"You can't talk to me like that. I'll tell my father. He'll fire you. Wait'll he sees the mess you've made. And the cake and time you've wasted." She flounced out the door.

Waves of fear, one right after another, glued me to the stool. I couldn't even clean up. The fear I'd lose my job and never save the money I needed, never get to ice another cake, grew huge, fueled by other fears too frightening to think about. Maybe I should rescue the dolls, wash them, and tuck them away in their box. I still had the plastic to rewrap them. I could throw the cake in the trash. I could deny the whole thing. As I washed the spatulas and bowls, I tried to convince myself to destroy the monster.

When I finished the dishes, I looked for something else to keep me busy in the back so I wouldn't have to face Antonia, something to make Tony know I was indispensable. Across the room my monster slept on the table. I wouldn't throw it out.

Tony blew into the bakery at noon, carrying a stack of empty boxes that towered above his head, blocking his view. "Wylie, help me out here," he yelled.

I dropped the cannoli shell I was about to fill with vanilla cream and ran to catch half the boxes. "Thanks. Cold out there." He dumped his boxes onto a stack in the corner and motioned for me to do the same.

"How is she?"

He pulled off his wet, suede gloves, unwound his scarf, stamped the snow off his feet, and checked his watch. "She's probably being cut open this very minute."

I put my hand on my hip and felt the bone. I shuddered.

"She seemed fine. Talking about coming back to work. I told her to hurry up, that we need her. She said you could do anything she could. Quite a compliment." He winked. "Not true, is it?"

"No, of course that's not true." But I began a mental checklist: fill donuts, yes, wait on customers, yes, clean up, yes, decorate cakes, yes. I tried to think of something Sofie could do that I couldn't. Sofie was better at working with Tony's kids. I would never get along with Antonia. I wished I'd kept my mouth shut about her makeup. What would she say to Tony?

"Things been quiet around here?" he asked.

"Antonia's out front. I finished everything back here and had some time so I hope you don't mind, I made an art project for school. I'll pay for the supplies." I pointed to my monster.

"Whoa!" said Tony. "It's a wedding cake for a mass murderer."

"Consider the supplies your tip for coming in on your day off." He approached the cake. "An art project, you say? For school?"

I nodded.

"You be careful they don't send you to one of those psychiatrist doctors. They might think you're crazy, coming up with something like that. They might think you have problems."

Problems.

"Do you think Sofie's son'll make it today?" I wanted mostly to change the subject, but part of me itched to meet a real person from San Francisco who had better things to do on Thanksgiving than spend it in Rivertown.

Tony looked out the window. "He's supposed to if the weather doesn't hold things up."

"You've met him before?"

"Sofie's son? A few times. When Sofie first started here he used to come for Thanksgiving or Christmas. But the last time he came must be ten or fifteen years ago now." Tony turned away from the window, kicked at the pile of boxes to straighten it.

"What's he like?" I still hoped he might have a ponytail and a beard. Some old guys did.

"Friendly, in a quiet way. Polite. Sofie likes to show him off. He's...Never mind."

"What? Tell me." Maybe he'd been in antiwar protests. Maybe he played the guitar.

"He's...well, you'll see. I shouldn't say anything." Tony pretended to zip his lips. "Sofie can't understand why he didn't stick around here." He shook his head. "Can't understand it myself. Kids don't realize how important family is. That's why this country's falling apart."

"He's not a kid. Isn't he older than you are?" If the country was falling apart, it wasn't because of the kids. I had a list of reasons, starting with disappearing fathers and mothers who drink too much.

Tony laughed. "Well, you're right about that. You are. You're right about that." Still laughing, he went to check the front before going home to bed.

I left without saying good-bye to Antonia, carrying two bags of trash to stuff into the trash cans. Snow was still falling slowly, in large flakes. The smooth, white cover on the parking lot was broken only by the tracks of the van's tires and Tony's path to the door. The streetlights shone, even though the sky was still light. Snowflakes flew around them like clusters of moths.

Looking up at the sky, I dropped the bags of trash and lay down in the snow. I moved my arms back and forth. I stood up, took a step, and repeated the whole process again and again until the parking lot was covered with angels caught in a tangle of boot prints.

CHAPTER 2

▼

MARTIN

I slid my fingers behind my mother's mailbox, feeling for the spare key on the same nail where it had been for the whole fifty years of my life. Sofie had sworn me to secrecy as soon as I could speak, ensuring my cooperation by describing in detail the unsavory people who might get wind of its location if I breathed a word to anyone, including my kindergarten teacher, and what these same people might do to me or the family's possessions. As a child, I'd worried about burglars stealing my father's tools and the radio. I feared disappearing like the Lindbergh baby. Even now, I looked up and down the tidy street to make sure no one was watching. I unlocked the door and slipped the key onto my key ring. Then I stepped inside.

Fifteen years since I'd entered this house and it smelled as it always had, of Lemon Pledge and Johnson's floor wax. Dust motes hung in the shaft of morning sun. They wouldn't dare land on Sofie's coffee table. Every surface with the potential to shine, did. Sofie's rocking chair, the one she'd rocked me in, the one my father had made for her, sat opposite the TV. She loved her wrestling. Her weekly phone calls always included an update on who'd beaten whom, her voice indignant as she recounted Killer Brooks' dirty moves, reverent describing the victories of "Chief" Jay Strongbow and Bruno Sammartino. I'd given up trying to convince her that the whole thing was fixed.

The plastic covered couch cushions resisted my weight. Everything was hard in my mother's house, even the pillows, and I'd never even realized it until I began baby-sitting for Ivy Jane, the little girl three doors down. My favorite part of that job was sinking deep into their sofa after I'd put IJ to bed. She still lived there. It was her hard-drinking, supposedly good for nothing son, John, who had found Sofie half frozen in the snow.

I should have gone straight to the hospital instead of sitting, remembering. When Tony called, I'd been at my workbench, where I'd spent every evening since Erich's death in May. Two lines of epoxy squeezed out, balsa strip poised to mix them, about to glue the engine mount to the firewall of an especially sleek model biplane, a stagger wing beech, when the phone jangled. My first thought on hearing Tony's voice was that Sofie had died. When I heard she'd broken her hip, my first thought, I kid you not, was 'Leave it to Sofie to resort to something like this to get me home for Thanksgiving. Surprised it took her this long to think of it.'

I went to my old room to lie down, just for a few moments, before going to the hospital. No one could rest on a plastic-covered couch. I lay down, taking care not to muss the chenille spread. Good thing my mother couldn't see me with my shoes on the bed. My Bleriot monoplane, a real beauty, covered in dark blue silk purchased more than thirty-five years ago with paper route money, still hung from my ceiling, faded but dust free. How did Sofie do it? With a vacuum cleaner and something to stand on? Perhaps the real question was why?

But I knew why. Since Erich died, I stayed later and later at work, "forgot" to buy toilet paper or mayonnaise so I'd have to make another trip to the store. I'd cleaned every slat on the Venetian blinds as carefully as Sofie would have, vacuumed the carpet when it didn't need it, duties to fill an empty life. My mother was lonely. Now she was lonely and flattened by a broken hip, and I was lonely and flat on my back in my childhood room, unable to force myself to go to her. It had taken everything I had to leave my apartment in Bernal Heights, arrange a leave from my job where everyone knew me as the engineer quickest with a slide rule, who never missed a day of work. Even when Erich was sick and dying quickly of melanoma, I'd gone into the office every day, done my job. No one knew my grief.

I had to rest, just for fifteen minutes, but my body ached and buzzed. My eyelid twitched. Downstairs, the phone rang and rang and rang. And stopped. And started.

Perhaps Sofie was trying to call. There was a time I would have rushed to the phone, but since Erich died I'd stopped hurrying. Instead, I put one foot in front of the other, my whole body tight, as if walking on a sheet of ice, sure I'd slip and fall.

I picked up the phone even though the ringing had stopped. I had dreams in which somehow I knew Erich was on the other end of the phone, but I'd answer too late or the connection was bad. The dial tone hummed, a faraway echo of the humming in my head. I remembered Erich on one of our Caribbean vacations with a shell to his ear, laughing—"People always say they hear the ocean. All I've ever heard is a toilet flushing." Now I heard flushing toilets in shells too. I should call Sofie, tell her I was in town, that I'd be over soon to see her. Instead, I hung up the phone.

I made myself a cup of tea. Even after fifteen years, even if I were blindfolded, I could find the tea bags in their canister, the teaspoons in their drawer to the left of the sink, the sugar bowl in the corner cupboard.

I was rinsing my cup when the doorbell rang. The neighbor, IJ's son, John MacKenzie, a small child when I last saw him, had noticed the rental car, and in the way people are compelled to talk about tragedy and disaster, especially if they've played a heroic role, wanted to tell about finding Sofie in the snow. I smelled beer on his breath. John must be in his early twenties. I heard he'd served in Vietnam. A pit bull panted and strained at the leash in his hand.

"Thought you should know she was talking about angels and shit." John raised his dark eyebrows almost to his hairline. "And 'while he...while he'...I said, 'while he what?' She kept repeating 'while he' and never finished the sentence. If you find out what she was talking about I'd like to know. Woke up wondering about it in the middle of the night." He leaned over to pat the dog's quivering side and smiled up at me, the smile of a drunk man who is handsome and strong and knows it.

I disliked dogs and drunks, but John's smile disarmed me to the extent that I might even have given the dog a tentative pat if the pit bull hadn't been quivering so hard.

"How's she doing anyway?" John asked. "Shredder, cut it out." He yanked the dog back from my crotch and smacked the animal. "Sorry. Dogs will be dogs. Anyway, it was old Shredder here who noticed your mother. I might have walked right by. You owe him a dog biscuit. Or even a box of dog biscuits."

"My mother has no dog. So, you see, she wouldn't have any dog food or biscuits or anything of that sort."

"A joke." John rolled his eyes.

A joke? Exhausted, I replayed the conversation in my mind. So tired, I missed things, missed the point. Why was this man—just the kind of man who had made my life here in Rivertown such hell I never wanted to come back—why was he at my—my mother's—door? Worse, why was this muscular mass of dog flesh lunging at me? Sofie. They'd saved my mother's life. John had asked how Sofie was. I hadn't answered. I'd do that. I'd answer. Then I'd ask John about IJ, he'd answer, and we'd say good-bye.

"She's broken her hip. I believe they operated on it already."

"She's out there all the time, shoveling snow, mowing her lawn. I offer to help, but no, she wants to do it herself. Hard for anybody to be laid up, but for someone like your mother…" He jerked the dog back again. Shredder growled.

"Yes, well…"

"My mother says if you need anything, give a yell. She'll probably be sending you more food than you'll ever be able to eat." John patted his stomach. "Since coming back I've been putting it on. She blames the beer, but her mashed potatoes will do it faster than Budweiser ever will."

IJ was a frazzled young mother the last time I saw her. She'd feed me even if I told her it wasn't necessary. I looked forward to unpeeling the foil from her meatloaf or lasagna. "She doesn't need to send food. But, please give her my best and tell her I'll give her a call." Thinking of Ivy Jane, I felt a momentary fondness for the son. "You know, I made more money babysitting for your mother when she was a girl than I made on my paper route. In fact, she'd help me with the papers." I didn't tell John how I was afraid to go to the houses with dogs or bullies and would send Ivy to the door instead, on her sturdy little legs, her knees always covered with scrapes and scabs she'd pick even though I told her not to, her dirty socks slipping down into her red sneakers.

He looked past me with an inattention Erich would have described as 'scanning the room for someone more important to talk to.'

"Yes, well." I cleared my throat. If the young man were sober he would know it was time to leave.

"She's talked about you," John said, looking me up and down with slitted eyes.

I stiffened. IJ had always liked me. She wouldn't have anything bad to say.

"I'm glad you didn't try to offer me a drink or anything," John said. "I don't have a problem with guys like you, but don't try anything with me."

"I have no idea what you're talking about," I answered. Don't flatter yourself, was what I should have said.

My first encounter back in Rivertown. I shouldn't be surprised. I wouldn't say anything to IJ. She'd be embarrassed by her son. Sons. Embarrassing sons. I should see Sofie. The reason I came. I'd see her and figure out how soon I could leave.

Driving to the hospital, I had that old trouble breathing. No matter what route I'd taken home from school I'd been chased, spit on, pummeled until I cried. For being a sissy with a German accent. A kraut-nancy boy. Memories of those childhood fights stirred my insides in a deeper place than memories of my time in the Pacific on the U.S.S. Montpelier. Images of Rivertown appeared in my dreams in black, white, and shades of gray with only an occasional splash of color, IJ's red sneakers, the orange-yellow punch at my mother's pinochle parties, the green basket my father used to collect mushrooms in the woods at the end of our block. The buildings, street corners, I remembered as monochrome, just as they looked now in the snowy winter twilight.

The bright light of the hospital lobby burned my eyes. Wheels whispered and squeaked across polished linoleum. Phones buzzed and rang. Overwhelmed, I fell into a chair, too low for my long legs. The last time I'd been in a hospital, Erich had died. Erich had never been to Rivertown. He'd grown up in the southern California desert among roadrunners and date palms, canyons and joshua trees, the only child of parents whose graciousness and good manners eclipsed any concerns they may have had about their son's love life. We slept in Erich's childhood room in a double bed, at the end of a wing of the sprawling, air-conditioned, one story house. No questions asked. When Erich died, his parents never challenged my authority to plan the cremation, the memorial service, the distribution of possessions. At the service, his father spent several long minutes clearing his throat before reading a few lines from an index card about Erich stealing the show back in Sunday School as one of the three kings. He'd tripped on the hem of his robe, dropped the myrrh, and made it seem part of the performance. He added that Erich had been voted most likely to succeed by his high school class, an honor Erich had never mentioned to me, even jokingly.

Back at the apartment, one of Erich's long haired English students, the student director of *Our Town*, Erich's last drama club play, plucked the coffee stained, dog-eared, copy of *Howl* signed by Allen Ginsberg himself, from a bookshelf and began to read the title poem. He passed the book to the next grieving student who passed it to the next. Before I could tell them Erich would have preferred W.H. Auden, perhaps "In Memory of W.B. Yeats," an unstoppable, full-length reading had begun. I still squirmed at the memory of Erich's pearl-earringed, gray-gloved, purse-lipped, mother passing the book to her husband who, without a glance, passed it to Jean Paul, who read with a booming voice, "who ate fire in paint hotels or drank turpentine in Paradise Alley, death, or purgatoried their torsos night after night/with dreams, with drugs, with waking nightmares, alcohol and cock and endless balls."

One learns a lot about someone when visiting the place in which he grew up. With the exception of our Caribbean trips, Erich had never been out of California. He'd never seen snow falling. If Erich could have met John MacKenzie and his dog, seen the dilapidated high school building and the perfectly manicured football field, heard the Saturday evening programming on the valley's radio station, Stas Wasniewski's Polish Variety Hour, followed by live coverage of the Lanes and Games Weekly Bowling Tournament, and Vito Mascone's Italian Music to Woo Your Wife With, he'd know I hadn't exaggerated anything. Mostly, Erich should have met Sofie. To really know someone you need to know his mother.

I wondered if I would have been more or less likely to bring Erich home if my father were alive. I pressed my forehead hard in a futile attempt to push my thoughts in another direction. No reason to think about my father now. He'd died in Yale New Haven Hospital, not here. Busy finishing my exams at the end of my first year at MIT, I had put off coming home, until my father was too sick to notice.

I'd found my mother sitting at my dying father's bedside, clinging to his limp hand. She didn't rant, scold or even pin me with her stormy eyes. I would have preferred it if she had. She only said, "I'm glad you're finally here," dropped my father's hand as if she couldn't have held on another moment, and slumped back in a chair, smaller and more exhausted than I'd ever seen her. My father's arm hung over the side of the bed. I held the dangling hand securely between mine and studied my father's unconscious face. While I'd been writing lab reports and scribbling my final exams, I'd missed Oskar Schmidt's last words. I'd missed the last moments of conscious, companionable silence. My father died that night without even squeezing my hand. I had to believe that he had felt the presence of his only living child, that coming home late was better than not coming at all.

I lifted myself out of the lobby chair and made my way down a hall, through bright glass doors decorated with gaudy paper turkeys. The last time I'd been back, it had been Thanksgiving too, 1960, just after Erich had followed me from the poetry aisle of a Berkeley bookstore to the cash register and out to the sidewalk where he invited me across the street to The Cafe Med for caffe lattes. I'd nodded and felt my life change. When Erich reached across the table to wipe foamy steamed milk from my neatly trimmed mustache, I decided to become a person who took chances, a person who could fall in love. Just two weeks after that, back in Rivertown, as Sofie dragged me to the bakery to show me off, talking for me as if I were a little boy, with IJ too busy being wife and mother to do more than stop by and assault me with a barrage of hungry questions about life in

California, I'd panicked. I didn't know what frightened me more—that no one knew me or that they did. Fifteen years later, in the hallway of Rivertown Hospital, I was no closer to understanding that fear.

I arrived at the door of my mother's room, unable to remember how I'd found it. I hadn't asked directions. One bed had curtains drawn around it. In the other, the one nearest the window, I saw her, tiny and old, leaning against a stack of pillows, eyes closed, her hair poking out from her head in haphazard wisps, her leg connected to a system of pulleys and weights. I touched her arm. Her eyelids flickered.

"I'm glad you're finally here," she said. "We have so many orders to do for Thanksgiving."

"Mother," I whispered. "It's me, Martin."

She blinked. "Plates and screws," she said. "Inside where only bones and blood and meat should be. I am like a robot now. Soon I will be having rust."

"I caught the first plane I could."

"They say I won't be here long," she said, voice slurred. "Feed the birds."

"Does it hurt?" I asked.

Her watery eyes focused on me. "Martin?"

Who did she think it was? "Yes, I came as soon as I could."

"No. Not soon. Fifteen years is not soon. And you said for Thanksgiving you were not coming." Her forehead wrinkled. "So long it's been. I wanted us to be having a nice visit, but now I am here, stuck in bed in this place."

"I came to help," I said, expecting her to tell me she didn't need it, the answer I was used to, the answer I thought I wanted to hear.

She closed her eyes. "*Danke sehr*," she said, voice small. She reached for my hand and stroked it. I waited, throat tight.

Her fingers stopped moving. She seemed to be asleep. "You're welcome," I said. Erich always laughed at my habitual good manners.

Back at the house, I unlocked the door, thinking I should have left a light on. Dark came so early—it was barely evening.

I unpacked my few clothes, arranged my razor, shaving brush, aftershave, dental floss, toothpaste and toothbrush in a row on the toilet tank, and ran a tub full of steaming bath water. I had one leg immersed when the doorbell rang. Instead of answering, I stepped in with my other foot. By the time I dried and dressed, surely the person would have given up. I slid into the heat. The ringing persisted. I submerged my head to blur the sound, stayed under until I had to come up for air. The bell again, followed by a door opening, and a woman's voice, tentative in tone, loud in volume, "Martin?"

It had to be Ivy Jane. "One moment," I said, hurrying to stand, to close the bathroom door, to dress.

"If you're resting," she called up the stairs. "Don't come down. I brought some tuna noodle casserole. I'll just put it in the fridge."

I fumbled for a towel. "No, wait!" I wrapped the towel around my waist, stuck my head out the half open door and called, "I'm in the bathroom. I'll just be a minute. If you're not in a hurry, I'd like to see you."

"I'll wait. Johnny's already eaten and off to the pool hall. I'll just put some of this on a plate for you."

I tried to smooth the suitcase wrinkles from my clean blue shirt, gave up, and covered them with a brown sweater vest. I combed my wet hair, thinning but still dark, off my forehead, peering at myself in the steamy mirror. Last time Ivy Jane had seen me I was thirty-five years old. I should shave but didn't want to keep her waiting. With my pocket handkerchief, I wiped my glasses on the way down-stairs. Erich teased me about my handkerchiefs, called them "Martin's security blankets," and gave me new ones on every occasion. This yellow and black plaid one had been a birthday present. Sick as Erich was, he had remembered my fifti-eth birthday and instructed our friend, Jean Paul, to buy the most outrageous handkerchief I. Magnin's had to offer.

Hooking my glasses over my ears, I blinked and entered the bright kitchen. IJ had set a place for me at the table. She turned from the stove, skillet in hand. "It was warm when I left the house, but it's so darn cold out there…" She landed the pan back on a burner. "Honey, look at you." She opened her arms wide and pulled me to her cushiony chest.

My chin rested on top of her head, and I was glad. Glad she was too short to see my face because I wanted to keep all I was feeling to myself and was sure it all showed, my confused despair.

"I'm so sorry about your Ma," she said. The warmth of her breath penetrated my shirt sleeve.

"Mmm," I managed. I wanted to tell her I needed her sympathy for so much more, other troubles, other losses. At least Sofie was alive, hurting but alive. She'd recover.

She released me, pulled out a chair. "Sit. What would you like to drink?"

The table stretched for miles around my place mat. "Will you eat with me?"

"I already ate with John, but I'll have a cup of tea." She dropped a spoonful of casserole onto my plate. She'd grown fat, comfortably fat. She filled the kitchen as if it belonged to her.

I blew on a forkful of food while she filled the teapot.

"I'm afraid I've spoiled that boy," she went on. "I was so relieved when he came back in one piece from Vietnam. But who am I fooling? It began a long time before that. Him being the only one." She laughed. "But you're the only one too. Are you spoiled?" She flashed a flirtatious smile. "Did Sofie spoil you, Mart?"

Mart. I remembered her at five, seven, ten, following me down the block on her roller skates, falling, getting up, falling, "Mart, Mart!" I hadn't even let Erich shorten my name. It sounded like a grocery store or a five and ten. "Wait, Mart." Ignoring her had never worked. I'd finally stop, let her catch up, and she'd have a spider to show, squashed in her hand or a melted candy bar to share. She was a pest and, though I never would have admitted it at the time, because she was a girl and so much younger than I, my only friend in Rivertown.

"I bet she didn't. Can't picture Sofie spoiling anyone." IJ poured the tea and served herself a plate of food. "Maybe I will have some," she said.

No, I thought. Sofie didn't spoil me. Sofie trained me.

"Mart, are you alright? I didn't mean anything by that. You know me—my big mouth."

"I'm tired," I said.

"You get some sleep. I'll finish this quick and leave you alone."

"No. Take your time." I was tired of being alone.

"Your mother will be okay, won't she? She's the type to heal fast. Won't put up with lying around for long. That woman does more in a day than I get done in a week. Remember when your father passed away, she wouldn't let anybody help with the food and dishes after the funeral? I'll never forget it. My mother used to talk about that all the time."

I remembered. I remembered that endless summer afterward. A healthy twenty-one year old college man, a veteran, and I squandered my days eating, building my planes, eating some more, playing a few hands of pinochle with Sofie and her friends, eating again. A couple times a week I handed things down to her from high shelves, dusted places she couldn't reach and lifted heavy objects. I couldn't wait until September when school would resume. Summers after that I stayed to work in Boston.

"I watched you that summer, had a big crush on you, man from the big city. Everybody talking about how smart you were, going to MIT."

"A crush on me?" I was surprised. "How old were you?"

"Eleven. But I had a thing for you long before that. Remember all the letters I wrote you when you were in the navy? Every night, before I fell asleep, I'd pray for you. I used to skip over my own family and spend all my time on you. My mother heard me once and asked me about it, but I told her you were the one in the war. You needed it most. You know I brought your letters into school. The teacher read them out loud to the class, that V-Mail. I still have them somewhere. I keep everything. I built up a whole story of how you'd marry me when I grew up, and then when you got back, I couldn't even talk to you. I was so afraid you'd know what I was thinking."

I remembered the first postcard I sent her, just before leaving the States. It showed the backs of two sailors, a flag pole between them. "Can you guess which one is me?" I'd written. I'd gone on to send her many letters, never correcting the idea the other guys had that she was my sweetheart. They never knew she was just the little neighbor girl.

"Every Saturday at the movies, I'd look for you in the newsreels, sure I glimpsed you now and then. There's nothing more romantic than being ten years old and in love with a sailor. I can tell you Johnny's time in Vietnam was a completely different thing. I got through the days alright, but I didn't sleep a full night the whole time he was gone. You can bet I prayed then too." She shook her head as if to clear it.

"I always thought you were so…elegant, different, made sense to me when you moved all the way to California. I'd be afraid to live there myself with all the earthquakes and what have you." She paused to take a bite and before she finished chewing asked, "You ever been in an earthquake?"

"Every so often there's a little one. Shakes the bed, rattles the dishes, knocks some cans off the shelves. Everyone here seems to worry about earthquakes in California. I suspect more people in New England are seriously injured and even killed, due to winter weather conditions than Californians in earthquakes. Look at Sofie."

"Maybe you're right. Doesn't mean a big one isn't waiting to happen." She scraped the last of her food onto her fork and put it into her mouth. "How's life been treating you anyway? You know my husband passed away, eight years ago now, Sofie probably told you. My prayers couldn't save him. But you know what it's like to lose family." My napkin fell. I hadn't told her about Erich. How did she know? With a little groan she picked up my napkin and handed it back to me. "Losing your father. All these men, dying so young."

I hadn't said anything. I could. I should. I could tell her about men dying young, or middle-aged anyway. Then she'd know the truth about how life had treated me. I spread the casserole across my plate with my fork, unsaid words blocking my throat.

"That's what John always did when he didn't want to eat my cooking," IJ said. "What do you like? I'll make something different next time."

"No, it's not that." I took a bite to prove it, chewing the mouthful of noodles until they turned to liquid to give myself time to think, expecting IJ to pick up the conversational ball as she always did. She said nothing. It was her uncharacteristic silence that decided me.

"Someone close to me died this spring," I said. "A friend."

She rested her chin in her hand and waited.

"More than a friend, really, my…"

She nodded, eyes wide, listening.

"My companion," I said. "We were together almost fifteen years."

"How did…uh…your companion die?" she asked.

I set down my fork. "You know it's not a woman."

"Mart, honey." She shook her head. "I wasn't absolutely, one hundred percent positive, but I had an idea. And when you say companion, well…besides, if he'd been a woman chances are Sofie would've known about her and told me, so…"

I pushed my plate away, knowing it was too late to stop myself from crying in front of her. "It's hard."

IJ blew her nose. "You said it."

I hid my face in my hands, letting my tears soak the napkin I clutched. Chair legs scraped the floor, and IJ stood, solid and warm behind me, rubbing my shaking shoulders until I summoned the strength to say good night and without looking back at her, climbed the stairs to bed.

At the hospital elevator, with my finger poised over the button, I heard a girl's breathless voice ask the woman at the information desk for Sofie's room. She pushed ahead of me jabbing at the elevator button as if she were trying to squash a bug that wouldn't die. Wylie Steele. The famous Wylie.

When we ended up at Sofie's bedside together, I knew I'd feel silly for not having spoken sooner, so I forced myself to say, "That won't make it come any faster." She looked over her shoulder, then up. Caught my eye and glared. Even with her masses of dark, springy hair, she was a foot shorter than I. Compact, vibrating with energy. Like Shredder, the pit bull, but not as menacing. A pit bull puppy. She continued to prod the button until the elevator arrived, then raised her eyebrows in an I-told-you-so. I wanted to laugh, to flatten her hair with a calming stroke of my hand.

As the elevator doors slid shut, I waited for her to push the floor number, and with a suspicious glance up at me, she did.

"You're Wylie."

"You're Sofie's son." Her strange eyes flashed ridicule, stopping my nod as soon as it had begun.

We exited the elevator. She followed me, a step behind, down the hall. I'd slow my step for her to catch up, but she'd slow hers, maintaining the small distance between us. I wanted to make conversation, but felt intimidated by the sheer number of details I knew about her and probably wasn't supposed to. And what had Sofie said to her about me? Whatever she said, it was most likely inaccurate, full of harsh judgment, Sofie's trademark.

"You haven't been here yet." I didn't have to make it a question. If she had, she wouldn't have had to ask for the room number. "I've seen her already today." I wanted to see her with my mother. I was deeply curious about their friendship. But once I saw them together, just for a few minutes, I wouldn't mind giving them some time alone. "I can get a cup of coffee while you visit. Let's just see how she's doing."

Sofie lay slightly propped up, gazing toward the wall. Without her glasses, she couldn't see much. The sinking sun painted a path across the linoleum, past the curtained bed of her wheezing, snorting roommate, over Sofie's slightly suspended leg.

I hesitated, hovering near the foot of the bed. Wylie leaned past me.

"Mother, are you awake?" I asked.

"Am I looking asleep to you?" Sofie jerked her head toward her roommate. "Do you think with noises like that anyone can be sleeping?"

"Ssh." I glanced toward the closed curtain, but the loud breathing continued unchanged.

"She doesn't hear anything. You don't need to shush me. Who's that? Without my glasses I can't see."

"It's me." Wylie approached her.

"And me here, without my teeth."

Sofie sat forward to rummage through the items on her night stand. I moved to help, but she waved me back. Wylie's face turned a blotchy pink as she stared at the dentures resting at the bottom of a water filled plastic container. She glimpsed over her shoulder at me. I suspected she'd never seen false teeth before and certainly never knew Sofie wore them. I must confess—a part of me enjoyed her discomfort. Only family should be privy to certain information.

"Wylie," Sofie said, teeth settled in her mouth. "My glasses, in all this mess, can you find them?"

Full of purpose, Wylie strode around the bed and gave Sofie her gold-rimmed glasses. "Sit here." Sofie patted the bed. "I am very tired, but I have things to say to you."

I retreated to the lone chair in the corner of the room, in the shadows behind the path of sun. Before I was excluded I'd been willing to leave. Now, I sat, determined to watch it all, to understand what this teenaged stranger wanted from my mother and what my mother wanted from her. Before settling back in the chair, I took out my handkerchief and wiped my glasses.

"You were there when I fell," Sofie was saying.

"No, I wasn't. You left me off. At the corner of my street. And Sofie, I feel really bad about it. I…"

"I mean in the snow, after I fell, you came, like an angel. You asked me if I wanted to die. I said, 'No, not broken and alone four meters from my front door.' From your back you had wings growing, silver like the foil wings on the butterfly girl."

Wylie flexed her back muscles and looked over her shoulder as if checking for wings, then rolled her eyes. "I left the butterfly girl at the bakery. I wanted to tell you. I made another cake after I found out you were hurt."

"Why? That was a good cake. You made another, what are you calling it? Picture of yourself?"

"Self portrait. A monster. My art teacher loved it. She said I'd used the tools of the kitchen, traditionally a woman's domain, to create a strong feminist statement." She laughed.

"What is her meaning?" Sofie frowned. "Feminist statement? Self portrait? This teacher, she sounds *ein bischen verruckt.*"

"A little crazy," I translated from my corner.

Wylie whirled around. She'd forgotten my presence.

"What did this feminist statement look like?" I tried to sound as if I belonged in the conversation. Sofie's and Wylie's silent stares told me I didn't. I transformed my instinctive apology into a cough. Erich always said my worst fault was my tendency to over apologize. I had a right to be in my mother's hospital room. I'd come all the way across the country, leaving important work on core memory, unsolved pulse transformer problems. I had my slide rule. I wouldn't go anywhere without it, but even so, I wasn't going to sit around in my mother's empty house and wait, working or not, while this needy waif visited her.

Wylie had turned her back on me. She sat close to Sofie. "You should have seen the other kids. They didn't know what to think. All my life they've tortured me."

"Torture?" Sofie asked. "Why? What do you mean?"

"Well, teased me, avoided me, because I didn't have the right clothes and the right house. Because I have the wrong family. Kids' parents wouldn't let them come over to play because of my mother's drinking."

I wondered if Wylie had told Sofie these things before. Something about the recitation seemed staged, for my benefit.

"Everyone knew about our problems," Wylie said. "Danny's the only person who ever bothered to get to know me. Besides you."

"Ach." Sofie patted Wylie's arm and smiled.

"Carrying that cake down the aisle I felt everybody staring. I worried for a minute they'd start teasing. Tim Pulaski, one of the worst bullies, looked the most shocked, not exactly afraid, but almost…"

"I liked the butterfly girl," Sofie said. "What is this monster business? You are now thinking you are a monster?"

"I'd like to see it," I said.

Wylie half turned in my direction. "My brothers ate it," she said. "Or I'd have brought it today."

"You can show him the butterfly girl," Sofie said. "She has a gift."

I inched my chair closer.

"I hope soon I will be out of here," Sofie said. "Back to work." Her eyelids flickered. "I am now so tired. Come back tomorrow. There is more to say, but right now I can't remember."

Wylie stood, accepted the glasses Sofie handed her, and placed them on the table. I straightened the sheet. When I looked up, I saw Wylie watching me with the longing of a little girl. I resolved to find out what it was she wanted. I understood growing up in Rivertown with only one or two people who bothered to be a friend.

"Close the blinds," Sofie murmured.

Wylie and I almost collided at the window. I reached the cord first, but the pink smeared sky, hills like black cutouts and the lights of the town flickering below us, gave me pause. The river snaked through downtown, dark, rose tinted, gray at its icy edges.

"Wylie," Sofie said. "Feed the birds. To carry the tray to the back is for everyone else too much trouble." She closed her eyes and in a moment was snoring.

"And she complains about the roommate," I whispered.

Wylie's little snicker encouraged me to continue.

"Who would think a dreary place could be so beautiful?" I said as we looked out over the town. "Like a postcard."

"I see the bakery," Wylie said. "Beside the bank."

Neither one of us moved in the changing light.

"Nothing to do here but drive around and drink. Or walk around and drink. Or go to football games and drink. Or go to the mall. Or burn things. I hate this place."

"That's a bit extreme." I felt her prickle. I remembered moving to Cambridge—the Charles River with sculls and sailboats, the subways, movie choices, theaters, lectures, museums, bookstores, libraries. And the people—so many kinds of people. "I know what you mean, though," I said. "When I was growing up, if you weren't a football player or at least a fan, you were nothing."

"That's not what bothers me." She pressed her forehead against the glass. "Or maybe it is."

"I hated Rivertown too. I was miserable every day of my life here. Yet I still don't know how much to blame it on the town. How much of it was my family? How much of it was me?"

Wylie's hands tightened into fists on the windowsill.

"I thought Sofie mentioned that you're a senior?" She nodded. "I know it feels like a long time but graduation isn't far off."

My own senior year had been so interminable that I'd rushed to join the navy the day I graduated. I'd walked through the hallways of Rivertown High alone. There must have been other people walking by themselves, carrying books over their hearts like armor, purposely holding their heads high, ignoring whispers and giggles bubbling behind them. I remembered clusters and pairs and groups. Every few months I'd work up the nerve to ask a girl for a date, a quiet, careful girl, or a girl who laughed too much, a girl with glasses or a weight problem or the wrong clothes, who would be grateful. But after the movie, at her door, she'd be waiting for something I never felt, and it made the loneliness I wore every day cut into me like a pair of tight pants to which I'd grown accustomed.

"And?" Wylie folded her arms. "Then what?" Her tone was harsh.

"That's up to you, isn't it?" I stammered in the face of her sudden hostility. "You can leave."

"Right." Wylie sounded bitter. "I plan to. I'm saving money for a car. But there's still the question of where to go. I'm not exactly college material."

"Now, who gave you that idea?" I pulled the blind on the darkening sky. "I'm sure if you applied yourself…worked hard…"

"I work hard," Wylie snapped. "That's the problem. I work too hard and not at school. When your mother is a drunk and your brother is setting the woods on fire and the only people whoever seemed to give a shit about you are angry or in the hospital, it's hard to care about trigonometry or building your vocabulary."

Sofie was snoring louder than her roommate now. Wylie stomped out the door and down the hall.

"Wait!" I hurried after her. She zigzagged past nurses and gurneys and patients pushing IV stands. I realized I was creating a scene and gave up. I wouldn't have known what to say if I caught up with her anyway, except that I was sorry.

Turkey and cranberry sauce in the hospital cafeteria. I treated myself to lunch before visiting Sofie. As I carried my tray to the cashier, I thought of Erich, a year ago, healthy, before we'd learned the word melanoma, bearing a platter heaped with turkey to a table full of applauding friends. No one who was with us last Thanksgiving even knew I was spending my holiday this year in Rivertown, Connecticut. As they all ate their dinners, were any of them remembering Erich? Quite likely. Were any of them wondering about me? Maybe a quick wondering, such as is the old boy holding up alright? A pity he never returned our calls, but what can you do? We tried. This turkey, so moist. The chestnut dressing, divine. A toast. To life.

I sipped my water. Life goes on. Yes, it does. If you're not dead. If the person you loved deeply isn't dead. Erich had insisted we make every bit of the meal from scratch, no frozen pie crust, no packaged bread crumbs, no cranberry sauce from a can. After our guests left, it took until two o'clock in the morning to clean the kitchen, but our dish washing was accompanied by strains of Madame Butterfly, the meal had been a triumph, and the leftovers would feed us handsomely for a week.

Three tables away from me sat a woman dressed all in crocheted purple yarn, spooning cubes of orange Jell-O, and filling in a crossword puzzle. Across the room a doctor gulped a cup of coffee and devoured an enormous sandwich. Otherwise the cafeteria was deserted. I poked the gluey apples in my pie. I laughed out loud, embarrassing myself. I felt the woman and the doctor watch me as I floundered from the room.

The elevator doors slid open and there stood Wylie, cake box in her arms, face tear streaked, eyes red. I stepped inside. She scowled at me, then forced a smile. I wanted ask her what was wrong or tell her she looked like I felt, but didn't trust my voice enough to say anything. We watched the numbers over the door. What a pair. I imagined the elevator breaking down between floors. We'd be stuck. No choice but to tell each other everything. We could survive on whatever she had in the box. Just as I decided to speak the doors opened at Sofie's floor. I closed my mouth.

Wylie preceded me down the hall at a rapid pace and, at the door of the room, rushed right in. I hung back a bit, wishing I were more comfortable asserting myself, more like Erich. He wouldn't have stood quivering just inside the doorway, always watching from a safe distance.

"I brought you something," Wylie was saying.

"A new body, I hope."

She thrust the box toward Sofie.

"Put it there on the table. I am not trusting myself to hold anything. So weak. Ach!" Sofie scrutinized her outstretched arms, turned them over, flexed her gnarled fingers, and scowled.

"It is heavy." Wylie pushed aside a flower arrangement from the ladies at the German hall. "Guess what it is."

"Not a pie."

"No."

I cleared my throat.

"Where have you been?" Sofie snapped, noticing me. "At home there was no answer."

I suppressed a pang of guilt. At fifty years old I needn't account for my whereabouts at every moment.

"I was waiting," Sofie persisted. "Wylie said she would be coming this afternoon. It is better when the visitors are spreading out, not everything all at once."

"Would you like me to leave?" I asked through clenched teeth.

Wylie chewed her lip as though suppressing a giggle.

"Stay," Sofie said.

Finally, an invitation to their little party.

"And see what Wylie is bringing me. Not a pie she says. Maybe a turkey cake."

"Warmer," Wylie said, turning the opening of the box toward Sofie. "Want a peek?"

Sofie bent close. "Something red? Am I seeing dolls in there?"

"Ta da!" Wylie flung back the cover and let the box drop to the floor as she lifted out a cake in the shape of a Volkswagen, down to the smallest detail, with silver wings sprouting from its sides.

"I had to make it a convertible," she said. "To fit the dolls inside. Can you guess who they are? We didn't have gray haired dolls, but that's you." She pointed to the blonde doll in the driver's seat.

"With a plastic spike she can drive," Sofie said, smile evaporating.

"And that's me." Wylie pointed to the dark-haired doll passenger.

"I like the wings," I said. "A flying car could go anywhere."

"And with two legs, I can't." Sofie's hands squeezed at her thighs through the sheet. "I am going no place."

"Mother." I tried to distract her. "Look at the license plate. It spells Sofie."

Debbie, the physical therapist, barged in right then, shoes squeaking like a litter of mice. "Mrs. Schmidt," she singsonged, "no holidays when it comes to PT. Time to sit up on the side of the bed. Feet on the stool. Legs apart. No sitting like a lady." She noticed the cake and stopped. "Is that…"

"It's a cake," Sofie said. "Custom made. One of a kind. This talented young lady made it special for me."

"Come on, Mrs. Schmidt. Up now…"

Sofie's fierce look pushed Debbie back a step. "I want to go home," she demanded. "Can you get me out of here?"

Debbie bustled around the bed. "You'll be on your way home as soon as you're moving around a little. Sitting up for this visit will be a good start. Show your son and your talented granddaughter what you can do!" Behind the therapist's uniformed back, Wylie gave me an odd glance. Guilty? Triumphant? Flabbergasted? I couldn't read it. Sofie snorted but allowed Debbie to assist her to a sitting position.

"Very good. Would you like to try a chair?" Before Sofie could answer, Debbie went on in a stage whisper to Wylie, "Some people have to be pushed. They want to stay in bed and be babied, but your grandmother is just the opposite. It won't be long before she's out dancing."

Sofie narrowed her eyes. She was not even going to pretend to be polite. I almost laughed; the entire situation suddenly struck me ridiculous. Wylie's eyes gleamed as she pressed her lips together; again, I wondered what she was thinking.

Sofie glared at the metal walker Debbie dragged from the closet and resigned herself to the physical therapist's arm around her as she slid off the bed, her knuckles white against the walker's black handles. With Debbie's assistance, she pivoted and lowered herself into the chair. Wylie stared at the floor.

Sofie studied the car cake, beaming as if she'd already forgotten the indignity of moving from bed to chair. Debbie followed her gaze.

"So where do they make cakes like that?" Debbie asked.

"I told you, if you were listening, she made it," Sofie said pointing at Wylie. I had never heard such pride in my mother's voice, not when I built a plane, joined the navy, or graduated from college.

"I'll go to the cafeteria and get some forks," I said.

"Can I order one?" Debbie asked. "On a fishing theme, for my fiancé? Do you take orders?"

"Sure she does." Sofie's voice gained strength. "Only it won't be cheap. A cake like this is costing five or ten times the price of an ordinary cake."

Wylie's mouth dropped open.

"But he would never forget a cake like that," Sofie continued. "Or the person who is giving it to him. Wylie, if you don't have your business card with you, write down your phone number."

"I have a pen here." Debbie pulled one from her pocket.

Wylie printed her name and number. It took a long time as if she couldn't quite remember them.

"Let me know when you get tired, Mrs. Schmidt," Debbie said as she left the room, the scrap of paper in her hand. I took advantage of her exit to leave in search of plates and utensils.

"Where do you think you're going?" Sofie asked.

"The forks."

"*Bis du ein Dummkopf?* This cake is not for eating. It's art."

My inability to do anything to satisfy her struck me once again. I stood, silenced, all but wringing my hands.

"It won't last forever," Wylie said. "You're the one who told me, cakes are to eat."

"Not until I am out of this place." Sofie patted Wylie's hand. "Some people have only flowers. I have a flying car. Now, tell me about Ida's. How you are managing."

"I'll come back later," I said.

Neither Wylie nor Sofie urged me to stay. I took my leave, but something stopped me, just beyond the roommate's drawn curtain where I could eavesdrop.

"Eat the car if you want," Wylie said. "It's chocolate inside."

"It's a good thing to keep things as long as you need them. I have had much practice with this. When my sisters and I were small, my mother took us and ran away. Away from our stepfather who beat us, away from the farm which was rightfully belonging to my mother. We left everything." Sofie's voice was flat. I had heard only of my grandfather's death in a mining accident. I'd never heard of a wicked stepfather.

"In the city, my mother found work as a housekeeper, and all day while she was working she closed us in the apartment, each with a slice of bread. My sister, Amalia, she tore hers in half, ate one piece at nine and the other exactly at noon She was proud she could tell time." Sofie paused. I thought of the *gummibaren* and *Steif* animals Tante Amalia had sent on my birthdays, the careful thank you notes I'd written in painstaking German. Sofie had told me stories of her life with her sisters, but she tended to tell amusing anecdotes, nothing about being locked in a room with too little to eat.

"Dora, my youngest sister, she gobbled hers up the moment our mother left. Why shouldn't she? I shared always with her later." Dora, the nun. When I wrote to her I had to use her nun's name, Schwester Gabriele. The notion of renaming oneself had always fascinated me. I couldn't picture a nun, even as a child, gobbling food.

"My slice I tore into small pieces, rolling each piece into a ball. I put them in a line on the windowsill and ate them through the day, never touching the last one until I heard my mother's key in the lock. I gave some to the birds, of course."

Sofie paused. I feared they'd hear my ragged breathing, then decided they would think it was the roommate. Sofie had never told me that story. Why not? She was my mother. Dora and Amalia were my aunts. The story belonged to me, not to some girl my mother had only known for a few months.

"I knew, even as a little girl, what I needed. I found ways to give it to myself. Of course, my mother, she gave me the slice of bread. You need something to start." Her voice trailed off. I rubbed my temples, took off my glasses and wiped them. Nothing helped to ease the tightness in my face or my suddenly blurring vision.

"So, how was your Thanksgiving dinner?" Sofie asked.

She hadn't asked about mine. Here I was, in Rivertown for the holiday after all, and my mother hadn't even baked me a pie, or brought one from the bakery. Of course, under the circumstances, I didn't expect her to, but she hadn't even noticed her neglect.

"*Was ist los?*" Sofie's voice, oozing sympathy. Sobs. The girl thought she had something to cry about. Sofie's comforting murmurs. If I could bring myself to peek around the curtains, I'd probably see her head in Sofie's lap, my mother stroking that tangle of hair.

"I cooked all morning," Wylie said. "My mother's idea of Thanksgiving dinner is a fifth of wild turkey. She put out her cigarette in the mashed potatoes I'd dished onto her plate. I forgot dessert and my brothers complained. Before I even sat down their arms were all over the food, spilling things. I made gravy, for the first time in my life, and there wasn't a lump in it. When I get home the sink will be full of dishes and clumps of food. I've got to get out of that house."

"Ach, *schade.*"

A pity. What a pity. The girl was young, talented and healthy with her life ahead of her. Sofie had mentioned a boyfriend who picked her up at work and drove her home. I couldn't stand there any longer listening. I had to say something. Instead, I left.

Shivering as I crossed the parking lot, I realized I'd left my coat on a chair in Sofie's room. I couldn't go back. I turned the heat on in the rental car as high as it would go and pressed my shaking hands between my thighs. Hot and noisy air rushed at my face. The windows fogged. I switched on the radio.

"Call in and tell us what you're thank—"

I snapped it off.

Somehow I drove from the hospital to the house, loneliness and cold indistinguishable. I missed Erich; I wanted to be a passenger; I did not want to be a person who couldn't think of anything to be thankful for on Thanksgiving.

IJ, foil covered plate in hand, met me as I drove up, as if she'd been on the lookout for my car. I watched her lips move. As the engine sputtered to silence, I could hear the buzz of her voice. She rapped on the window, smiling when I finally opened the door.

"You must be exhausted. Why don't you just come on in? I'll heat this…Where is your coat? You're worse than John. Now, come on." She took my arm. "You're going to get sick. That would be a fine thing. Then you'll be needing someone to take of you." She reached behind the mailbox for the key.

Had Sofie told her about the key? I never had. Did her son know about it?

She propelled me to the table and prepared the meal as if it were one in a lifetime of nights, a long marriage, like my parents'—Sofie bustling, talking, Oskar silent at the table, waiting to be fed. Had he ever listened to his wife?

"I asked you how Sofie is doing." IJ set the plate in front of me and handed me a fork. If I opened my mouth she would probably start feeding me.

"She's…"

"Does she want visitors?" IJ patted my hand. "I'd be glad—"

"She has visitors," I said, sounding bitter even to myself. "Or a visitor. A girl she worked with—Wylie."

"You mean that Steele girl, Wylie Steele? I could tell you some stories about her family. I don't know the girl myself, but I knew her mother and father growing up. Lucy Lovett and Joe Steele. Joe, the football hero, everybody's darling, until he tore his Achilles tendon. Couldn't adjust. Lucy should've known better than to marry him. We could all see he had a drinking problem. At least she should've known better than to have his babies. But then Lucy had her own problems, raised by her aunt, Beryl Lovett. You remember her. The lunch lady at the high school? The one who doled out loud, nasty comments along with the food. Really personal remarks, remember? How you shouldn't even be thinking about eating the dessert, you were so fat. Or you were such a scrawny, pipsqueak you needed extra protein if you were to ever to grow into a man. Or with that acne, you'd best leave the chocolate pudding and French fries alone. Can't think of anyone in town who liked that woman.

"When she died I remember people celebrating...quietly...but still, celebrating. That Lucy was a lonely little girl. Kids afraid to come over to her house. No wonder she moved in with Joe right after high school. When Beryl died she left her house, the house Lucy had lived in with her for most of her life, to some distant cousin who sold it. Right up until her marriage, Lucy had always worked hard, waitressing. She was a tough one. Had to be. She could have used that house. I think she had the daughter and one son at the time. Joe working, in construction I think, trying to make it. That house might have made a difference. But then again, Lucy hardly knew love and when you don't know love...well, I don't think there's much hope then." She paused for breath. I stabbed a pea with the prong of my fork. "Those kids, you could say they never had a chance." I liked the sound of her talk filling the room, but what she was saying bothered me. Generous, give-everyone-the-benefit-of-the-doubt IJ. If she was saying such things, what were other people saying? No wonder Wylie wanted to leave.

"Came back twice after moving to North Carolina and don't you know Lucy's got that younger boy to show for his visits. And a drinking problem of her own. Joe died a few years ago. I've got the obituary some place. I clip them when it's people I know. Hit by a car, it said, changing a tire on the highway. Unemployed. No address. Everything he owned in his rusted out Ford wagon. They didn't mention that in the paper. I knew the car from when he came to town. He'd park down in the vacant lot, before they built the mall there, and he'd cook on a little camping stove, like a hobo. No one bothered him. People more sorry for him than anything. Left behind a former wife and three children, the paper said."

"That's a lot to leave behind." I imagined Wylie crossing the street to avoid her own father, probably shunning downtown altogether. No way to escape the talk. Now, if Joe Steele were homeless and drunk on the sidewalks of San Francisco, crowds could pass him in the span of a day, and no one would ever think about whose father he was. I yearned for the pastel houses on hills draped in fog, for my workbench, for Sunday afternoons flying my planes in Golden Gate Park, for the throngs of people who didn't know or care that I was fifty years old, from a dying Connecticut mill town, of German descent, homosexual, Sofie and Oskar Schmidt's son, valedictorian of my high school class, World War II veteran.

"Are you alright?" IJ asked. "Is the food okay?"

"I'm curious." I kept my voice steady. "What does 'everyone' say about me? I suspect they have some interesting opinions."

I half-expected her to hem and haw, but then again, IJ had always been direct.

"They talk about why you're not married, why you hardly ever come home. Some people guess you're homosexual. Other people think your mother is so difficult you can't stand to visit."

"People pity me."

"Feel sorry for you," IJ said. She looked uncomfortable. "I brought you some pie. Apple. I have mince too, but not many people like it so I brought the apple. I can run home and cut a slice of the mince if you'd rather…"

I folded my hands and stopped her chatter by staring hard, over my glasses. "What exactly is the difference? Feel sorry for, pity? Wylie's father, poor man— he's a homeless drunk. Martin Schmidt, poor man…he's a fairy. Do you know, IJ, when I was a little boy and the kids beat me up for being German, my mother called the ringleader's mother? She told her that her son was beating me up. Do you know what that woman's response was? 'I told Timmy the little boy can't help being German.'" I waited for my words to sink in. IJ shook her head.

"The old man can't help loving men. The old man can't help having a difficult mother who broke her hip. The old man wants to go home to his work, his apartment, his life, as lonely as it may be right now. I have a life, IJ."

"Wait a minute," she said. "I know you have a life. In fact, I think you should get back to it. Have you thought about who will care for Sofie when she comes home?"

"I haven't been able to think."

"I could do it," she said. "If you wanted me to. I could use the money."

"That might work," I said, amazed to have a solution to a problem I'd only that moment discovered I had. "You know what Sofie's like. Could you manage with her?"

"Sofie's all bark and no bite. Do you want the rest of this pie?" When I shook my head, she pulled the plate toward her. "She won't bother me. How long have I known her? My whole life, forty years."

"I guess that's long enough to really know someone," I said. "I think I will have another slice of that pie." For the first time all day, I really did feel thankful.

My relief lasted for two and a half weeks. During that time I settled Sofie into her new downstairs den-turned-bedroom, purchased my return ticket and packed my bag. It lasted until IJ announced in a whisper, so that Sofie wouldn't hear, that she was quitting.

"Martin, I'm so, so sorry. You know I'd stick it out if I could, if for no other reason than to help you, but I can't. She is determined to drive me crazy. I'm a good housekeeper. I've kept a clean house all my life, but nothing I do is good enough. She scolded me this morning for putting sheets on her bed upside down. The print on the top sheet is supposed to be inside. Did you know that? Of course you did. She told me you did. Martin would know that the sheet is laid out so that when the top is folded back you can see the design. He would know that the stems of the flowers point toward the foot of the bed. He would know an egg sits in an egg cup, toast should be sliced straight across, not on a diagonal, butter on the side in a covered butter dish. He would know which TV show to put on when, without being told. No one else will satisfy her, Mart. She's all yours. I'm sorry." IJ untied her apron and hung it over the back of the chair. "I've got to leave before I scream at her. I have to live two doors away. I don't want to make an enemy of a neighbor. I'm sorry."

Her words fell like a blizzard, piling drifts of snow against the house, the doors, the windows, stopping traffic, closing airports, cutting me off from the rest of my life. I wanted to grab her arm. Instead I clutched at my forehead.

"You know I'd do it, if I could."

Determined to leave, IJ still seemed to want something from me, my permission, my blessing, even a nod or grunt.

I closed my eyes. I would give her nothing. I stood in the kitchen, in my own private darkness, until I heard the door shut.

"Martin!" Sofie's voice wavered from the back of the house.

I would talk to Sofie, explain how much we needed IJ, convince her to apologize. Sofie sat in bed, small and fierce, against a stack of pillows, the edge of the sheet folded back to reveal its small pink flowers.

"Martin, I have to ask you to fire that woman. She is meaning well, but no one ever is teaching her the right way to do things, and she is too old, how do they say, old dogs are not learning new tricks. Not like you knowing how to do things because since you are small I am teaching you. You know the right way."

I flushed at a momentary twinge of pleasure, swallowed by fury.

"She quit, Mother. There's no need to fire her."

"Quit? Why?"

"You drove her to it."

"And I thought I could not drive." She giggled at her own joke, then bit her lip when I didn't smile with her.

"IJ is a decent person who's known our family for a long time. She is available at a moment's notice in an emergency. Would you rather I hire a stranger?"

"No," Sofie said. "I'd rather you are staying. Every day for myself I am doing more. Soon I will be back at work. I only need you for a little longer time. Your work can wait."

"No," I said. "No. It can't. I have a ticket. I intend to use it. You need to apologize to IJ and convince her to come back or I'll hire someone else. Your choice."

I stiffened my spine and envisioned myself on the plane, tray table folded down, pencil and slide rule in hand, scratching numbers onto a napkin.

Sofie pressed her lips together and rolled her eyes toward the ceiling.

"Don't you see you're acting like a spoiled child?"

"You, you are acting like a spoiled child! All these years you are not coming home. Finally you are here and all you are wanting is to leave. Go ahead. I will be fine. Call Wylie. Pay her something to look in on me."

Wylie. I hadn't thought of her.

"You need more than someone to look in on you."

"Call her," Sofie said. She struggled to move her legs to the side of the bed. "Or I will go to the phone and call her myself."

"No, stay there, I'll call her." I hastened to the kitchen and looked up the number. A slurred voice told me Wylie was at work. I'd call Ida's. No, I'd go talk to her in person, where Sofie couldn't overhear. I'd tell her everything. I'd offer her so much money she'd have to say yes.

The door to the bakery was already locked. Inside, Wylie swept the floor, her hair escaping from her stubby braid, her uniform smudged with raspberry jelly and chocolate. I pounded on the glass. She looked up, annoyed, mouthing 'we're closed.' Then, recognizing me, she approached.

"It's winter," she said. "Below freezing. Where's your coat?"

"Listen." I went straight to the point. "My mother wants you to take care of her."

Wylie leaned on the broom and frowned. "Oh, she does? Well so do my mother and my little brothers and my boyfriend. And then there's Tony who expects me to do Sofie's work and my own. And I'm sure you've already heard about my brother being arrested for setting the woods on fire. His court date is tomorrow, and my mother will probably be too drunk to go with him which will alert the state to the fact that we all belong in foster care so you can see that I have a lot on my mind and a lot to do. Too much to help Sofie. Even if I wanted to."

"Wait, I said it all wrong." The words to persuade her had to exist somewhere, but I couldn't find them. I'm upset...I..." Thinking it might help to sit down I crossed to a stool at the lunch counter leaving a trail of muddy footprints. Wylie smeared them with the broom.

"I've got to go home," I said. "To San Francisco. To work. You're the only one who understands her. I'll pay you, anything you want, within reason."

She sat, listening.

"Quit this job. Take care of my mother instead. I'll pay you twice what you're making here. Three times."

She picked a crumb from the counter and rubbed it between her fingers. "Then what do I do when she's better? Tony would be so mad at me for quitting; I doubt he'd give me my job back."

"Make your cakes. You can use our kitchen. Start your own business." Hope and desperation had me leaping from my seat. "This is an opportunity." I looked toward the doors to the back of the bakery and slapped a hand over my mouth. "Goodness, is anyone back there? I assumed..."

Wylie laughed. "No, it's just me." She spun on her stool. "I think you're right. An opportunity."

"So you'll do it?"

"I need to talk to Sofie first."

"Okay, of course, but you think you'll do it?"

"My brothers need me. My mother too."

"You'll still have time to spend at home. It's not as if you were moving across the country."

"I'll talk to Sofie. I'll think about it."

She smiled as if she was leaning toward yes. I cautioned myself against begging.

"I've missed Sofie," Wylie said. "This way I'll get to see her. You said she asked you to ask me?"

She'd heard me the first time. I resented having to repeat it. Wylie and Sofie would be icing cakes together, laughing, while I came home from a long day at work to a mailbox full of junk mail with Erich's name on it. I thought of IJ's son, parading past the house twice a day, Shredder straining at the leash, and remembered how badly I wanted to leave. "Sofie said to call you."

Wylie smiled. "I'll come by tomorrow."

Driving back to the house to prepare supper—Sofie liked it promptly at six and it was already ten of—I remembered the first time Erich cooked for me. I'd never eaten so late. Thick spaghetti sauce simmered in a skillet. I'd been shocked. Didn't you need a deeper pot? Erich had julienned the carrots for salad instead of cutting circular slices and he left the peel on the cucumber, striping it with the tines of a fork. One dinner and my world had filled with possibilities. There wasn't just one right way, Sofie's way. Back in Rivertown it was too easy to forget that.

CHAPTER 3

▼

WYLIE

Our case worker's pen, pinched between perfect, purple fingernails, looped across her yellow legal pad. Since Robbie's day in court, Miss Jennings showed up once a week, on Wednesdays, to make sure our family was "making positive changes" in our lives. Lucy and I, exhausted from cleaning, sat straight, doing our best to make a good impression, TV turned off for the occasion.

"And how is the younger boy?" Jennings wore an eager look of concern. "Um…" She flipped through her pad. Lucy, hands trembling, lit a cigarette.

"George," I smirked.

"Yes." Miss Jennings stopped rustling papers, flashing me a grateful smile. "George."

Lucy inhaled quickly, choking on the smoke. She flashed me a warning look and would have kicked me if we hadn't been across the room from each other. Behind the case worker's back Lucy called her a skinny do-gooder, but in front of her it was all perfect manners and sucking up.

"Miss Jennings," Lucy said, catching her breath and raising her eyebrows at me. "She's joking. My younger son's name is Kevin. He's fine. Robbie and him are at the playground. He worships the ground his big brother walks on. And he's doing real good in school. Ask his teacher. He was the turkey in the Thanksgiving pageant. You should've heard him gobble. And speaking of Thanksgiving, Wylie here made a meal you could've fed the president." She didn't mention she'd been too drunk to eat it.

"Ah hah." The case worker widened her eyes at me in a hurt puppy expression. She pressed so hard with her pen, the paper tore. I imagined her writing "Wylie Steele, oldest daughter, pathologically hostile, needs residential program."

"There was concern about Kevin's tardiness. The school reported…" she flipped through her pages once more, "eleven days late in less than a month."

"Are you sure about that?" I asked.

The social worker jammed the cap onto her pen and stuffed it and the pad into her briefcase. "I think that's all for today. Do a better job of getting Kevin—" She glared at me. "To school on time."

She teetered toward the door on her high heels shaking her head. Lucy followed her, not to be polite, but to make sure she drove off. We'd be real once the car was out of sight, Lucy pouring a drink or swallowing straight from the bottle, me figuring what we could scrape up for dinner.

The phone rang. I leaped to answer. Jennings' visits shrunk and dirtied the living room, the whole house, in spite of all the polishing and sweeping we did.

"When are you coming over?" Martin didn't even bother to say hello or identify himself. "To talk with Sofie. About the job." He sounded frantic. I told him I'd come right away.

As soon as I stepped through Sofie's front door, I knew I was in a house where they never ran out of toilet paper. All the surfaces—coffee table, shelves, floor—gleamed, uncluttered, like a commercial for Lemon Pledge which I'd never believed anyone really used. Plastic covered the front room furniture, except the chair Sofie was sitting in and an empty rocking chair made of golden brown wood with flowers and birds carved into the back.

Sofie looked smaller. Her fingernails, thick and yellow, curving over the ends of her shriveled fingers, were the most solid part of her. I could imagine her shrinking until her fingernails were the only things left.

"Sit down," Sofie said. "Martin, bring us some coffee."

Martin hadn't said anything after 'hello' and 'may I take your coat?' Maybe he worried if he said more he'd let everyone know how angry he was. He acted more like a butler than a son, and Sofie seemed used to treating him that way. Maybe he was afraid if he started yelling or crying, he'd never stop. She waved a hand, dismissing him.

The sofa crackled when I sat.

"So," Sofie leaned forward. "Did that girl pay you big money for her fancy, schmancy cake?"

"Sure did," I grinned. "You should've seen it. A lake. With boats and docks and people fishing. And a shadow of a sea serpent lurking just beneath the surface. A little guy, meant to be her boyfriend, about to hook it with his little fishing rod. Everyone loved it."

"Thirty-five dollars she paid?"

"I've never seen a more satisfied customer. She would've paid more. Now her friends all want custom made cakes. Ida's is swamped with orders."

"Ha!" Sofie slapped her thigh, beaming. "*Wunderbar! Ausgezeichnet*! I told you. With all that talent you will be going places." She frowned. "But Tony should be giving you a raise. How much of that money are you keeping for yourself?"

"I wanted to ask your advice. I kept twenty-five dollars of Debbie's money. Seemed like leaving ten for Tony more than covered supplies. It wasn't like she came into Ida's to place the order. But now, with people phoning up, I don't know what to do."

"I thought Martin told you. In my kitchen you make your cakes. I have a decorating kit, pans, all you would be needing. That way you keep all the money for yourself. Why should Tony be the one getting rich?"

"I don't know how to tell Tony I want to quit."

"Listen." Sofie shook her hooked finger at me. "Tony can find someone else. In this valley are plenty of people needing jobs. Don't be worrying so much about other people. Do what you want. That way it turns out best for everyone."

I didn't believe her. My brothers and I would have better off with a little more worry. Lucy always did what she wanted, hardly giving any of us a thought.

"Who will feed the pigeons?" Of all the responsibilities in my life I didn't know why I thought of that.

"I will. When I go back," Sofie said. "Until then? Pigeons are tough. They'll survive. And while I am not at the bakery I am still feeding the birds here in the yard. Everywhere is something to feed."

The slippery fabric of Sofie's dress fell in shiny folds over her lap and knees. I wanted to rest my cheek against it, knew it would feel just like the edge of the blanket I'd carried around until it dissolved into separate threads.

"So, will you stay for a few weeks here with me until I can better get around?" Sofie asked.

Do what you want. Her words looped through my head, over and over. Do what you want. What did I want? I wanted my mother to stop drinking and be a responsible adult. I wanted to forget that I'd lost my father without ever really knowing him. I wanted to get out of my crazy house and suffocating town before

I was too tired to care anymore, before blue veins spread all over my legs, before I had a house full of kids, no money for heat, and my own drinking problem. Making custom cakes at Sofie's I could earn real money. Especially if I was getting paid for helping Sofie too. I could buy my own car. Any car as long it worked. And I'd drive away. The black lines on the maps I'd been studying all my life would become real roads, paved with real asphalt, with real things to see along the way. Things I didn't know enough about to even imagine.

"I would love to stay here," I said. "It'll be hard for them without me at home but I want to be here. With you."

Martin brought the coffee. With the three of us in the same room the air thickened, time slowed to an ooze. I had no idea what Sofie and Martin talked about when I wasn't around, if they talked at all. I started worrying about how to tell my mother, Robbie, Tony. No one was going to like the idea of my moving. Even Danny who I hardly ever saw anymore. I'd spot the Bonneville outside school, passing Ida's, or parked at the mall, and my heart tore a little worse every time. Nights, before I fell asleep, after working late to keep up with the flood of cake orders—after my first dragon cake that breathed real fire, every seven to ten year old boy in Rivertown had to have one—my body ached to curl around Danny's warm back, but I was too exhausted to talk, even to him, too tired to bother tiptoeing up his stairs, past his snoring father.

Did I really know how to take care of an old person? Remembering Sofie's teeth in the jar I imagined other personal things I wouldn't want to see, underwear drying in the bathroom, weird and old-fashioned with lots of mean looking hooks and buttons and who knew what else? I slurped fast, a whole cup of coffee, burning my mouth, set my empty cup and saucer on the tray, and said good-bye.

"*Nein*," Sofie said. "Stay to eat."

I tried to think of a good reason to leave. Martin went to the kitchen. I moved from the couch to the rocking chair. It held me like a nest, the seat just the right distance from the floor for my short legs. "I never knew a wooden chair could be this comfortable," I said, rocking back and forth.

"That is a wonderful chair, no?" Sofie said. "Oskar made that for me, when we first came to this country. So I could rock our baby. He said I should sit more. I don't like to sit. Now, look at me, sitting all the time. And not even in that chair. Nothing so exciting as rocking for me. Nothing to do but watch TV."

"You could knit or something," I said.

"Never learned. I am never sitting long enough."

"Didn't you have to sit in school? That's all school is as far as I can tell—sitting, sitting, and more sitting."

"I didn't go long to school. We had no money for a copy book." Sofie stared at the ceiling. I sensed a story coming and sat back.

"The teacher hit us for not doing our homework. So my sister and I, we stopped going. We went instead to the edge of town where a bridge crossed over the railroad tracks. All day we would lean over the railing waiting for trains. When they passed under us, we spit. We spit on people going places while the bridge shook. When school was over for the day, we went home. To our little sister who every morning wanted so badly to go with us. No one knew how we spent our time. After what would be here the third grade I never went to school."

Where were social workers back then? Times had changed a lot. "If they'd had malls, you and your sisters would have been hanging out on the benches." I laughed. "No, I take it back, you wouldn't be sitting. You'd be roaming back and forth in a gang of three." I wished I had a sister to be friends with instead of two brothers to worry about. "Wait a minute. How did you learn to read and write and figure out math?"

"My writing, even in German, is not so good." Sofie adjusted a sleeve, then looked right at me and in a more cheerful voice said, "But school isn't the only place to learn." Then, fussing with her sleeve again, "I sometimes wish I went to college. You will go to college."

I shook my head.

"Why not? You're a hard worker. And no *Dummkopf!*" She tapped her forehead.

Why not? Because I didn't even know how to get an application. I hadn't signed up for the SAT. Even if I got in who would pay for it? There was nothing college could teach me that I wanted to learn.

"Martin told us he loved college. In high school, he was not happy. But college he liked. The first year he wrote us long letters about all he was learning. Oskar read them out loud to me. I wish he could have seen Martin graduate. I was so proud. My son, the engineer. Alone I took the train to Boston for his graduation. On the train ride home he tells me he is moving all the way across the country for a job near San Francisco. Then I was glad his father was dead and didn't have to hear this news."

Martin entered the room with a platter of bread, meat, and cheese and a handful of knives and forks. I imagined him young and on the train, holding his square graduation cap; did they let you keep it? Maybe just the tassel. He would have been twisting it, sliding it between his fingers. I could see it as if I'd been there, Sofie glaring, Martin playing with the strands of a gold tassel, the way Robbie still twisted his hair when he was nervous.

He handed me silverware and a small board. He stooped in front of Sofie, holding the tray while she speared a slice of liverwurst and laid it on a piece of dark bread.

Sofie and Martin ate their sandwiches with knives and forks, fork in the left hand, knife in the right. I tried it. The chewing together, the rustling of napkins, the satisfying sound of knives against wood as we sliced off each bite ended the earlier awkward silence. I liked eating tomato on my sandwich without the seeds and juice running out the sides and over my hands. I felt like I was in another country and again, I wanted to stay.

"You could help me with the cake orders," I said. I saw us working side by side again, Sofie mixing colors, encouraging me, admiring my creations.

Sofie swallowed a mouthful. "What could I do? You're the artist. I'm the old lady with the broken hip."

"Are you kidding?" I set my empty board on the tray and sat on the low stool by her chair. "You're the one who got this all started in the first place. You taught me decorating. You had the nerve to ask Debbie for thirty-five bucks. If you hadn't been there I would've given the cake away for nothing."

"We're like a team?" Sofie sawed at her sandwich. Martin dropped his knife and bent to pick it up.

"How soon could you start?" Martin's voice sounded as though it were being squeezed through an icing tube with a very small tip.

"After Christmas," Sofie said. "Martin, for Christmas you are staying. It's not even two weeks away."

Martin almost choked, eyes bulging behind his glasses. He cleared his throat instead. I wanted to tell him to say no to her, to use her line about people doing what they want to do, but he'd been out of the room when she said it. I could bring it up except that I wanted him to stay through Christmas too. I'd have more time to tell everyone about moving, get them used to the idea. If he couldn't stand up to his mother, that was his problem.

"Wylie," Sofie went on, paying no attention to Martin. "We always celebrate on Christmas Eve. If your family is celebrating on Christmas Day, maybe you can come on Christmas Eve by us."

I waited for Martin to reinforce her invitation. He didn't.

"I'll see," I said. Sofie's forehead wrinkled. "Probably."

"Could you start the day after Christmas then?" asked Martin. He loaded the tray, trying to act as if my answer didn't matter.

"Fine."

Sofie beamed. "Wylie, turn on the TV. I think it is time for the wrestling."

"Would you like to see your room?" Martin asked.

I hadn't even thought about where I'd sleep. A real bedroom. I clicked on the TV and fiddled with it until I found the right channel while Martin brought the supper remains to the kitchen. He led me upstairs.

"She won't believe that wrestling is all a fake," he said, loud enough for Sofie to hear over the cheering from the TV.

"My brother likes it," I said. "He says it's real."

"Well it's not." He sounded more bitter than I'd ever heard him. "It's all fixed. Winners, losers, all predetermined. She won't believe it. This is it." He flicked the light switch, illuminating a small, blue room with slanted ceilings, a fairy tale room with a colorful braided rug, a desk and chair in a windowed alcove, a bed with a fuzzy patterned, white spread. Martin could only stand straight in the middle, but I could walk through most of it without even ducking my head.

"The closet is small," Martin said, holding open the door.

Everything I owned would fit in a couple of shopping bags. "It's big enough," I said, rubbing the raised lines on the bedspread.

"This wasn't your room, was it?" I asked.

He seemed angry and not just at Sofie. "No, mine is across the hall, exactly as it was when I was a boy, waiting for me to move back in. This was always the spare room. For company we never had."

Or the baby that died, I thought. Your sister. But I didn't say it. "Well I love it," I told him.

He gave a nod, formal and stiff. "I should be helping Mother get ready for bed."

"That's not true," I said surprising both of us. "She just started watching her show. You just don't want to talk to me. Or maybe you don't know what to say."

His eyebrows flew up, high over his glasses. He began to laugh. I hadn't heard him laugh before, not like that. He pulled out the desk chair and sat, laughing harder.

"So what do you want to talk about?" he said between chuckles. He cleaned his glasses and wiped his forehead with a bright red checked handkerchief.

I said the first thing that came into my head. "Where'd you get that wild handkerchief?"

His laughing stopped, surprising me as much as when it had started.

"What is it you really want to talk about?" he asked. "Sit down."

I decided to get right to the point. "You don't like me, do you?"

He adjusted his glasses and looked at me, concerned, confused. I couldn't tell what he was thinking. I never knew what I would say until I heard it myself. His words seemed to leave his mouth planned, whole, fully formed. "What makes you say that?" he asked.

"Oh, never mind." I picked at the bedspread.

"I have no reason not to like you. I appreciate all you've done for Sofie. I'm glad you're able to move in for a while. It will be advantageous for everyone. Sofie will appreciate your company. Helping with the cakes will give her something to do. That will help her heal faster than anything else. You'll earn what you need to leave. That's what you want, right?" Martin was smiling like he felt sorry for me, as if I were a little kid with a long list of Christmas presents I really believed I'd get cause I didn't know yet that Santa Claus was really my mother who didn't have any money.

"You don't think I can do it! You don't think I'll ever get out. You think you're so great cause you have nice clothes and live in California!" Why was I yelling at him?

"Wait a minute." Martin crossed the room to sit beside me on the bed. Then he said, "You're thinking I don't like you. You're thinking I believe you're stuck here. You're wrong in both cases. The person who thinks those things is you."

"No sir!" I blurted out, sounding like a kindergartner, but I replayed his words in my head and thought about them the whole time I said good-bye to Sofie and walked home in the cold dark. I thought about them at home that night after putting Kevin to bed while Lucy dozed on the couch and Robbie struggled with homework at the kitchen table, the first I'd seen him do all year.

He held a stub of pencil in his fist, never having learned to hold one the right way. "Do you remember much about Dad?" he asked.

"Why?"

"I'm supposed to write about someone who influenced me."

"Why him? If you can't remember him he couldn't have influenced you very much."

"I remember him," Robbie said. "I remember a lot of things. I just wondered what you remembered."

"I remember fighting," I said. "Lots and lots of fighting. Mom would send us out to the store for things we didn't even need just to get us out of the way. If she didn't have any money she'd hand us the salt shaker and send us out to catch birds."

"With a salt shaker? I don't remember that." He put down the pencil. It rolled to the edge of the table and stayed.

"Salt on the tail feathers would tame the bird, Mom said. We'd spend hours on the porch steps, waiting, Mom and Dad screaming, dishes breaking."

Robbie chewed his lip and twisted a knot of hair. "I don't remember any of that."

"You're lucky. I'd get mad at you for moving around too much. You were only a baby. But I really wanted a pet bird. I thought if it weren't for you scaring them away, I'd have a whole flock. I had names all picked out. That's how I put myself to sleep at night, chanting lists of names for my birds."

"I can't believe salt tames birds," Robbie said.

"It doesn't." I picked up the pencil. Robbie or someone had chewed the eraser. "She lied. All those hours we sat out there. Waiting and waiting." I pushed the pencil at him. "I'm tired of waiting. Come June I am out of here."

Robbie flinched. "You're lucky." He sat, pencil hovering over the paper. "I don't remember any of that. I was going to write about the time he gave me that magic box that turned pennies into quarters, and you told me how it didn't really and ruined the whole thing."

"It was a trick!" I saw the scene as if it were happening in front of me. Robbie clutching his penny jar and the black, plastic box with a slot for a penny in one side, a quarter in the other, thinking he could change all the pennies and be rich. "I just showed you how the trick worked. Reality. The truth."

"I liked having it be magic. I'm not stupid. I would have figured it out sooner or later."

Our father taught us about magic. He made himself disappear. "Setting those fires was pretty stupid," I said.

"Yeah, well...I guess I learned my lesson about that." He scribbled a sentence. I couldn't see what he wrote, but even if I could it was probably too messy to read.

"I love watching things burn, the whole woods on fire, knowing it all started with one little match and these." He rubbed his fingers and thumb together in front of my face.

His future gleamed in his eyes.

He stood and began pacing. "Fire is a live thing. The crackling, the heat, even the smoke. It eats, breathes, moves. It's not right to keep it trapped in a small, paper matchbook. Look at it this way. It's like having a seed and not planting it."

"You're crazy," I said.

"No, I'm not. I told you I learned my lesson. If I was really crazy, a pyromaniac or whatever, I wouldn't be able to stop."

"Robbie! Wylie!" Lucy's voice from the living room. "Could somebody turn off the TV?"

Robbie leaped up. I sat where I was. I could hear them talking.

"Did you see your probation officer today?"

"Yeah."

"Good boy." Maybe he had. Maybe he hadn't. But she believed him.

If she'd been awake she could have heard our whole conversation. I wished she had. Then my mother would know I thought she was a liar. She'd know her son was a danger to himself and society.

"Jennings came by today." Lucy's voice sounded hard and awake. "Pushing her AA stuff again. I told her when I decided to quit drinking I'd do it on my own. She said if I wanted to keep all you kids I better decide soon. I told her not to threaten me."

Silence.

"Do you think I drink too much?"

My mother had never asked me that question.

"Maybe," Robbie said. "Maybe a little. Sometimes."

Sometimes. Sometimes. I pressed my fingers against the Formica so hard they should have left an imprint.

"It's not easy," Lucy was whining. "God knows, it's not easy. If I drink a little…"

She wouldn't dare talk to me like that. She knew what I would say. I'd called my mother a drunk more than once.

Robbie returned. He wouldn't look at me, went straight for the refrigerator where he stood, swigging milk from the carton. He wiped his mouth. "Don't say it. I know. Use a glass."

"Why should I care if you use a glass or not?" I said closing myself into my pantry, leaving him there, wasting electricity with the refrigerator standing open, his germs swimming around in the milk.

"So you're quitting Ida's." Danny nodded approval and cocked his head, listening to the engine. He never started driving until the Bonneville warmed up. I rubbed fog off the windshield.

"Don't do that!" Danny grabbed my hand. "I've told you. You smear it. Can't you wait a minute? That's a perfectly good defroster. Let it do its job."

I pulled my hand away. Two small half moons of cleared glass appeared above the dashboard. He was always harping about streaks, but I hated waiting without being able to see. "Let's go. Take me to Ida's. I'll tell Tony this afternoon. Before we pick up my skates."

"They need us for the hockey game." Danny shifted, peered through the slowly clearing windshield. "Does this mean we'll have more time together?"

"Yeah. No more leaving you alone in bed on Sunday mornings." I suspected it would be harder to sneak out at night if I was supposed to be caring for Sofie, but I'd worry about that later. We had so little time together these days. I moved close to him. "Come on. Let's stop at Ida's. It won't take long. We drive right by. You don't have to go in, if you don't want to." I flip-flopped between dreading to tell Tony and aching to blurt it out and hop back into the Bonneville, leaving the words behind like a bag of Lucy's empties left on the curb for the trash collectors.

"So, you quit the job. What'll you do for money?" Danny turned onto Main Street. "Depend on me to support you? Right now, keeping the car running is about all I can afford but someday…"

"I'm going into business for myself." The words sounded so good I said them again, louder. "I'm going into business for myself."

"What kind of business?" He pulled to a stop at the curb in front of Ida's. I had pictured going in the back door. In the front, I'd have to suffer Antonia's glare from behind the counter.

"What else? Custom cakes." Too late I heard the pride in my voice. Danny narrowed his eyes.

"Excuse me." He leaned back, folding his arms. "I forgot. Rivertown's Picasso. Is that the guy's name? Am I saying it right?" He hammered away. "And where will you make these custom cakes? At home?"

"Sofie's," I whispered, furious I'd given him an answer. I had nothing to feel embarrassed about. "I think I might even move in there for a while."

"With that old bag? What about her son? The old bag and the old fag." He slapped his leg. "Great."

"What's the matter with you?" I said. "I thought you'd be happy. I'm quitting the bakery to have more time with you."

"Are you quitting to be with me, or is it because the old lady isn't there any-more? Are you making money for our life together or for your life apart from me? Why don't you tell the truth about what's happening here?" Danny turned his face away, pressing his hands against his chest as if his heart hurt.

"If this is how it is when we're together, maybe we should forget the whole thing." I considered leaving him then, slamming the car door behind me. But Danny DiBona had spent many months convincing us both he needed me. On the list of people who had achieved that distinction, he was the only one whose need appeared in the shape of desire, in his gentle grin, his arms around me. I remembered; I loved him.

"I thought we were going to have fun this afternoon. Skating. Right?" I pleaded, stroking his bluejeaned thigh. He caught my hand under his and rubbed each of my cold fingers with his warm ones.

"You're freezing," he said, voice thick as cake batter. "I'll turn the heat up."

A customer exiting the bakery reminded me of my mission. "I'll be right back. I don't want to miss Tony."

Danny pulled me close and covered my mouth with a kiss that didn't stop. Photos from *National Geographic* flashed through my mind, pictures of snakelike creatures, all mouth on one end. They attached to the side of a fish while the unsuspecting victim went on with its swimming, its life. They didn't let go until the fish died, everything sucked out of it.

"I'll come in with you," he whispered as if his kiss had fixed everything. I shrugged. If I told him I wanted to go alone we'd be fighting all over again.

As I opened the door to Ida's Antonia looked up from a stack of unfolded pie boxes and frowned. "What are you doing here? I thought you said you couldn't work today."

"Where's Tony?"

She jerked her head toward the back, put a hand on her hip and pushed out her chest, grinning at Danny as though he were the only one there. "Hey Danny DiBona."

"Hi." He grinned back, swaggering toward the counter. I coughed, and he threw me a pleased look of exaggerated innocence.

"Can I help you with something?" Antonia leaned on the counter, offering Danny her widest smile, her big breasts. "Dad's back there," she said to me. Danny stopped trailing behind and waited, fingers tapping on the counter top, pretending to want a cupcake or a donut. He'd told me he was sick of bakery food. I shoved the swinging door out of my way.

"Who's the richest man in the world?" Tony hollered over the grinding of the mixer. I knew the answer. He told the same jokes over and over. If something was funny once, it was funny every time. He turned the mixer off. "What, you don't know? A baker. Cause he's got a lot of dough." He lifted the mixing bowl to prove his point, and laughing, set it in a warm corner, near the oven to rise.

"I don't know how to tell you this except to just come out and say it," I said.

"You've fallen in love with me." He winked. "Don't worry. I understand. Happens all the time. I won't tell my wife."

"Seriously," I said. "You're not going to like this. I'm quitting."

His face fell. "My two best girls. During the holidays. It's too much." He bent over, using his hands to wipe flour from his boots, something I'd never seen him do before.

"I'll work until after New Year's," I offered. "I'm sorry, but Martin wants me to help out at Sofie's so he can go back to San Francisco. They're hiring me."

"And those cakes of yours?"

"I'll be making a few of those too I guess."

"Name your salary," he said, straightening up. "You name it. I want you to stay." I hesitated, wondering if I'd make more money at Ida's or on my own. I'd miss Tony's bad jokes, his faith in me and the work I'd learned to do. I was sick of disappointing people.

I thought about serving Officer Belinsky. I thought about Antonia, wondered for a moment what she was doing with Danny up front. "Do what you want," I heard Sofie say. I thought about working at Ida's without Sofie and knew what I wanted.

"No, I'm quitting."

"Between now and New Year's," Tony said, his voice cheerful again. "I'm going to find a way to change your mind."

"I don't think so." I'd never have to work with Antonia, never even have to see her unless I went to a Rivertown-Spelton game or came into Ida's as a customer. I'd never have to empty the muddy wash water or scrub a film of donut grease from my skin or drag myself out of Danny's warm bed at four a.m.

"You'll see," Tony said, pushing an empty flour bag deep into the trash. I decided not to argue. He'd be the one to see.

Up front, Danny said something. Antonia giggled. He jumped when he saw me.

"We still going skating?" I asked as if I didn't care about the answer.

"Sure." Danny dragged himself away from the counter, from Antonia DiMartino. DiBona and DiMartino. Teresa and Tony would approve of a nice, hard-working Italian boy.

I remembered something Sofie had said way back in the fall about Ida, the original owner. "Too busy working." What was it? Too busy working to have babies, to get married. That was me. But I didn't even want marriage or babies. Ida had saved all that money and didn't even get to where she wanted to go. No one wants to die alone, all worn out. There had to be another choice.

"We better go, I guess," Danny said. "People are waiting for us."

"I like to skate," Antonia said. "Whenever my father, the slave driver, gives me time off. I'll see you around."

"Okay." I pretended she was talking to me. I clung to Danny's jacket.

Back in the Bonneville, I sat on my hands to keep from wiping the windows and chewed the insides of my cheeks to keep from kissing Danny too long and too hard. On the short drive to my house to pick up my skates the only sound in the car was the roar of the defroster.

In the living room, Lucy and Miss Jennings drank tea. Lucy with a steaming mug in her hand. Tea instead of vodka. They turned toward me, Jennings' pen hovering over her pad.

"Hello, Wylie." The social worker's voice sounded like a warm vanilla milkshake. "How are you?"

"I am fine," I answered. "Can't talk. Someone's waiting for me."

"Where are you going?" Lucy asked. "Do you think you can just go out without letting me know?"

"Oh come on." The bomb ticking inside since Danny picked me up exploded. I pointed a finger at the social worker. "Because she's here, you want to know where I'm going. Stop trying to impersonate a real mother." Lucy's mouth opened and closed. "By the time I get home you'll be passed out anyway. What do you care?"

Jennings' eyes popped. "Go ahead." I jabbed a finger at her notes. "Scribble that. She's a drunk. She's not going to quit because you tell her to go to AA. She even said she'd never go."

I took four careful steps out of the room, then ran to my pantry. I couldn't breathe. I heard Lucy and Jennings jabbering as I dug around for my skates. Rushing past them before they could turn into anything more solid than a babbling blur of color, I dove into the Bonneville and Danny revved the engine.

"What's the matter?" His voice folded around me.

"Just drive, okay. Get me away from here." My scuffed skates rested in my lap. The blades needed sharpening.

I'd taken the bomb from inside me and hurled it, saving myself, destroying everything else. I would be okay. I'd live with Sofie. Robbie and Kevin would have nowhere to go. Jennings would be filling out the paperwork for foster care the minute she returned to her office.

"Is it too hot in here?" Danny fiddled with the heat.

"It's fine."

"I love you." His hand rested warm on my neck like a scarf. No way was I going home. We'd spend the night together.

Danny unloaded two hockey sticks and his skates from the trunk. We walked across the snowy gravel lot, the pond spreading silver in front of us. The sun, sinking behind the dark pine trees, spilled fading light over it all. Skaters tore around the pond, laughing, yelling. Hockey sticks scraped at the speeding puck. Robbie whipped by in a long, navy blue coat he'd found in the neighbors' trash. Unbuttoned, it flapped out behind him.

"Wylie's on our team," he shouted. He always wanted me for goalie.

"We get DiBona," someone yelled.

Danny and I laced up our skates and played hockey on opposite teams until the first stars came out and our fingers and toes had moved through pain to numbness.

"Robbie," Danny called. "Got any matches?"

"Ha. Ha. Very funny." Robbie skated over and punched Danny's shoulder.

"I'm serious. We need a bonfire right now. Here on the beach. Or we'll have to leave in search of heat." Danny rubbed his gloved fingers together and blew on them.

Robbie tossed him a book of matches. "When the cops come, remember, I had nothing to do with this."

We spread out in the dark, staggering around on our skates, picking up wood and dumping it into one big pile. Danny arranged it carefully, as if he'd been a Boy Scout. He knew how to make fires, take out splinters or fix broken stereos. Crouched over the dry wood, he held a match under the thinnest pieces. They crackled. Looking at his face lit by the glow of the fire, I knew that if we stayed together he'd shovel the sidewalk, wash dishes, and keep the car running. He'd wear rubbers until we were sure we wanted a baby. He'd change his fair share of diapers.

I skated away from the warm circle where people were passing around joints and bottles of wine and sloe gin. Someone else broke away and followed me. Danny. I led him to the darkest edge of the ice, near the cattails and reeds. Our skate blades slashed across the ice. We breathed hard. I stopped suddenly with a spray of ice chips.

"Whoa!" Robbie ran into me. We fell in a heap.

I untangled my legs from his. "You!" I stood, offered my hand.

He let me yank him to his feet. "Danny said you're moving. Is that true?"

"When did he say that?"

"Before, over at the fire." We stood close, without touching, our faces shadowed. He kicked at the ice with the sharp tip of his skate.

"He had no business saying anything. I was going to tell you."

"How can you do that?" Robbie seemed to strain to keep from whining. "How can you just move in with someone you worked with…for what? Three months. She doesn't even know you. Where does she live anyhow? This Sofie person." He growled 'person,' making her sound dangerous, evil. The fire was a small orange blur, far away in the dark.

"Did Danny explain it's a job? I'll take care of her while her hip heals." Resting my hand on his arm, all I felt were the layers of mitten and coat between us. "And at the same time I can make my special cakes there. So many people want them. I can make lots of money."

"For what?" Robbie spit the words and pulled his arm away, skated off a short distance in the darkness, then came back.

"For…" I hesitated. "For a car. We could use a car. For grocery shopping and things. My driving test is next month."

"Yeah." Robbie spun around, hands in his coat pockets.

"You and me could drive places too." I skated around him in a slow, tight circle.

"Sofie only lives a couple minutes from our house. I could pick you up and we could drive into New Haven or up to Hartford for concerts. Look, did you expect me to stay in that house for the rest of my life?" He chopped at the ice again instead of answering.

"Tell the truth," I persisted. "If you were me, if you had the chance to get out, you'd do it."

From far away, people laughed. Close up sounded the steady thwacking of Robbie's skate.

"You would!" I shouted. "Anybody would. Say you would." I jabbed him hard in the chest. He struggled to keep his balance. "Or maybe you wouldn't," I went on. "Maybe you'd stay. Sometimes," I mimicked him. "Sometimes? Sometimes she drinks too much? She asked you. You could've told her. Made her listen. She might've believed you."

"What would you want me to say?" Robbie asked, his voice wobbly.

"Yes!" I said. "I wanted you to say yes. Maybe she'd listen if you said it."

"She wouldn't. She'd just get mad. It's not worth it."

"You should button up that coat," I said.

We skated back to the beach where people recruited Robbie to lead a game of crack-the-whip. Danny held out his hand to me. I loved my turn at the end of the line when after skating as fast as we could skate, the leader stopped, the line whipped across the ice, and I'd wait for the right moment to let go. I loved the sensation of gliding, flying, into the dark, everyone's screams fading behind me.

"It's my long lost daughter." Lucy, stretched out on the couch, in her pink, quilted bathrobe, raised a can of beer in a lazy toast. It was nine o'clock Sunday night. Kevin was in bed.

I edged toward my room, glad not to have to lift my brother from the living room floor. I couldn't tell how drunk my mother was, how angry about the incident with Miss Jennings.

"Wait a minute." Lucy patted the sofa cushion near her hip. "Come here."

I stood over her, waiting. "Well, sit down," Lucy said. "We can't have a talk when you're looming over me like that. Like you're waiting to pounce." She set her beer on the coffee table, sat up against the arm of the couch, and folded her hands in her lap. "Turn down the TV. Turn it off."

"Forget it, Mom," I said. About once a year Lucy tried to have a real conversation with me, usually after she'd seen a heart to heart, mother-daughter talk on one of her soap operas. She always began with her memorized lines right from the mouths of the TV moms, but when I didn't follow her script she'd get all fuzzy, distracted by the phone or Kevin or anything. She didn't know how to improvise.

"Turn the TV off, will you? And sit down." Lucy hugged herself as if she were cold. Her glare forced me into the nearest armchair. I landed with a crunching sound, pulled a bag of potato chips out from under me, ate a handful of crumbs, and stared at the blank television screen, waiting for my mother to say something. Lucy licked her lips, rubbed the worn elbows of her robe. She didn't seem drunk.

"Robbie tells me you're planning to move." When I didn't say anything, she went on. "He told me Friday night. He was pretty upset."

I nodded and swallowed, my mouth dry and salty. Robbie knew he'd have to start doing more work if I left. That's all. I didn't say it out loud.

"I've been thinking about it all weekend," Lucy said. "You moving. I know you think I'm a lousy mother. I guess I can see how you might think so. But I love you. I love all you kids." She squinted her green eyes. I wondered where the conversation would take us. It matched our life circumstances too well to be TV inspired, though it might make a good show. Mother, panicked by threat of oldest daughter leaving, tries anything to make her stay, even going as far as to say the "L" word.

"Having a mother who loves you, even one who makes some big mistakes, is better than not having a mother at all. You know, I was seven when I lost mine. When I went to live with my father's sister, my Aunt Beryl. She hated me but believed in doing her duty. My father was off looking for oil in Alaska or somewhere. No forwarding address. You're lucky you never met Beryl. She died when you and Robbie were small. I did my best to avoid her once I'd moved out."

I'd known my grandmother died when Lucy was a girl, but I couldn't remember how I learned it. Lucy never talked about her. I hadn't known my mother had been so young, just a little older than Kevin.

"Beryl worked in the high school cafeteria. Strange job for someone who hated teenagers. I guess she hated people in general. She hated my mother in particular—blamed her for getting pregnant with me and not marrying my father. The shame that brought the family." Lucy picked at a cuticle until it began to bleed. "She even blamed her for dying."

"Why didn't Beryl blame your father? And why didn't your mother marry him?" I really wanted to know. It had been a long time since I'd asked my mother anything and cared so much about her answer.

"The guy was a jerk. She knew he didn't love her. She didn't want to marry him. But in those days, that didn't matter. A woman with a lousy husband was better off than a woman with a baby and no husband at all."

"Didn't you just say the same thing to me about mothers?" I crumpled the empty potato chip bag and held it tight. "Aren't you saying exactly the same thing? That it's better to have a lousy mother than none at all? Maybe what you really mean is that it's better to have a lousy mother than a lousy aunt. Maybe a nice aunt would be better than a lousy mother."

"Or a nice old woman who works at Ida's?" Lucy swung her legs from the couch to the coffee table and leaned forward, challenging me. Her robe gapped open exposing her thin chest. Her collarbones stuck out.

I thought for a minute before answering. Something important was happening. I wanted to go slow. "Sofie," I said.

"Is that her name?" Lucy knew it was. "Listen, what you don't see is all that I have done for you. I left my lousy family. They never had a chance to poison you kids' lives the way they poisoned mine. I've kept a roof over our heads, food in your mouths. I've never hit you or let your father lay a hand on you, even when he was raging drunk. I don't bother you about school work. Have I ever said anything bad about Danny?" She pressed her lips together and waited, probably for me to say thanks. "Not that you have to go around being grateful all the time or anything.

"That was the worst thing about Aunt Beryl. I couldn't take a step without her saying something. Criticizing. I promised myself I'd give my kids room to be who they were. To do what they wanted so they wouldn't ruin their lives making stupid choices just to get out of the house." She narrowed her eyes. "And look. The first chance you get, you're leaving."

"What I'd like to know," I said, uncrumpling the potato chip bag and smoothing it over my thigh. "Is why everyone knows about my plans before I've even said anything. And why no one asks me about it or gives me a chance to explain without having a big fit."

"Am I having a fit?" Lucy asked, voice shrill. "I could be. Most kids who called their mother a drunk in front of the social worker would see a lot more of a fit than you're seeing right now."

"Alright," I said. "Listen. It's a job. I've been offered a job."

"You just got a job. At the bakery. Why do you need another one? There's enough to do around here."

"If you'd listen to me, I'd tell you," I shouted.

She sat back and took a long swallow of her beer. "Okay, I'm listening."

Part of me wanted to give her the long version, the whole story of Sofie and the goddess cake, the butterfly and the monster, Sofie's fall and the angel, the steady stream of strange cake orders only I could fill, Martin. Part of me felt I didn't owe my mother even the shortest explanation.

"I've been decorating these made to order cakes. For big bucks. I can make more on them than I make at Ida's. I want to quit and start my own business. I can use Sofie's kitchen. At the same time Sofie needs someone around to help her while she recovers from a hip operation so…"

"So you move in with her and live happily ever after and what happens to us?" Lucy rolled her empty beer can between her palms. "What's wrong with our kitchen?"

I stood up. "I have homework."

"I didn't want it all to work out this way. I didn't think my life would be like this." She held my sweater so I couldn't get away without shaking her off. "You'll see. You have an idea how your life will work out, and it won't happen that way. I guarantee it."

"Wait." She tugged at my sleeve. "Sit down, please. One more thing. Then you can go. Do your homework, screw your boyfriend, take care of your old lady, whatever you want." She took a deep breath. "I have one more thing to say to you, and I've been waiting to say it since Friday when you stormed out of here. So sit down." She slid over to make a space on the sagging couch and pulled me down beside her.

"Don't look so mad. I just want to tell you a story." I rolled my eyes. "Really. I told it to you when you were little. But you probably don't remember. I should have told you more stories. I'm sorry. My mother told me this one, and it's one of the only things I really remember about her."

Stories. This was new. The only story she'd ever told was the one about salting birds' tails. I called that a lie.

"Once upon a time there was a seal-woman."

"Like a mermaid?"

"Sort of." Lucy folded her long legs underneath her.

I put on a bored expression.

"There was a farmer who lived by the sea. One day he took a walk on the beach and heard a beautiful song. It stirred him up inside. He followed the sound and found it was coming from a woman resting on a rock near shore. He hid himself and listened and watched and fell in love. When evening came he tore himself away and went back to his farm and his work. But he was obsessed. He couldn't stop thinking about her."

"Well, he asked everyone he knew about her and no one knew anything until finally the oldest woman in the town said, 'Ah, the selkie girl! She'll come again. Watch for her. When you see her, look for a bundle beside her. Her selkie skin. If you can grab her skin, and take it from her, she'll be forced to stay in her human form and won't be able to return to the sea. So the guy did just that. And he married the selkie girl even though she was crying and begging for her skin back.'" Lucy stopped, her face hard.

"That can't be the end?"

"No."

"Well, tell me the rest."

"She had a bunch of kids. She worked on the farm. But it never felt right because she belonged in the sea. One day one of the kids saw her father take the skin from where he'd hidden it. She watched while he laid it out in the sun and oiled it, then put it back in its hiding place. She asked her mother about it. The mother, of course, knew right away that the girl had discovered the skin. And that night the woman found it, brought it down to the sea, slipped it on, and was gone forever."

"What happened to the farmer? And the kids?" I asked in an unfamiliar squeaky voice. "That can't be the end."

My mother squinted at me, perplexed. "That's all. That is the end."

"It's not. It can't be."

"The guy stole her skin, her skin." Lucy's eyes glinted green as wet sea glass. "How could he expect to have a decent life with her when things began like that? And the worst of it is that the whole time, he knew right where it was and even though he could see she was miserable he wouldn't give it back."

"Why are you telling me this?" I stood up. "What are you trying to say?"

"I never pictured my life working out this way." She lit a cigarette.

"Did the selkie woman ever look for her skin? Why did she sit around waiting for her daughter to find it?" I asked. "If I were her, I wouldn't have stopped searching for a minute."

"I don't know." Lucy blew a smoke ring and picked a tobacco flake from her tongue.

"It's pathetic," I said, trying not to shout. "She should've held onto the bundle in the first place if it was so important. She should've grabbed it away from the guy when he tried to take it. She should've looked for it when it disappeared."

"It's easy for people to tell other people what they should've done," Lucy said. "It's the easiest thing in the world."

"I'm taking a bath," I announced.

"When are you moving out?" Lucy yelled. She never worried about waking anyone up.

"Soon!" I wished it were the next day.

"Fine. Don't worry about us." My mother's words followed me down the hall. "We'll do alright without you. You take care of yourself."

"I will." The bathroom doorknob came off in my hand. I jabbed it back in and turned it. I'd tried to fix it so many times. It would work for a while, then loosen and pull out again.

"Wylie." Lucy's voice came from the other side of the bathroom door. I concentrated on the sound of the running water, pretending I couldn't hear. "All I had to drink today was three beers." What did she want? A cake with congratulations written on it? The day wasn't even over yet. "You don't believe me? You can go check the six pack in the fridge. There are three cans left."

How did I know my mother hadn't polished off another earlier? Or a bottle of vodka? She did seem more sober than usual. Not only was the desperate mother using the "L" word, she was actually trying not to be drunk. Big deal. One day. I sat on the covered toilet, still dressed, and held my head. The water gushed into the tub.

Lucy went on and on. "I'm going to stop drinking. But I can't just stop cold turkey. Three beers a day for a week. You watch. Then one. Then I'll stop. I'll never drink again."

Sure. The tub was almost full, but I needed the sound of running water. I opened the drain.

"You don't believe me. Have I ever said I'd stop drinking before?"

She hadn't. Never.

"I'm going to do it." I pictured my mother pressed against the chipped white paint of the door, her long fingers on the broken doorknob, her bare feet cold on the floor. If those three beers were sitting in the refrigerator when I got home the next day, I wouldn't move out. That's how sure I was they'd be gone.

"Listen," Lucy said. "If you don't believe me, you take that beer and hide it. Search me. Search the house. Prove to yourself I don't have anything stashed away." I turned off the faucet and watched the water slide down the drain with a whispery sound. Lucy's breathing was loud. She could open the door. It wasn't locked.

"I've thought about it all weekend," she said. "The state is ready to put you all in foster homes. What would I do then, the three of you spread out across the valley, living with strangers?" Her voice caught. "I'd have to stop drinking anyway to get you back. The only choice I have is how I quit. I won't go to AA."

The water gurgled away. I clung to the sink.

"Wylie?" Lucy said. "Can I come in?"

"No."

The girl in the mirror shook her head. "Tell her to go to AA," she whispered. "Tell her it's not your job to hide her beer. Tell her."

"What?" Lucy asked. "I can't hear you. Come on. Open the door so we can talk."

"No," I said.

I wanted to be in my mother's lap, pressing my face against the cool, smoky satin of her bathrobe, feeling her arms around me. I wanted my mother to hold me until I stopped struggling to get away. That door wasn't even locked.

"Have it your way," Lucy said, shuffling back to the couch.

I reminded the girl in the mirror that I'd taken care of myself for years, what my so-called mother did or didn't do made no difference.

On Monday, after school, I went to Sofie's to make a birthday cake for IJ's son, John. Martin seemed to think I had the power to make a cake so special we could convince IJ to help out some with Sofie after he left, so I would have time for my family and school. Martin said he'd pay for the cake himself and had suggested a pool table design. I fingered the bag of gum balls in my pocket. They were just the right size for billiard balls on a nine by thirteen inch cake.

My mother's birthday was next week. I tried imagining a cake for her. Flowers, dragons, emerging butterflies, pool tables, nothing seemed right. The three beers were still in the refrigerator that morning. I'd scratched a little x on the bottom of each can to be sure they were the same ones. Lucy, up early, paced the house smoking, ashes falling unnoticed from her cigarette.

Four different characters lived inside my head and never stopped arguing about where my body belonged. One thought I should be at home, another wanted to be close to Danny, a third pushed for living with Sofie, and a fourth couldn't decide between running away or climbing into bed and hiding under the covers. The voices were so evenly matched none could stay in control longer than a few hours and so loud, Janis Joplin's loudest screams couldn't drown any of them out for more than minutes.

Martin answered the door as soon as I knocked, as though he'd been standing there waiting. "I'm glad you're here," he whispered. "Sofie's been asking for you every time there's a commercial. She's been ready since noon to begin on that cake." He took my coat. "Asking me to find pictures of a pool table."

"I've got one," I said. "But maybe we should use this as an excuse to get her out for a while. We could all head over to Rivertown Billiards. I bet Sofie's never been there." Martin wiggled his mouth into what he probably thought was a smile. Poor Sofie, with a son born lacking a sense of humor. She said she talked to Oskar every morning before she got out of bed. Maybe she joked around with him.

Sofie dozed, slumped in her chair. So much for being ready to decorate a cake. With his ironed handkerchief, Martin daubed at a string of spit dangling from the corner of her open mouth. I looked away, thinking of all the nights I'd found Lucy passed out on the couch snoring, drunk, drooling, surrounded by ashes, cigarette butts, maybe a knocked over glass. I always stopped to clean her up so the boys wouldn't see their mother like that.

I sat down in the carved rocker, leaning back.

"My father made that chair for her, when she was pregnant with me," Martin volunteered.

"I know," I said, rocking. "Sofie said."

"Did she tell you…"

"How he wanted her to sit." He didn't need to tell me things I already knew about Sofie, things I told myself.

Martin stood, silenced, and I regretted interrupting him. "I guess you should wake her up."

He squeezed her shoulder. "Mother, Wylie's here."

Sofie stirred, opened her eyes, yawned and adjusted her glasses. "*Ach du liebe*, the dreams I am having. I had a wedding cake, three tiered, all decorated, and had to deliver it to the hospital of all the places! For a very important doctor's wedding. Carrying it to my car, across the parking lot all ice and deep snow, I dropped the cake. On my hands and knees I tried pushing the broken parts back together. My fingers were so cold. Birds came to eat and I kept trying to shoo them off and they were speaking German, squawking, *Wir haben hunger. Wir haben hunger.*" She hunched her shoulders. "I am still feeling them flapping." She forced a laugh.

"Wylie brought a picture of a pool table," Martin said.

Sofie breathed the deep breath of someone who's just made a big decision. "Alright. I'm ready to walk to the kitchen." Martin set her walker in front of her. She gripped the handles and stood.

"You go on," she said. "Start mixing the icing. By the time I get there, you'll have it all ready."

I slipped past her.

"You're moving more quickly every day, Mother," Martin said. "Do you want to try the cane?"

She waved him aside. "When I'm wanting to use the cane I'll be letting you know. Now, move. Right in my way you're standing."

Martin avoided my sympathetic glance. He scurried out of Sofie's path. A tall man should never scurry. When I did as Sofie told me, I did it because I chose to, not because I was afraid of her. How could you be afraid of your own mother, especially when she only came up to your armpit?

I considered myself fearless. I stopped being afraid of my mother and even my father as soon as I learned where they kept the loose change and how to walk to the store for groceries. I could take care of myself.

The chocolate sheet cake waited in the refrigerator. Sofie had baked it that morning with Martin's help. He'd set the mixer and ingredients at the table so she could do the baking sitting down. He'd carried the full pan to the preheated oven, taken it out when it was done. He kept the kitchen clean. No dishes in the sink, no soggy Cheerios or carrot peelings clogging the drain.

"On my own, I can manage," I heard Sofie complain as I drizzled a tablespoon of water over a mountain of sugar in a large, blue bowl. I pictured her shuffling through the dining room, Martin hovering behind, wringing his hands. He should threaten to leave, to go home to California. Sofie couldn't or wouldn't remember Martin had a good job and his own life, miles away from Rivertown.

"Martin, why don't you go to the store?" Sofie said. "We have work to do here."

"I won't bother you," he said. He talked like a marshmallow, a pillow, a snowman on a warm day. Didn't he ever get angry? "I'll be down in the basement."

Sofie settled herself into the chair. I moved the walker and pushed her close to the table. "What's he do down there?"

Sofie sighed. "With all Oskar's tools, you'd think he'd do woodworking or fix something. But no." She slapped the edge of the table.

I divided the icing into small bowls and mixed a green and a brown. I showed them to Sofie. "What do you think?"

"A little more yellow in that. And mix some black. Black we are needing, for details."

I handed her the yellow paste and the green icing. "You do this one. I always add too much." I scooped white into a cup and made black. "So what does he do down there?"

"Model airplanes he builds." Sofie snorted. "A grown man spending time with toys. In California he says he has a whole room for building models. In a four room apartment. Can you imagine?"

I couldn't, at least at first. Then, the more I tried, the better I pictured Martin's fingers, the same careful fingers that smoothed Sofie's blankets in the hospital or wiped spit from her mouth, fitting together pieces of wood or plastic or whatever models were made of. Again I felt an urge to know him better. I imagined an apartment with airplanes hanging from every ceiling. From the doorway of his room, I'd seen the planes he'd made when he was young, but I hadn't realized adults built models, especially someone as serious as Martin.

"He flies them." Sofie stirred the bright green icing. "That's what he is doing with his time. When he's not working, he is making and flying planes. A fifty-year-old man."

"They really fly?" I stopped between the counter and the table, a bowl balanced in each hand. "Do they have engines or what?"

"Why don't you ask him?" Sofie slammed her bowl down on the table, her anger sudden and startling. "Go right over there to the basement door and holler down to him. And while you are asking, you can be finding out for me why he never was marrying or having children. With his cutting and gluing and flying, maybe he is so busy he is forgetting all about it. Like old Ida with her bakery. Ask him. Tell him how sorry he will be."

I looked for Sofie in the twisted face of the woman beside me. I replayed our conversation, trying to understand what had upset her.

"What's the matter?" she asked. "You're the artistic one. Cut pockets into this pool table so we can start with the icing."

I picked up a knife, put it down, and picked it up again. It was none of Sofie's business why Martin decided not to get married. And none of mine. "I think it's amazing he can build planes that fly," I said. "I'd like to see them."

"Are you going to cut that cake or not?"

I studied the sheet cake, trying to position pockets without measuring.

"Get a ruler," Sofie said.

"I don't need one!" I shouted.

Sofie leaned back, surprised.

I dropped onto the chair next to her and sat, elbows on the table. "I can't do this right now."

"Why not?" Sofie reached for a well mixed bowl of icing and beat it some more. "You have to do it now. Ivy Jane is coming tonight to pick it up."

"What I want to know," I blurted. "Is why you treat your son worse than a dog when he's come all the way from California and taken time off from work to help you out? He cleans your house, does all the errands, waits on you. How can you be like this? So what if he wants to build airplanes?"

Sofie stared.

And so what if he's not married? I thought. Maybe he never met the right person. Is it a son or daughter's job to give parents grandchildren? Maybe he's seen too many bad marriages.

"He's trying so hard to please you and you're never satisfied," I went on. "It just makes me sick. A man fifty years old trying so hard.

"I'm sorry," I added, suddenly uncomfortable.

The door to the basement creaked open. Both of us turned to stare at Martin. "Sound travels." He pointed to the heat register, a rectangular piece of slotted metal in the floor near the refrigerator. "I'd be glad to show you my airplanes, Wylie. Any time."

"Oh." I picked up a spatula and stared at it, my face red. "Sure."

All three of us seemed to be waiting for him to say more. He frowned and took a step backward.

"Wait," said Sofie. "Is that all you can say?"

He edged toward the basement stairs. Sofie glared at him. I was glad Sofie wasn't my mother. He looked at me. I managed a shaky smile.

"I'm not the pathetic old bachelor you seem to think I am. I've had plenty of love in my life. I had a lover for almost fifteen years. We didn't live together, but we might as well have. We lived in adjoining apartments."

Martin, with a lover? Hard to imagine. He was not a sexy guy. Lover. The word brought to mind wide beds with satin sheets, lacy lingerie, steamy nights, ending in breakfasts in bed. Martin could do the breakfast part, silver coffeepots and single red roses. The nights were harder to imagine.

"What happened to her?" I asked. I liked the idea of being lovers next door to each other. I could suggest it to Danny. Forget marriage.

"Him," Martin said. "He died." He took off his glasses, wiped his eyes, then concentrated on polishing the lenses with his handkerchief.

"Him?" I asked. "Your lover was a man?" Two men kissing between those satin sheets? I couldn't believe Danny was right. Martin was a fag. I should have known. I'd heard San Francisco was full of them.

"Well," said Sofie. "Well." She looked up at the ceiling then closed her eyes. She looked like a statue you'd see in a church.

Her hand gripped an icing bag so tightly that black icing oozed from both ends of it. Martin kept rubbing his handkerchief over his glasses with small, perfect circular movements of his thumb and fingers.

Martin, a homo. I had heard about those guys but didn't think I knew any. Men kissing each other and who knew what else they did. I couldn't picture Martin kissing anyone, never mind another man.

He leaned against the wall and wiped his face with his handkerchief. He looked pale.

"How did your lover die?" I asked, partly because it seemed someone should say something, partly to feel the word lover on my tongue. I'd never had a reason to use it before.

"Melanoma." Another new word. "Skin cancer," Martin explained.

Martin looked at Sofie. Her turn to speak. "Well," she said again. Her mouth moved like she was about to say something else, then she tightened her lips. A thousand wrinkles surrounded her puckered mouth, her nostrils flared.

I willed the outlines of six pockets to appear on the surface of the cake so I could start cutting.

"I think we should talk about this later," said Sofie looking at Martin, tilting her head sideways toward me. "We have a cake to finish here."

"No," said Martin.

"Later." Sofie's voice was sharp. She studied the cake.

The refrigerator hummed. Martin shifted his weight, a floorboard squeaked. I wanted to leave but didn't know how. Some silence holds you. Some freezes you. Some makes you squirm. The silence filling the kitchen was that kind, but worse. It made me itch.

"Come here," Sofie ordered Martin, finally. She pointed to a chair across from her. "Sit." Martin sat, but in the other chair, the one across from me. "All these years I've waited for you to get married." Noticing the drippy icing bag in her hand she wrinkled her nose in disgust. I rushed to hand her a dishcloth. *"Alter schützt vor Torheit nicht.* You made a fool of me, Martin." She held the dishcloth like she didn't know what to do with it.

"You're not a fool, Mother." Martin rested his head in his hands. Busy sculpting the cake, I tried to make myself belong. I was working.

"How could you do this to me?" Sofie said, shaking her head. She gazed at the table, the floor, the ceiling, around the room, everywhere but at Martin.

"It is what it is," he said. "It's nothing I've done."

"In high school, those girls you went to the movies with, the dances? What about them?" Sofie asked.

Martin didn't answer. I scooped green icing from the bowl and plopped it onto the middle of the cake.

"And even IJ. She is, how do you say it, not the brightest bulb, but she needs a husband, and you two were always liking each other. I thought maybe you and she—Why are you telling me this?" she interrupted herself. "Why now? This I don't have to know."

"You asked why I never married. Now you can stop wondering. Erich never met Father. He never met you. Father never really knew me."

Sofie's eyes blazed. *"Bist du ein Dummkopf?* He knew you. He was your father."

"No. Whole parts of my life, he never knew."

"Parts like that, better nobody knows," Sofie spat the words. I pictured her at Ida's urging me, yelling at me, to talk about my problems, things that hurt the heart.

"You are so very wrong about that," Martin whispered.

In the next silent moments Sofie's face changed expression more times than I could count. Martin stood still, waiting. Nobody knew what to say. I thought of Sofie's dead daughter, Martin's sister, and wondered how much Sofie had said to him about her, what he remembered about the birth that was a death, the long silent years afterward.

"Fifteen years you are together?" Sofie asked. "Cancer, he died of?" Her face had settled into sadness.

Martin nodded. "After the diagnosis, it happened so fast."

"It's hard after so many years to be losing someone." She must have been thinking about Oskar. "Losing someone is very hard.

"Erich," she said. "How is he spelling it?"

"With a c-h. His parents were German. Like you. Like us."

I smoothed green over the cake's surface.

"Wylie," said Sofie. She tapped the cake board twice with her crooked finger.

"Hmm?" I spread the thin layer of brown crumb icing onto the sides of the cake.

"Look here." Her eyes shot me a warning. "It's like you're part of our family. I hope…"

"I mind my own business," I said. "I told you. I don't talk about other people's business."

I finished crumb icing the cake. Martin sat, shoulders hunched, clutching his handkerchief. Sofie's eyebrows and lips moved as if in an argument with herself.

"Always I was hoping you would marry a nice German girl. At least you got the German part right."

I laughed. I couldn't help it. Sofie looked at me in surprise. Then Martin started, a small laugh, then a louder one from way down inside. Laughter ricocheted off the walls of the kitchen. A sound halfway between a chuckle and a sob escaped Sofie's tight lips.

Martin wiped his eyes. "I'll make some tea." It was getting dark. The conversation wasn't finished. I knew the rest would happen without me. Sofie fingered the teaspoon Martin set in front of her.

I finished the cake while Martin collected the tea things. I didn't have to watch to know where he found the saucers, the cups, the tea bags. Already I knew where things were in Sofie's kitchen better than I knew where things were in my own. Everything had a place.

Martin poured tea. Sofie's absentminded, steady stirring created a small whirlpool in her cup. I worked quickly, arranging the gum balls. The world was stranger and more full of possibility than I'd realized. If a man from Rivertown could sleep with a man and come back and tell his seventy-year-old mother about it, anything could happen.

"Next week is my mother's birthday," I offered, just to say something. "I want to make a special cake for her. I don't want to just cover a cake with flowers. But I can't think of anything."

"What is she interested in?" Martin leaned forward, eager to keep the conversation going.

I pictured a vodka bottle and a deck of cards. "Nothing much."

"Before she had children?" he prompted. "There must have been something she enjoyed."

"I don't know. She liked her waitressing job. She liked going to the movies. Musicals."

"Maybe something from a musical then," he suggested.

"Maybe." There had to be something better, more significant. I emptied my teacup.

Sofie put down her spoon. "I'm tired," she said abruptly. "Martin, give Wylie a ride home. Then come make for us a little supper." Us meant Martin and her, not me. Sofie didn't even comment on the cake, didn't smile when we left.

Until we were out of the driveway, Martin and I were quiet. I looked back at the dark window of the upstairs blue room. Once I moved in no one would have to take me "home."

"So now you know." Martin said, eyes focused straight ahead.

"I guess." Neat lines of stitching crossed his leather gloves. He turned the wheel.

"And?"

"It's your business," I said. "I mean it, it's your business. I'm sorry he died." He wanted more from me, but I was thinking of Sofie's warm kitchen and empty good-bye.

Unable to get to his handkerchief, Martin pushed a gloved finger under his glasses to wipe his eye. I handed him a clump of tissues, swallowing my own tears.

"It's just been in my pocket a long time," I said, noticing his hesitation.

Nodding, he swiped at his face.

He pulled over in front of my house. The moment when I could have naturally touched him, a hug, a pat on the arm, passed. "Take it easy." I climbed out of the car as fast as I could, before he could open the door for me, before I started crying too.

Careful not to slip on any icy spots in the dark, I watched the ground, and tried not to think about Martin and Sofie sitting together, talking in the front room, cutting up their sandwiches into bite sized pieces.

In the kitchen, Lucy was burning pancakes. With a spatula, she pushed a smoking mess off the frying pan and carried it to the trash. She looked up. "Oh, Wylie!" She was drunk.

"Three beers, huh?" I snatched the spatula from her hand. "Let me do this. Get out of here."

I turned the heat off and waited for the frying pan to cool. Lucy followed me around the kitchen. "I'm sorry, Wylie. A day is a long time. Especially the afternoon." I scraped charred drops of pancake batter from the pan. "I just didn't expect a day to be so long. And one after the other. Too many long days stretching out all in a row on and on. But I am going to stop drinking. I promised you and I will." Tears sounded in Lucy's voice, but her eyes were dry.

"If you expect me to feel sorry for you," I said, washing the spatula. "I don't." I felt sorry for myself and Robbie and Kevin. No stupid seal woman story was enough to change that.

"Wylie," Lucy whined. "You have a right to be mad. I'll get help. I'll go to meetings." She put a hand on my shoulder blade.

"Don't tell me what you're going to do," I shouted, whirling around. "Just do it. Don't talk about it."

I threw out my mother's pancake batter and started over. Lucy melted away to her room in a haze of cigarette smoke.

"Is dinner ready?" Kevin yelled. The music bouncing down the hall announced the end of his show.

I yelled back. "Turn off the TV and come get the dishes out."

He rushed in, slapped down some plates and wriggled into a chair. I set a stack of perfect pancakes in front of him and poured the last of the milk.

Martin, as spineless as he seemed around his mother, had escaped, had a lover, an apartment, a job, his model airplanes. He had his place in San Francisco. I washed the frying pan while Kevin chewed his food. It seemed crazy to think I would ever leave Rivertown or even my house. My family would all starve without me.

Danny and I drove down Main Street under tinsel garlands that looked like a pack of stray dogs had chewed them. He was leaving the next morning to spend Christmas in Maine with his Dad and a cousin I'd never met.

"Why we have to go a week ahead of time, I have no idea," Danny complained. "Dad makes these odd plans and won't let go of them."

"I'll just be working anyway. The days before Christmas will be crazy."

Danny frowned.

"I'll miss you," I added quickly. "I'm glad we have some time together now. It's been awhile. I'm sorry about that."

We pulled into Danny's driveway. "The old man won't be back for hours," he said, pocketing the keys.

In his room he held me close, the heat of his body melting into mine. He covered my mouth with his. He put me right in the center of a blurry, spinning universe. Nothing else mattered. Hours passed. Mr. DiBona stumbled up the stairs.

"Shh." Danny traced my lips with his finger. "After he takes a piss he'll go to his room and pass out. We won't hear from him again." He lifted my hair, gave me a necklace of soft kisses.

When Mr. DiBona's bedroom door opened and shut with a final slam, Danny sat up. "Time for your present. Since we won't see each other again until after Christmas."

I'd been so busy I hadn't done any shopping yet. "Sorry, I haven't had a chance..."

Danny didn't seem to hear me or didn't care. He tugged on his jeans, picked his way through our scattered clothes, rummaged in his desk drawer, practically leaped back across the room.

Suddenly I knew what he held in his hand behind his back. I saw every-thing—the small velvet box, the hours he'd spent rehearsing his lines, Mr. Panetti boasting to him, as he did to all his customers, that Panetti's Jewelers had never sold a diamond that hadn't been accepted, as Danny handed over a folded wad of bills.

A muffled click and there, in his open palm twinkled the ring I was supposed to accept, exclaim over, slide onto my finger. Hippies in Haight-Ashbury wore wooden beads on macramé strings, silver peace signs, crystals maybe, but not real diamond engagement rings on a particular finger on a particular hand. I couldn't do it. I could never do it. I pulled the covers tight around my neck. Danny met my eyes for an agonizing second then stared at the elegant, little box in the center of his outstretched hand, grease around his fingernails, small scars from the sol-dering iron, palm callused from shoveling snow and pounding out fenders to earn money for a ring I wouldn't take. He snapped the box shut, threw it across the room.

"What is it that you want?" he shouted. "What do you want from me?"

"Shh," I said. "You'll wake up your dad."

"So what?" His eyes burned full of angry hurt.

"I love you," I said.

"I don't think so." Danny paced the length of the small room hating my weird ideas and my weird cakes, and my weird relationships with old ladies and their faggy old sons, hating himself for needing me so much.

"I do love you," I said again. "Come here."

"I don't think so." Danny stood at his window, pulled back the edge of the curtain, and looked out over the dark yard. "When people love each other they get married."

"Not always." I wanted to walk to him, wrap my arms around his strong, bony shoulders, pull him back to bed, but his hand balled into a fist kept me where I was. "I love you more than anybody, Danny." It felt true.

Three long steps brought him back to my side. "Then take the ring. We don't have to get married until you say so."

"It wouldn't be fair to you." I squeezed my eyes shut. "Taking that ring is like promising to get married, and I can't say for sure I'll ever want to."

He retrieved the box and shook it in my face. "How can you make love like we just did? How can you be with me after all this time and not want this ring? I don't understand you. Most women would die for a diamond like this.

"Just listen to me." He stroked the soft velvet box lid with his thumb. "I have it all figured out. My father's friend, George Swan? You know, Swan's Auto Body on West Main?

"George said I had a guaranteed, full time job after I graduated. Decent pay too. No minimum wage bullshit. We could save money, live here until we had enough for our own place, a house."

"Houses are expensive," I said, shivering.

"Well, what is it you want?" he shouted. "I don't know what you want."

"A car." I said the first thing that came into my head and felt the truth of it cut through the tangle in my guts.

"Why do you need a car?" He grabbed my shoulders, put his face too close to mine. "I have a car. I'll take you anywhere you want to go."

"You have a car," I said. "Exactly. You have a car. What about me?"

"What's mine is yours." His fingers dug into my arms. "You know that!"

"I don't want a house." He was right. Most girls we knew would love that ring. Most girls we knew wanted to get married. Not long ago I might have said I wanted that too. Who wouldn't want a house, a guy like Danny? What was wrong with me? I began to shake. I would lose him over this and then what? How could he understand when I didn't understand it myself?

"Alright," he said as if he were granting me a huge favor. "We won't get a house. We'll live here and have two cars."

"I'm sorry," I whispered.

"What do you want?"

I pulled away from him and a strange voice said, "I want you to keep your hands off me right now. I want my mother to stop drinking. I want to get the hell out of this town." I wanted to make magical cakes for strangers, dripping with flowers and fancy borders—cakes to inspire awe and appetite—mouthwatering cakes people could bear to cut only after taking entire rolls of pictures.

"You think you can run away from your problems," he said.

"Maybe I do." Sometimes you have to run away. Some problems you can't solve. All you can do is put distance between them and yourself or they'll swallow you whole.

"I don't believe in running away," he said. He was thinking of his mother, and I almost reached out to him.

"I want you," I said, through tears. "Really. I want you, the way we are…were. I don't want to get married."

He tossed the box from hand to hand.

In his silence I breathed deeply. "Your father's going to wonder what's going on."

"He wouldn't wake up if the house was burning down." Danny sat on the bed. "What do we do now?"

"I don't know. Just believe I love you, okay? You do, don't you?" I touched his cheek.

He jerked away, threw the ring into his desk drawer and slammed it shut. With his back toward me he said, "I'm good enough for you now, while you're stuck in Rivertown, but you just said it yourself, you want out. Come graduation, it's see ya' later. Right?" He stood over me, waiting to hear he was wrong.

I pictured the hippies. I wasn't a bad a person. I wanted something different. I'd die if I stayed in Rivertown. Danny didn't understand, and I didn't know how to explain it. I managed a weak, "I love you."

"Fine. Great. With your love and a dime I can make a phone call. Big deal, Wylie." He stepped back, shoved his hands into his back pockets. "You love me until graduation. What's that? Six months until June. Six months of your so-called love. You leave. What do I do then?"

"Who says I'm leaving?" Panic filled my throat. "It's just a dream. Where would I go?"

"Don't ask me!"

"Come back to bed." I reached toward him, the covers slipping down to my waist. "Please." I felt my heart pulsing just under my skin. I could almost see Danny's beating under his. I wanted to press my ear against his chest, to feel his hands in my hair. He stood where he was.

"Do you want me to go home?" I asked.

He swallowed, then shook his head.

"Then come back in here." I lifted the covers, inviting him into his own bed. He slipped in without looking at me. "Try to sleep."

"I can't," he said into the pillow.

"Try." I rubbed his back the way he liked it, from his shoulders to his thighs, long, light strokes. We made love as if we would be together always, but afterward curled together, Danny's breath warm and even on my neck, I lay awake wondering when he'd return the ring, hoping he'd get all his money back. When he woke in the morning, I'd be gone, filling donuts at Ida's, exactly one pump of jelly in each. I dreaded Mr. Panetti's look of confusion at the sight of my naked finger when he came in for coffee, all ready to congratulate me.

$$*\qquad*\qquad*\qquad*$$

Martin came around to open the car door for me, Sofie's car, not the rental. She wanted it driven to be sure it hadn't stopped running. Lucy's birthday cake weighed heavy in my hands. "So you'll move in two days after Christmas," he was saying, as if we hadn't already been over it in detail twice on the short ride from Sofie's house. "Only four days from now. Today's the twenty-third."

"Martin," I said. "I know the date. It's my mother's birthday. I told you I'd move in on the day you leave and I will."

"I leave on—"

"The twenty-seventh. I know."

"I'm sorry." He couldn't believe I hadn't already moved any of my things, though I'd told him I didn't have much.

Robbie and Kevin's pale faces bounced in the living room window. They pressed against it, flattening their noses, trying to see the cake.

Martin patted my shoulder. Robbie rapped urgently on the pane. He didn't approve of my friendship with Martin. Jimmy Daley teased him about it. I still couldn't figure out how everyone in Rivertown but Sofie and I seemed to have known for years that Martin was homosexual or why it mattered so much. Robbie's knocking grew more insistent. If I didn't go in soon, he'd break the glass. 'One minute,' I waved.

I turned back to Martin. "So stop worrying. You'll catch your plane. Sofie and I will be fine, especially with IJ's help. Everything's under control."

"And you'll come Christmas Eve?"

"Yes! I told you I would. Do you ever listen to me?"

"I'm sorry." He never missed a chance to apologize. "Bring your family, if you'd like."

Lucy had a marathon AA meeting. I assumed Robbie would be home watching Kevin. He hadn't been invited anywhere. "Maybe," I said, trying to picture my brothers in Sofie's house. They could always turn on the TV. If I brought

Kevin, Robbie would be alone. He'd die before he set foot in the house of the enemy, the people plotting to lure his sister away from her rightful home.

"Give your mother our best wishes." Martin touched the middle of my forehead with a gloved finger and grinned. "I'm sure she'll love the cake."

Kevin hammered at the window. I started up the walk. When I turned to wave from the top step Martin was busy with the door handle, double-checking to be sure the door was shut. In the streetlight's glow, exhaust billowed around his long, bent form and the squat and shiny red car. He and the Volkswagen were disappearing before my eyes in a cloud of smoke.

"We want to see the cake." Kevin flung open the door, almost knocking the box from my hands.

"Look at our sign." He pointed to a torn paper bag with 'Happy Brithday, Mom,' colored on it, hanging over the kitchen door.

Robbie stood behind him, glaring, his hair twisted into impossible snarls, angry he'd missed an afternoon of skating to supervise the decorating.

"Watch out." I nudged them away, set the box on the kitchen table, and lifted out the cake. "Ta da!"

Kevin leaped to a chair for a better view. "It's Mom's bag! Everything's the same, the flowers, even the worn out spots. It doesn't even look like a real cake."

Robbie hadn't said anything.

"Well," I asked. "What do you think?"

Lucy loved her carpet bag. She'd had it longer than she'd had Robbie. It had held diapers, vodka bottles, gum, makeup, magazines, and food stamps. In the hours we'd spent as kids waiting, at the clinic, at the welfare office, at bus stops, I had memorized every detail of that bag. So had he. We'd both heard Mom wail, "My life is in that bag!" when she forgot it somewhere. We were always blamed for her mistake, if we hadn't been whining for candy, if we hadn't pestered to pull the cord on the bus. Once she'd even left us on Main Street while she retraced her steps looking for it. He was in a baby carriage so I couldn't have been more than five or six. I remembered how heavy it felt, rolling off the curb, and how he almost bounced out, into the street. A lady in a fur-trimmed coat helped me. She asked where our mother was in a voice that made me feel I was bad for not knowing.

"What's all that gray stuff spilling out of the top?" Robbie asked. He hadn't even bought our mother a present and couldn't stand it that I had made her the perfect cake.

"It looks like a blanket," said Kevin. "Cloth."

"Good," I said, widening my eyes at Robbie. "That's what it's supposed to look like."

"Why?" Robbie asked. "What's a blanket got to do with anything?"

"Don't worry." I stuffed the cake box in the trash. "Mom'll know what it means."

Before Lucy had stopped drinking eight days ago, when she and I were still at war, all Robbie had to do was choose a side. He could switch back and forth to whoever gave him the best deal. He was never alone.

"Here." Kevin shoved a handful of balloons at Robbie. "Blow these up, quick."

Robbie smoldered, looking like he wanted to smash the cake or me. Instead he accepted a balloon, stretched it, then blew so hard his face turned colors. He never fussed or raged when he was small. To get what he wanted he just held his breath until he turned that same purplish-blue. He even passed out a few times. I remembered the relief I felt when he opened his eyes. And the envy. Throwing a fit seemed ridiculous, laughable, and ineffective next to the drama of silently turning blue or falling to the floor.

"That's big enough!" shrieked Kevin. "Do a red one. Here."

Robbie tied the balloon, launching it with a snap of the knot. I caught it before it landed on the cake.

Instead of tying off the next one he aimed it at me and released it. It spluttered in a clumsy circle instead of hitting me as he'd hoped. I stuck my tongue out at him. Kevin batted the first balloon, keeping it in the air.

"Come on, Robbie," I said. "Don't be mad. Mom will be here any minute."

He grimly blew up balloons, one after another, until the bag was empty.

"Get out the forks, Kevin," I said, pretending nothing was wrong. "Does anyone know what happened to the candles?"

"Look at me!" Kevin held a long balloon over his head, making his hair stand up straight. "You try it."

He took a flying leap onto Robbie's back, almost knocking him down. Kevin held on with his legs and rubbed a balloon through Robbie's hair. Static electricity crackled. Robbie tried to smile.

"The door!" I said. We froze.

"Anybody home?" Lucy called.

Kevin slid off Robbie's back. "Surprise!" he screamed as Lucy stepped into the kitchen. He wrapped himself around her.

She looked over him to Robbie and me. "A party." She shook her head, gave a tired smile. "You guys."

Spotting the cake, she unpeeled Kevin and walked toward the table. "Every flower, every leaf. How did you do that?" She reached for my hand. Robbie stood at her elbow waiting to be noticed. "The whole texture of it, everything. So real."

I could've mentioned Robbie, reminded her he'd helped too. I saw his anxious hair twisting, his trembling lip. But it had been years since my mother had shown such interest in me, and I couldn't share it.

"And what's this inside?" Lucy asked. "The gray stuff?"

"She said you would know." Robbie's voice was bitter.

"Think about it," I urged, clamping my lips shut to keep from telling. Lucy had to figure it out herself.

"It's cloth," said Kevin. "I guessed it was cloth."

"No." Lucy's eyes misted. She knew.

"Who cares what it is," said Robbie. "Let's just light the candles and eat it." He grabbed a book of matches from the counter, ripped off a match, rolling it between his finger and thumb.

"Skin," whispered Lucy, giving me a look that closed the black hole inside me for a moment.

"Skin in a bag," I said. "So you can have it with you all the time. So that when you need it, it's there."

"What are you talking about?" Robbie struck a match, shook it out.

"Skin?" Kevin squealed. "Gross. I don't want that part. I want a purple flower."

Robbie lit another match.

"Go ahead, firebug. Light the candles." Lucy laughed. He scowled and blew out the flame.

"Thirty-eight candles should make a big enough fire to please you," she teased. She pushed his hair back from his forehead, gently picking apart a tangle. "Thank you," she said, looking at each of us. "This has to be the nicest birthday I've had. The nicest I can remember for sure."

"Sit down," Robbie said, jerking his head away. "Close your eyes while I light these." He lit all the candles with one match.

Kevin switched off the lights. The cake glowed.

We bunched together around our mother and sang happy birthday. "Hurry," I said. "Make a wish and blow them out before they melt all over the cake."

Lucy thought for a minute. Wax dripped. Kevin sucked a finger full of icing he'd sneaked in the dark. "I don't know what to wish for," she said finally. "Can you believe it? Right now, this minute, I feel like I have everything I want."

Robbie scowled at the flickering candles. "Don't waste your big chance," he said. "Think about tomorrow. Think about tonight."

"One day at a time," Lucy whispered and sucked in a huge breath.

CHAPTER 4

▼

MARTIN

Christmas Eve without Erich. I was pleased when Wylie called to say she was bringing both of her brothers. More work for me. More distraction.

"I am in your way," Sofie said, up even earlier than usual, honey, molasses and eggs in the basket I'd attached to her walker. She had decided to bake a batch of *pfeffernusse* for our guests.

"I don't mind." I stood at the sink peeling potatoes. Sofie seemed easier to get along with since Wylie had agreed to move in.

"Your father loved these cookies," Sofie said. "Before I had a chance to roll them in sugar he was eating them. Never did he eat any other cookies, *kuchen, torte*. Nothing sweet for him. He'd rather have a mushroom."

I remembered my father off to the woods with a basket in his hand. Oskar was a man of gentle and silent habits. He'd come home from work, take a solitary ramble through the woods and fields behind the house, eat his supper, and then help me with my arithmetic homework or my latest model plane. We spoke only when the task at hand required a word or two. Upstairs Sofie talked enough for both of us. Quiet was a part of being together.

Sofie measured a teaspoon of pepper into the dry ingredients. "These may be too spicy for Wylie's brothers but it wouldn't be Christmas without *pfeffernusse*."

"I haven't had any in years," I said.

"I could have sent you some," Sofie said. "But I didn't want to make it easy for you to be staying in California. If you wanted my cookies, you could come home to get them. But you never came."

I took a deep breath. Sofie hadn't said any more about my being homosexual. The conversation had stopped. I could continue it now or let it be. In a few days I'd be home, away from here, whatever my mother's reaction.

"You never came," she repeated. I listened and heard more sadness than blame.

I sat beside her at the table. "I didn't want to leave Erich."

"Why didn't you bring him?" Sofie said. "All these Christmases I have been alone. Tony's best worker coming in on all the holidays because I have nothing to celebrate, no one to celebrate with. I have thought many times on going to Germany for *Weinachten* but spring is better for traveling. Sometimes I am thinking I should move back to the old country, but with Dora in the convent and Amalia's house full of grandchildren, where would I be finding a place for myself? Anyway, most of the time I think I am not anymore a German. So long in a strange, new country it stops being new and strange."

"What would you have done if I brought him here?"

"I would have cooked for him good German food. Was he skinny, this Erich?"

"Not as skinny as I am."

"Ach!" Sofie threw up her hands. "No one is as skinny as you. All your life people are looking at you thinking, this one's mother doesn't feed him."

"Really." I pushed back my chair and stood up. "If I had brought him, what would you have done?"

"What would you have done?" Sofie countered. "Would you have said he is your friend? Or what?"

At the sink, my back to Sofie, I let the water run, filling the pot of peeled potatoes. Sofie had stopped her sifting and stirring. The water overflowed, and still I stood at the sink. Or what? I didn't know what I would have said. I'd never figured that out. I'd never introduced Erich to people at work or at the field where I flew my planes. I'd never introduced Erich to anyone. I had one life, my real life, with Erich and our friends, Erich's friends, really, and my other life—all the rest.

I turned off the water and looked at her. "I would have said he was my friend."

"And I would have welcomed him as your friend." She gave a nod full of her belief that she'd given me the answer I wanted, the right answer.

"That's just it." I barely recognized my own tired voice. "He was so much more than my friend. The whole visit would have been a lie."

Sofie shook her head and shuffled to the stove. "I would have made for him *sauerbraten*. And cookies. A house of gingerbread like we made every year when you were small."

I could see myself at four, ten, and fourteen, dripping white icing off the gingerbread roofs, Sofie, opening bags of candy we bought by the pound from bins at the five and dime, my father watching, having done the manly job of constructing the house from slabs of cookie, ready to steady the roof if it started to slide or straighten a tilted wall. I had never thought to question why my father never decorated, my mother never built.

Sofie's head bent over the saucepan heating honey and molasses. Pink patches of scalp showed through her wispy white hair. In an hour and a half, she had an appointment at the hairdresser. I could pick up candy and anything else we needed for a gingerbread house while she sat under a dryer.

"Let's make one of those houses right now, for the kids," I proposed. "Put it together ahead of time and let them decorate it."

"Too much like work for Wylie."

"We'll decorate it then."

"You and me?" Honey and molasses dripped onto the floor from the spoon Sofie held in the air.

"Why not? After the hairdresser and a nap."

"Ach! Clean that up, will you? A mess I am making." She plunged the spoon back into the pan and turned off the heat. "After the hairdresser a candy house. Yes. Why not? You and me. Like when you were small."

Sofie touched my back as I bent to wipe the floor. "Sometimes a lie is not such a bad thing. Sometimes a lie is the best we can do."

✳ ✳ ✳ ✳

I heard Wylie and her brothers coming up the front walk and hurried to plug in the outdoor Christmas lights. As I fussed with the extension cord that passed through a small hole in the door that my father had drilled expressly for that purpose, I could hear them talking.

"Don't Germans eat all those weird sausages, made with blood and ground up pig eyeballs and stuff like that? What if that's what they made for dinner?" An adolescent, boy's voice, must be Robbie's, just outside the door. "Nazis."

"Shut up," Wylie said. "You didn't have to come."

"I don't want to eat blood." The younger boy. "Whoa, look at the lights in the bushes."

"Is a fag a bad thing, Robbie?" The younger voice continued. "Scary?"

"Both of you, shut up." Wylie's words, full of frustration. The doorbell.

For one long moment I considered not answering. Wylie, by herself, would have been good company. Why had I included the brothers? Some foolish, romanticized notion of children and Christmas I supposed. I thought of the gingerbread house. I thought of the model plane, how between all the mixing and stirring and slicing in the kitchen I'd chosen one of them, unpinned the fishing line from my ceiling and wrapped it. It waited under the tree with Robbie's name on it. The doorbell rang again. I straightened my red sweater vest and gray flannel trousers, took a deep breath, and opened the door.

Robbie stood an inch taller than Wylie, sharp-faced like a weasel with dark, heavy eyebrows, in a long, blue, wool coat, unbuttoned and much too big for him in the shoulders. No hat. His ears must have been frozen. Kevin, bundled so thickly I couldn't tell what he looked like, huddled close to Robbie and Wylie.

"Welcome," I said. "Merry Christmas."

Wylie nudged them all through the door. They crowded into the vestibule where, with a lot of bumping against each other, they removed their coats and boots. I stayed close to the wall, out of the way, holding out a hand every few moments to accept a coat. Wylie arranged the dripping boots on the towel I'd provided, and they followed me into the living room in a messy clump.

"You look nice," Wylie told Sofie, planting a kiss on her cheek.

"Martin took me this morning to the hairdresser." Sofie patted her white curls. A gold Christmas tree pin with jewels for ornaments sparkled against her green dress.

The boys hung back. Robbie eyed the pin as if he planned to steal it.

"Say hello to Sofie, you guys," Wylie ordered, ushering them forward. Robbie grunted. Kevin gave a singsongy hello.

"You must be Kevin," Sofie said. He beamed his pleasure at being recognized. "I wonder if you like candy."

He nodded. "In the kitchen you might be finding some. Martin will show you where to look. And you..." With narrowed eyes she regarded Robbie. "The boy who is in the newspapers with his fire making." Robbie made his face blank and stared at the floor, fists clenched. Wylie, brow furrowed, glanced at me, as if for an explanation. I gave her a look to say I had no idea Sofie planned to bring all that up.

Sofie stuck out a hand toward Robbie who stepped back as though expecting to be hit. I would have pulled my hand back immediately upon realizing Robbie hadn't anticipated a handshake, but Sofie let hers hang in the air until Robbie, embarrassed, figured out he was supposed to shake it, and did.

She seemed to surprise him with the force of her grip, pulling him close, compelling him to meet her gaze. "I hear you are making for your sister a lot of problems with this fire business." He scowled. "I hope you are stopping all of that. Now, don't be angry. I am an old woman. Old people believe they have the right to say what they are thinking. I am pleased to have Wylie's family as guests for Christmas."

Robbie pocketed his hand.

"Candy?" Kevin whispered to Wylie.

"Kitchen is this way," I said.

"Robbie, put these presents under the tree." Wylie swung the shopping bag at him, her attention focused on Sofie inching across the living room behind the walker. Robbie, smoldering, took the bag.

"She talks like Colonel Klink," Robbie muttered. When he frowned his eyebrows came together in one heavy line.

"You take Kevin to the kitchen, Wylie," I suggested. "We have a surprise. For you too, Robbie. I'll help you with the presents, and we'll join them."

Robbie clutched the handles of the bag, glaring suspiciously at me, probably looking for a telltale wiggle or exaggerated wrist movements. I told myself not to take offense. A fourteen-year-old boy, raised in Rivertown, couldn't help his attitudes. His scraggly, knotted hair made his thin face look even thinner. Pale skin fit tight to his sharp bones. I would win him over with compassionate understanding. This boy's sister was my saving grace, my ticket back to San Francisco, where I would reach out to some of Erich's—Erich's and my—old friends and mourn properly, with other people. I'd call Jean Paul and Mark, our old pinochle partners and wish them a Merry Christmas. Maybe I would even begin mentioning Erich at work. If Sofie could accept me as a homosexual, there were other people in my life who could too. I'd be careful. I was always careful. Too careful. A fault. What was that saying—your greatest strength is also your greatest weakness? Being careful was mine. Careful and deferential and apologetic.

Robbie, as unpleasant as he seemed, was Wylie's brother. It was Christmas. I knelt beneath the tree, rearranging packages, flushed with the possibility of miracles. Robbie released his grip on the bag but stood rigid and scowling as I emptied it, package by package. Everyone else had disappeared into the kitchen.

"If I didn't come I would have been home alone. My Mom went out. We celebrate Christmas on Christmas Day," Robbie muttered.

"We've always celebrated Christmas Eve," I said. "I'm glad you came." Sometimes a lie is the best we can do.

Robbie examined a glass ornament. Again, I had the feeling the boy was only waiting for the opportunity to pocket it. So what? We had boxes of the things. I turned my back and led the way to the kitchen.

Kevin, mouth pink from a candy cane, thumped the table. "Hurry up! She won't show us the surprise until you come." Sofie stood in front of the counter, shielding a paper towel covered lump with her body.

"Wylie, move this to the table."

"No." I stepped past her. My idea. My creation. I'd pieced it together so it stood firm under the strokes of Sofie's spatula, the pressure of her fingers. I would unveil it. "I can do that." Sofie moved aside.

Kevin stared at the candy studded gingerbread. Icicles of white icing dripped from the eaves.

"It's gorgeous," Wylie said. "Why didn't I think of making one of those?"

"A family tradition," I said.

"Didn't a witch live in a house like that?" Robbie broke off one of the icicles. Kevin protested.

"It's for all of you," Sofie said. "You can take it home."

"We can show Mom," Kevin said. "Don't wreck it, Robbie."

Robbie pried a gumdrop from the chimney.

"Stop it," Wylie snapped. "That's enough."

I put a bowl of leftover candy on the table. "You can eat this," I said. "But it's time for dinner. Save some room."

Robbie stuffed a handful of candy into his mouth. Cheeks bulging like a rodent's, he chewed and chewed while Kevin stared at the house. Sofie beamed.

"I remember when Martin was that small," she told Wylie. "He would pick from the house a little every day, thinking his father and I are not noticing. Every day, a little more. Finally, I have to say something. 'Martin, someone is nibbling on the house. Who could it be?' 'I think we must have some mice,' he says. 'Maybe we should get a cat.' Always he is wanting a cat. What is that saying two birds with one rock? He is explaining the disappearing house and making an argument for a pet at the same time. He should have been a lawyer."

"I want a cat," said Kevin. "But Robbie has allergies. And we can't afford one anyway, Mom said. We had to get rid of the ones we had."

"The table is ready," Sofie said. "Then presents. Please, go into the dining room before eating any more candy."

Robbie, with a loud swallow, grabbed another handful, emptying the bowl.

In the dining room Robbie had to struggle to keep the bored look on his face when he saw the spread. Wylie and Kevin looked awed. The best white china and heavy silverware gleamed in the light of many candles. Shadows crisscrossed and stretched over the walls. Sliced meats, cheeses, breads, potatoes, salads, cookies, cakes, nuts, a steaming soup tureen, covered the dark green tablecloth.

"In the old country we are putting candles even on the Christmas tree," Sofie whispered. "Beautiful, neh? We had none of the colored lights. No need."

"Candles on trees?" Robbie snickered. "Bet some people ended their holiday with nothing but ashes."

Sofie glared. "Beside the tree we kept a bucket of water. We were not dumb."

"Sit please," I said. "Anywhere."

Wylie helped Kevin to food. He tried everything and ate and ate without talking. Robbie helped himself to seconds, then thirds, then more.

"I like to see people eat." Sofie smiled.

Wylie flushed. "That's good. These guys don't know about leftovers. In our house we finish everything. No little plastic containers like you have in your refrigerator."

"No wonder you're leaving us," Robbie said. "If someone offered to feed me like this I'd leave too, even if it was two old people I hardly knew."

"I'm not moving in here because of the food," Wylie snapped. "I hope no one thinks that."

I shook my head and hid my annoyance by patting my mouth with my napkin.

"Can I stay here too?" Kevin asked. "Just sometimes. With Wylie."

"Of course," Sofie said.

"Aren't you guys forgetting about somebody?" Robbie asked. "What about Mom?"

"Maybe she could come too," Kevin said.

Wylie coughed. "Sorry," she said, looking first at Sofie, then me. "Listen, I'm moving in here because Sofie has offered me a job. I'm going to help out." Her gaze flitted from one brother to the other, settling nowhere. I wiped my glasses.

Sofie scolded, "This is an opportunity for your sister. We are going to pay her very well. You should be happy for her, not giving her a hard time."

Kevin stopped eating and looked to Wylie for a cue. Wylie studied her plate. Robbie fumed.

"I think they're worrying about losing you, Wylie," I said. "Maybe you could reassure them that you're still going to be around. You're still their sister."

"Yeah, right," Robbie sneered.

"Of course I'm their sister," Wylie said.

"You don't have much choice about it," Robbie said. "I wonder what would happen if you did."

"What do you think?" Wylie asked glaring at him.

He helped himself to another slice of bread.

"You can't stop being a sister," Kevin said. "Even if you want to."

"If you can stop being a father," Robbie said, mouth full, "seems you could stop being anything else."

"Would anyone like more soup?" I asked, ladle raised over the bowl.

Wylie shook her head. Kevin slid down in his chair. I looked down the table to Sofie, wondering how to save the evening.

Robbie ate and drank, with complete disregard for anyone else. I felt an urge to snatch the food away, pound his back until the bite he was chewing so loudly flew from his greedy little mouth.

"I think it's time for the presents," Sofie said.

"Presents!" Kevin hopped out of his seat.

"Robbie and I will help clear," Wylie said. "Thank you for this meal. A lot of work."

With a quick nod I hoped they'd interpret as polite, I grabbed the soup tureen and beat them to the kitchen where I splashed cool water on my face. Sofie entertained Kevin with a German dice game. Robbie and Wylie carried dishes. Scraping, rinsing and stacking, I tried to relax. I always enjoyed washing dishes. Over the running water, snippets of whispered arguing reached my ears—Wylie hissing shut up and ordering Robbie to behave, Robbie defending his behavior with words like rich old people, Hogan's Heroes, homos, Nazis, buying off my sister.

I almost cracked a plate. Easy, I told myself. Compassion. The boy needs compassion. His sister is my mother's closest friend right now. The reason I can go home. Easy. Easy. The boy doesn't know any better. I accepted the last bowl from Wylie and wiped my hands. "I'll wait to wash these," I said. "Sofie still tires easily. We should open presents, then I'll drive you home."

"We can walk," said Robbie.

Wylie winced. I kept my expression neutral.

When I was young, Sofie had insisted gifts be opened one at time. Now, she sat smiling as Kevin tore into the presents, ruining wrapping paper that had been in the family for years, used over and over again. I'd bought lots of little plastic toys from the five and dime so they would have plenty to open. Robbie sat on the couch, arms crossed. Kevin found the presents with Robbie's name tag and stacked them beside his brother. The pile grew, untouched.

Kevin and Sofie opened gifts, smiling, enjoying themselves, oblivious to Robbie's sullenness, Wylie's discomfort, my ambivalence and the rage all three of us shared but couldn't express. Wylie gave me handkerchiefs and Sofie a bird feeder.

"Look Robbie." Kevin dragged the plane, a large wrapped object, from beneath the tree. "You have to open this. Look how big it is!"

"Careful." I almost leaped to my feet, then caught myself and sat down. "That's fragile!" I should have known better than to give the boy one of my planes. I still cared about those models. Even after so many years.

Robbie couldn't resist. Everyone watched as he peeled off the tape piece by piece, the way I had been taught, but then crumpled the paper, instead of folding it. Robbie lifted out a thirty-four inch model of the Spirit of St. Louis I'd built when I was his age.

"You're kidding," Wylie said.

Robbie held the fuselage in hands as careful as mine, his eyebrows arching to his hairline, mouth open.

"That's thirty-six years old," I said. "Thought you could hang it in your room or something. It really flies, but once it crashes, that can be the end. I never flew it."

"Wow," Robbie breathed. Until that wow I didn't understand why I'd chosen to give away my best model to a boy I hardly knew. The beautiful plane, never flown, hanging in my childhood room, providing surfaces for Sofie to dust saddened me. I'd wanted more for it. A wow.

"Did you make it?" Wylie asked.

"You bet he did," said Sofie. "Always hiding in the basement making airplanes. Go out, I'd tell him. Get some fresh air. But no, he'd rather be in the dark by himself."

"How do you make it?" Robbie asked. "It looks complicated."

"It is, somewhat," I said. "Every piece cut by hand. It takes hours just to carve the propeller." Kevin stared without touching.

"When we're finished here," Sofie said. "You can show him the workshop downstairs. But first, Wylie must open her present."

I pushed the largest box across the carpet. Wylie knelt beside it, close to Sofie's chair. Everyone crowded close to watch, even Robbie, the Spirit of St. Louis, set aside. She tore off the paper in wide strips and unfolded the flaps of a cardboard carton. She grinned as she lifted out a stack of stainless steel bowls and a handful of spatulas. They reflected the colored lights of the Christmas tree. A smaller box held an assortment of decorating tips, row after row of metal cones, each snug in its numbered cubicle.

"I tried to think of everything you'd need," said Sofie.

"Thank you." Wylie ran the surface of a spatula across her cheek.

His curiosity satisfied, Kevin went back to playing with a set of plastic soldiers. Robbie stared, blinking hard, into the smallest mixing bowl, his reflection distorted and full of yearning.

"Some day you might be starting a bakery of your own," Sofie said.

Wylie hugged the mixing bowls in her lap.

Robbie returned to the couch and his gift. I settled beside him, the plane across our laps. "It's covered with Japanese tissue," I said though Robbie hadn't asked. "Coated with something called dope. And aluminum paint. Expensive hobby. All my baby-sitting and paper route money went toward it."

Robbie's thin shoulders relaxed. His arm grazed mine, and he didn't seem to notice. He wound the propeller part way.

"I think I have the plans for this very plane downstairs in a drawer. Would you like to see them?" I offered.

Robbie nodded.

"We can't stay too much longer," Wylie said, repacking her bowls and spatulas.

"Martin will drive you home," Sofie said. "I bet you'll be glad when you can drive yourself."

"She doesn't have a car," Robbie said.

"She'll use mine," said Sofie, meeting his defiant stare with one of her own.

Robbie looked away first. "So where's the basement?"

"I'll just show him the plans," I told Wylie. "It won't take long."

I flicked on the fluorescent light over the workbench.

"This doesn't seem like a basement," Robbie said. "There's no dust or anything."

"My mother doesn't believe in dust," I said. The yellowing papers lay in the same drawer I had put them years ago. All my airplane plans were filed there, in chronological order. My tools hung on a pegboard, each over the appropriate outline my father had drawn, then painted in white. "I suppose I don't believe in it either."

"Dust?" Robbie asked.

I unfolded the plans.

"My father thought this one might be too difficult for me," I said. "He didn't want to discourage me so he wouldn't say so. I knew though. I knew from his face when I first showed him these drawings. He humored me, nodding as I explained each step."

Robbie bent over the paper, smoothing the brittle folds. I remembered the warmth of my father's arm next to mine and the urge to grab it, to peer into my father's lined face and tell him how much I loved him, how much I treasured our time in the basement, how the hours together had shaped the rest of my life. My lips moved. I tried to find words powerful enough to say what I felt and couldn't, so what did it matter that my father wasn't really there to hear?

"I'd like to build my own plane," said Robbie. I ran a hand over the paper, not knowing how to respond. "Something simple." Robbie rushed to add, to fill in the space where I was supposed to offer to help. "Maybe you could just show me...help me...get me started, and I could do the rest."

I remembered with the suddenness and force of a blow to the belly that Robbie had no father. I wanted to give the boy something now, felt I had to. More than the model itself. "I'd like to," I said. "But there's not enough time...I leave the day after tomorrow. I'm sorry. If I'd known you were interested..."

Robbie clenched his jaw. His eyes went blank. "No problem," he said. "I don't have the time either, really."

Fathers and sons. If I'd a son, or a daughter for that matter, or even a niece or nephew, I could have passed along the Spirit of St. Louis to family. Martin Schmidt, the last of my father's line. I'd spent so much of my life pretending to be someone I was not without even a child to show for my efforts. All those years before Erich. I could have had a family. All I would have had to do was pretend a little more. Pretending. Lying. Sometimes a lie is the best you can do. Had I done better not lying so much, not pretending so far? I'd done the best I could with what I knew at the time. So had Oskar, and Sofie. And the desperate boy beside me. The best he could.

"If I were you I'd start with a kit," I said. "And here..." I stooped to pick up a neat stack of model building magazines and held them out toward Robbie. "Take these. And if you need to borrow any tools."

The magazines slid into Robbie's waiting arms. He clutched them to his chest.

"I'm sorry," I said, reaching to touch Robbie's shoulder.

"Why?" Robbie jerked away. The magazines tilted and slid to the cement floor, slithering over each other. "I don't care. I've got to go." He bent, grabbing at the pages. The magazines refused to stack.

I picked up several, aligned the edges, and tried to hand them over.

"It's okay," Robbie said edging away. "I don't need help. I don't need any help from you."

"Tomorrow the stores are closed," I said to the boy's hunched back. "But early the next day, before I leave for the airport, we can go to the hobby shop and choose a kit. They used to have some good ones."

"Forget it," Robbie said. "No thanks."

Robbie said nothing else, not a word, as Wylie helped Kevin gather his things. Sofie packed some leftover food.

"The plane won't fit in the car with all of us," Wylie said. "We'll have to get it another time."

"I can deliver it tomorrow," I said. "Just tell me when."

Hangers jangled and clattered as Robbie grabbed for their coats.

"Does everyone have everything?" I asked, buttoning mine.

"What do you say to Sofie?" Wylie said.

Kevin said good-bye and thank you. Robbie was silent. Wylie jabbed him with an elbow and flashed him a stern look, and he still said nothing.

*   *   *   *

As I fit my clothes into my suitcase I let myself think about the changes I would make in my life when I got home. I would invite the medical students downstairs to dinner to thank them for bringing in my mail. Jean Paul had insisted on picking me up at the airport. I'd inquire about his New Year's Eve plans. I'd dreaded and resisted visiting Sofie and Rivertown, yet it had turned out to be just what I needed. I hummed along to Debussy as Sofie dozed downstairs. I'd closed her door and turned the music up. The afternoon sun sank low in the sky but the days would grow steadily longer, an appropriate time for new beginnings, renewed hope.

I tucked the package of handkerchiefs from Wylie into a shoe, a space saving trick Sofie taught me. IJ had stopped by with yet another package of handkerchiefs wrapped in Santa Claus paper. I slid those into the other shoe.

"Mart," IJ had said, hugging me good-bye. "I wonder if I could visit this spring. Johnny should be able to manage without me for a week or two. I've always wanted to ride on one of those cable cars they show in the Rice-a-Roni commercials."

I pictured IJ at Fishermen's Wharf, the Golden Gate Bridge, my apartment.

"I've never left New England," she said. "Unless New York City counts."

"Of course," I said, imagining her at the botanical garden, admiring the floating leaves broad enough to hold a child, the aquarium with its manatees munching on whole heads of lettuce, the Japanese tea garden. Everywhere we went she'd exclaim, snap photos, buy postcards and souvenirs and affirm I'd done the right thing leaving Rivertown to build a life in a city so lovely it teemed with tourists.

I smelled something burning. I hadn't heard Sofie climb out of bed. I turned the music down, listening for sounds in the kitchen. Nothing. The burning smell, stronger than ever, piney, like a campfire. Leaving the suitcase half packed I went downstairs to investigate. Sofie's door still shut. Kitchen empty. Odor of burning wood too strong, no longer pleasant. Smoke outside the kitchen window, clouds of black smoke, seeping in. I'd heard how quick fire could spread. Before looking further, I dialed the fire department. When I opened the back door, the azalea bush was on fire, just a few feet from the house. I glimpsed a familiar figure running away, long dark coat flapping.

Snow filled my slippers as I chased Robbie Steele. The fire alarm blared as the boy tripped, fell, and lay whimpering, covering his face with his arms. Panting, I yanked him to his feet by the collar of his coat.

"Don't turn me in," Robbie cried. "I'm sorry. I'll go to jail if they catch me. Please, let me go, it's only the bush."

I checked the progress of the fire. Flames licked at the house. Sofie!

"Help get my mother out of the house unless you want murder on your record," I told Robbie. Sirens began to wail.

Robbie raced to the house, beating me by several long moments, and disappeared inside. Fire fighters sprang from two fire engines, attached hose to hydrant, drowning the fire, as I approached. Robbie and Sofie were still inside.

"Just a little scorched paint," the firefighter said. "Lucky. How'd it start?"

"You fellows got here faster than I ever would have thought." I avoided the question, trying to decide what to say about Robbie Steele. "I've underestimated you. Never thought a volunteer fire department could be so quick. And on Christmas Day."

"The guys want to get back to their families, so tell me, for the report, how did the fire start?"

I thought. How could a fire conceivably start in a bush outside the kitchen door? "Well...I was...cooking something, using a dishtowel for a pot holder. The edge of it touched the flame and poof! Fire. I should have thrown it in the sink, I suppose, but I panicked, threw it out the door, and before I knew it, the bush had begun to burn. I called you right away. Thank you for coming so quickly."

"Martin!" Sofie's voice, unmistakable from inside.

I walked the firefighter to the street. Neighbors had gathered on the sidewalk. John MacKenzie and Shredder. IJ rushed over. "Look at you, your feet are soaked. What happened?" I stopped her with a frown and a jerk of my head. The firefighter jotted a few words in a palm-sized spiral notebook and shook my hand. "Feel free to show your appreciation with a generous contribution to our next fund-raiser," he said. The other men were already in position on the trucks.

I waved, praying they'd be gone by the time Sofie made it to the front door. I wondered what happened to the boy.

"Just a bush," I said to the crowd. "Barely touched the house, foolish mistake, burning dish towel. Now, if you'll excuse me, my feet..." I backed up the front walk. The front door was locked. Although the neighbors began to disperse, I felt like a character in a situation comedy, locked out of my house in my slippers, letting everyone think I'd started a fire. Why hadn't I announced the truth?

"I'll go around the back and let you in," IJ offered. "Your feet must be freezing."

"No, no." I pressed the door bell again and again. I didn't want to use the hidden key with John MacKenzie watching. Shredder barked.

"Sofie must be scared to death," IJ went on. "I'd be glad..."

"We're fine!" I shouted.

IJ cringed.

"Sorry." I patted her arm. "I'm a little overwrought. Everything's alright. Stop by later, if you'd like."

IJ shook her head. "But your feet..."

"His feet are fine!" John yelled. "Let's go home. He said he's alright."

"Clean that up!" I said, noticing that Shredder had deposited a pile on the snow near the sidewalk.

"Oh, John!" IJ rooted in coat pockets as if she'd find something she could use to pick up the mess. All she found was a crumpled tissue. "I'll run home and get some newspaper."

"It's his dog, isn't it?" I asked, rattling the door again. "He should get the newspaper. You've spoiled that man, IJ."

"Mind your own business," John muttered.

IJ laughed. "You're right."

Sofie unlocked the door, leaning on her cane.

"Sofie," IJ called. "Merry Christmas. Can I borrow a piece of newspaper? Shredder here..."

I swooped around Sofie, edged her away from the door, closed and locked it, sagging against the wall.

"Martin, tell me what is going on." She tapped my wet ankle with her cane. "Fire engines. Wylie's brother behind the sofa."

"Let me dry my feet," I said. "Sit down."

"Young man," Sofie said to the couch. "Come out right now and explain what you are doing, pulling me out of my bed, hiding in my house."

"Mother, wait," I said. "At least until my feet are dry."

Muttering, Sofie limped to her chair.

I put on the pair of socks I'd laid out for the day. I took my time tying my shoes. I wanted to talk with Wylie before facing Robbie and Sofie in the living room, but she wasn't there. I'd take Robbie home, tell Wylie and her mother what happened, and let them decide what, if anything, to tell the police or probation officer. I didn't want to be responsible for putting a child behind bars.

Sofie disagreed. "Why, when we give you a nice dinner, a nice Christmas, are you wanting to burn our house down?" She wagged her finger at Robbie, perched on the edge of the couch, still wearing his coat. Snow had melted onto the plastic cover. Sofie didn't seem to notice. "What are you thinking? You belong in jail. You are a criminal, all this fire business."

Robbie looked at his feet. "It was a bush," he whispered.

"I'm taking him home," I said.

"I am calling the police. Martin, why are you not telling the firemen you caught this boy?"

"I want to talk with his mother first," I said. "Wait."

"You make sure the police are knowing about this," Sofie said. "People need to feel safe in their houses. We can't be thinking there is a fire setter running loose."

"Get in the car," I told Robbie. "Mother, please wait until I get back before you make any phone calls."

"Why did you do it?" I asked, waiting for the car to warm up.

I'd driven down the block before Robbie spoke, startling me. "If your house burned, my sister couldn't live there."

"So you were trying to burn the house?"

"Yeah, but I couldn't. I figured I'd do the bush, and let God decide about the house."

"God?"

"The boy nodded. I turned onto Wylie's street.

"Would you say God decided the house should be left standing?"

Robbie pressed his lips together. A muscle in his jaw twitched.

"So your sister can live in it?" I pressed on.

He didn't answer.

I stopped the car, opened the door for Robbie who sat unmoving. "Let's go." The boy hid his face in his hands.

"Come on." I rested a hand on Robbie's shoulder, felt a tremble.

The door to the house burst open, and Kevin appeared on the porch. "Martin!" Kevin called. "Where have you been? Did you bring the plane? Why did Robbie get to go with you? I wanted to come over to your house."

Lucy stepped out behind him. "What are you doing with my son?"

"This boy just set a fire in our yard." I leaned against the car, arms folded. "Very close to our house. Before I reported him, I thought I'd consult with you."

Wylie raced down the sidewalk, dragging Robbie from the car. "Are you crazy?" she hollered. "You moron. You idiot. You're more stupid than I thought." She shook him. He went limp. I did nothing to stop her.

"Come inside," Lucy yelled. "Everyone just come inside."

"What?" Wylie faced her, still gripping Robbie's shoulders. "Are you afraid of what people will think? You never worried about that before, drunk at City Hall, fighting with Dad. People see this, they won't be surprised. Just those trashy Steeles at it again."

"Please," Lucy begged me. "Come on in." She removed Wylie's hands from Robbie's coat and helped him to the house.

I couldn't find a seat in the cluttered living room. Wylie pushed a heap of wrapping paper off the couch. "Here."

The shabby room felt small, hot, and full of people. Lucy sat at one end of couch, arm around Robbie. Wylie paced and glowered. Kevin rolled on the floor, picking up toy soldiers and putting them down, attending to every word.

"You should've had him arrested on the spot," Wylie said.

"That's what Sofie said." I wiped my sweating forehead. "I wanted to discuss it with your mother,"

"I appreciate that," said Lucy.

"What if the house had burned?" Wylie asked. "What if Sofie hadn't made it out in time? She doesn't move very fast, you know. This isn't like a baseball through a window or a smashed jack o'lantern or even burning the woods. This is serious!"

Lucy removed her arm from behind Robbie to light a cigarette.

"You can't keep this a secret," Wylie continued. "When Jennings finds out, you're off to the Farm or maybe Cheshire."

"Don't tell on me," Robbie pleaded, twisting a clump of hair.

"He could kill somebody, Mom, if he keeps this up," Wylie said. "I don't want my brother put away, but you have to do something. He's dangerous. He doesn't even know how dangerous he is."

Robbie certainly didn't look dangerous, huddled against his mother, trying not to cry.

Lucy smoked her cigarette. Everyone waited. "Wylie's right," she said. "Thank you for bringing him home. I'll let the probation officer know."

Robbie's face crumpled. "You can't. I'll run away."

"I won't press charges," I said.

"They'll lock me up anyway," Robbie said. "You watch."

"If they do, you deserve it," Wylie said.

I edged toward the door, tripping over Kevin's leg. How had I become involved with this troubled family? Where would the involvement end? I was glad I hadn't yet delivered the model plane.

Wylie followed me to the car. "You're helping me move my things tomorrow, right? Before you leave?" She touched my arm to stop me from gripping the door handle. "We could do it now."

"I can't," I said. "Tomorrow."

"I'm really sorry," she said. "You probably regret hiring me, but I promise I'll do a good job. My family's crazy, not me."

"I don't regret hiring you," I said. I hadn't had much choice. I wanted to be home in San Francisco, alone in the peaceful space of my apartment.

CHAPTER 5

▼

WYLIE

Sofie's VW shrunk as Martin drove off. I wanted to run after him. Danny was away. Ida's was closed. I had nowhere to go to get out of the cold except back inside. I could pack. I would go straight to my room and pack everything.

Lucy was waiting for me at the front door. Robbie sat small and sullen in the corner of the couch. Kevin was already setting up another war. I shrugged off Lucy's hand, found a stack of bags and an extra pillowcase, and locked myself in my room, blasting Janis Joplin while I sorted clothes. How could our mother be so matter-of-fact about everything? Her son had attempted to burn someone's house down. She'd been about to leave for another AA meeting when Martin showed up with Robbie. I didn't know much about Alcoholics Anonymous, but missing a meeting seemed like a bad idea even if she had gone to a long one the night before.

I stuffed the pillowcase with clothes until it bulged with shirts, underwear, and my bulky black sweater. I held the stuffed dog I'd had since I sucked my thumb. One eye hung by a thread. I'd picked off all the fur. I couldn't leave something that sad and pathetic behind so I jammed it into the pillowcase with all the rest. The huge, lime green teddy bear Danny had spent a week of gas money to win for me at Saint Anthony's carnival wouldn't fit in any of the bags. I left it for Kevin.

I counted my money. Nine hundred and thirty-five dollars. Once I began selling cakes, my stash grew fast. Almost a thousand dollars that no one knew I had.

I knew I should open a bank account—Robbie could've set my room on fire and burned it all—but I liked to count it, keep it close. A wad of bills so thick I could hardly wrap the rubber bands around the cigar box was more real than a printed number in a bank book.

Behind my tapes, I discovered a fifth of vodka I'd hidden from Lucy, back when I thought if I could only keep a step ahead of her, find her bottles and pour the contents down the drain, she'd stop. Finding her drunk, I'd blame myself and figure I had to work harder, remember to feel under the couch cushions.

The neck of the bottle grew warm in my hand. The clear liquid sloshed. Janis launched into a new song. Janis, a small town girl who made it out. Port Arthur, Texas. Rivertown, Connecticut. What difference did it make? Janis drank. Busy trying to stop my mother, I had ruled it out for myself. When people I knew gathered at the Rock with tango and sloe gin and Annie Green Springs berry wine, I passed the bottles without tasting any of it. Maybe I'd missed something. I unscrewed the cap.

How could something that looked cool and clear as water taste like fire, scorch your throat, and keep on burning where it landed in your stomach? How could my mother drink something that tasted like heavy duty toilet cleaner? How could I? I forced myself to take another swig. Mixed with coke or juice it might not be so bad, but I didn't want to run into my family in the kitchen. I could hear them out there between songs. Lucy coaxing Robbie to play cards, asking him what he wanted for dinner.

I stretched out on my mattress, head on the green bear. I held my money box against my chest and raised the bottle to my lips. Vodka dribbled into my mouth and down my neck, each slug easier to swallow. The burn faded to a warm glow. I unstuck my poster of Janis, unpeeling the rolled tape, careful not to tear the corners. I took down my hippies, too, and rolled the pictures together. They'd hang on my new slanted ceilings, over my bed.

I gulped more vodka. The hard edges of my tiny room softened and opened out. Surprise. Drink enough and you didn't have to go anywhere. But what about when the bottle was empty? Or when I had to pee? I'd sneak out to buy more, with a bathroom stop on the way. I had enough money for a hundred bottles, five hundred even.

I pushed a handful of bills in my back pocket and drained the bottle. Holding it like a microphone I sang a few more bars with Janis, reeled backward and landed sitting on the mattress, the wad of money in my pocket so thick I sat higher on one side. I stuffed the rest of the bills in my empty pocket to balance things out. I could buy some Southern Comfort, Janis' drink. Just the name warmed me up. With the music blasting, no one would notice I was gone. Forget the bathroom, forget my coat. I'd sneak out the back door. I layered on some long sleeved shirts and the sweater I'd just packed, spilling socks and underwear across the bed.

"Lord, won't you buy me a Mercedes Benz," Janis pleaded. She didn't ask for any old car. She made the mistake of asking too much. If she'd asked for a Volkswagen, nothing fancy as Sofie said, still a good German car, maybe she'd still be alive. I closed the door with a click so quiet I couldn't even hear it while Janis begged for a color TV. Wanting too much. That's what'll kill you. She should have asked for a black and white.

Safe on the back porch among the dented trash cans, I sang, "Oh, Lord, won't you buy me a Volkswagen bug?" Sounded okay. I was almost to the foundry before I remembered, Christmas wasn't over yet. Package stores were closed. I veered left, up the hill, to Avery field. They had rest rooms there.

Streetlights reflected off old snow. I pushed myself up the hill. I had to pee so bad that walking hurt. The cold air hurt too, like breathing poison. No one walked the streets. It could have been early morning. I could've been walking to Ida's.

The dark green cinderblock cube of a rest room was locked for the winter. I squatted behind it and let loose, the hot stream melting a huge patch of iced over gravel and ending in total relief. Perfect happiness until my ass began to freeze, reminding me to pull up my pants.

One lone swing dangled from the skeletal swing set. I sat on the wide wooden seat worn smooth by countless rear ends. I kicked the ground to start moving, chains freezing my fingers until I couldn't feel them. When I was little I thought if I could swing high enough I could jump off and land in God's lap. I swung up into the starry skies and back down again and again and again, until exhausted, I stopped pumping and threw up everything I'd drunk and eaten all day.

The walk home seemed an impossible distance, especially in boots spattered with vomit and pants wet with pee. My mouth felt like a sewer. The tears came and the runny nose. I was a leaky container, fluids spilling out every opening. Poor Janis, who drank and poured her heart out in her singing and her messy, wild life that ended long before it should have. Poor Lucy who drank and kept it all inside. Poor me spending my whole seventeen years taking care of other people and not knowing how to care for myself. If I did, I wouldn't be trudging home from an empty playground, on Christmas, in the middle of winter, without a coat.

I dragged myself through streets emptier than my vodka bottle. I had money, but so what? All along I thought it would make a difference. I sneaked onto the back porch. Empty yard. Empty heart. Empty mind. I made up a song about emptiness, then remembered to be quiet. I didn't want Lucy to catch me. I sat on the back steps, planning my entry, debating whether or not to risk a trip to the bathroom. I sat on flat pockets. My money. Empty pockets. I shoved a fist in my mouth to keep from wailing.

Something so disastrous had to be a sign from whoever was running the show. I was supposed to stay in Rivertown, take care of my brothers, my mother, and marry Danny. I stretched out on the cold step, frozen hands folded on my chest like a corpse and stared at the sky.

And what are you thinking you are doing? A voice hissed in my ear. I turned my head but no one was there. For that money you are working so hard only to be leaving it on the ground.

"I don't know where it is," I sobbed. "I'm too tired to get up. Who cares?"

Anyone who isn't drunk would know that when you were swinging or peeing the money fell out, Sofie's voice reasoned.

"You find it, then," I said.

What's the matter with you? You are not a lazy girl. The voice was furious. I still couldn't see anyone, but I felt something force me to sit up. Now valk! Sofie sounded like a German drill sergeant. I stood, my head clearing as I walked, then ran.

The money lay by the rest room, some of the bills soaked in urine and plastered to the ground. I peeled them up, pushed them deep into my pocket, thanked Sofie and even the Lord. I promised I'd buy my own car, my own TV instead of getting drunk and begging for them.

*   *   *   *

True to her word, Lucy told Robbie's probation officer who sent him packing. After four months of good behavior, Robbie would be eligible for weekend passes. I offered to visit him, but was relieved when Lucy said no visitors the first two weeks. Martin went home to San Francisco. I spent the rest of the Christmas vacation arranging and rearranging my things in the blue room. IJ stayed with Sofie while I stopped home each day to watch Kevin so Lucy could go to her meetings. When school started up again Lucy wouldn't even need me for that.

Danny came back from Maine complaining about a week spent at his cousin's trailer, shooting squirrels, watching TV and missing me. Neither of us mentioned the ring. We didn't mention much of anything, agreeing without words to talk and listen with our bodies. I couldn't spend the whole night, but after I'd put Sofie to bed, I'd sneak out to be with him for a couple of hours. I hated leaving him, half asleep, curled in the warm spot I left behind.

During the last minutes of my last day at Ida's, Antonia posed against the mop handle, wet linoleum glistening around her feet. "Your hunky boyfriend's here, Wylie," she said as if I couldn't see for myself. Danny had promised me a driving lesson. Antonia watched him through lowered eyelashes, throwing him a smile as sweet and sticky as the icing we smeared by the handful on trays of cinnamon buns. He blushed, jangled his keys.

"Your car's real nice," Antonia said. "Do you know a lot about cars?"

"Enough," he muttered. "Come on, Wylie, let's go."

"My father's buying me a car," Antonia said. "I need someone to help me find one. I don't want to get ripped off. I don't know a thing about cars."

Danny stared out the window. The Bonneville glittered blue in the pale winter sun, the only car on the empty Sunday street. I stacked coffee cups as fast as I could, wishing he'd stayed behind the wheel and honked the horn like he usually did. Why hadn't he?

Antonia tiptoed across the wet floor to stand beside Danny. Her shoulder brushed his. The coffee cups crashed to the floor behind me. I'd stacked them too high. Danny and Antonia jumped; the thin slice of air between them crackled.

"Whoa," he said.

"I'd love to go for a ride sometime," Antonia said, as if ten cups and saucers hadn't just shattered.

I gathered thoughts and broken dishes at the same time, tossing the shards in the trash can.

Danny watched, his face anxious. If I'd asked him to help, he would've rushed to my side, leaving muddy footprints coming and going, for Antonia to mop up. Before the ring, he would've come without being asked.

"Tell Tony I'll come by next week for my check," I said.

"He'll take money out for those broken cups," said Antonia.

"Fine." I had planned a little ceremony for myself. I wanted to feed the birds for the last time, think of Sofie, and appreciate all that my months at Ida's had meant, but I was too upset. Antonia DiMartino had ruined the day and more.

Until Danny opened the car door to join me, I wasn't sure he would. He started the engine. "Where do you want to go?" he asked.

"I don't know," I said. "Away from here. Can't you think of someplace? Why do I always have to do the thinking?"

He didn't answer.

"What was going on in there, anyway? Will you please tell me what's going on with you and Antonia?"

Danny screeched to a stop just in time to keep from going through the red light. "I wasn't doing anything," he mumbled. "I was waiting for you."

"I'm sure Antonia would love a diamond ring," I said. "And a house for that matter."

"Shut up," Danny said.

Too hurt to pay attention to the anger thickening his voice, I kept pushing. "Why don't you just turn around? Go back and ask her. A diamond would look perfect on her beautiful hands. Imagine those long, red fingernails running across your back." The light turned green. He pushed the accelerator to the floor and headed out the River Road, a route so familiar the car could drive itself.

"Stop it," he breathed through clenched teeth. The engine purred. The heater blasted. Danny gripped the steering wheel. "You know I don't care about her. But you're jealous. You're jealous because Antonia's normal. And you're not."

"What are you talking about?" I asked. "Who appointed you to decide what normal is? What the hell is that? Normal?"

We careened around a curve.

"Normal is what you are not," Danny shouted. "You are abnormal. You hang around with old people. You don't have any friends. You say you love me but you won't get married. You don't know what you want."

"Lots of people don't know what they want." I huddled next to the door. "And I'm too busy working and taking care of everything all the time to make friends. You're my friend." Whether I meant 'you are' or 'you were,' I didn't know.

"I know what I want," Danny said.

"You're lucky then."

I knew what he wanted too, but he told me again anyway. "I want a job, a life. I want to marry you. But," he slowed the car, "I'm starting to figure out that maybe I can't have that."

His sidelong glance begged for reassurance, willed me to say he was wrong. When I looked away, curling tighter around my tucked up knees, he checked the rearview mirror for cops, gunned the engine, and drove even faster along the curving River Road, past the Rock, to a small, unmarked lot by the river. Part of me wished he'd drive until we crashed and burned.

"I'm ready to give up," he said. He turned off the motor, leaving the keys in the ignition. "If you don't want to marry me, I'll look for someone else. You're using me. I'm sick of being used." He rested his head on the steering wheel.

"No." My stomach leaped into my chest. I reached for his arm.

He pushed my hand away. "All you think about is leaving. I don't know what makes you think it's going to be so much better somewhere else." His father could have said those exact words as his mother walked out the door.

"You never even thought that I could go somewhere with you, did you?" Danny asked. "All you think of is yourself."

"You like it here," I said. It took more imagination than I had to picture Danny without the valley as his backdrop. He knew every pothole in the roads, the cheapest place to buy gas. People respected him. He had a job waiting when he graduated.

"With you here, I like it," he said. "Without you...I don't know what I'll do."

"But if I stayed, you'd stay. You don't really want to leave."

Danny was too honest to try to fool me about that. "I like it here," he admitted.

"See. I don't want you leaving because you want to be with me. What if it doesn't work out? What if we go somewhere and you hate it?"

"Then we'd come back."

I hit the dashboard. "*We* would not come back if *you* hated it.

"Take me to Sofie's," I said.

Danny threw the car into reverse and backed up without even a glance behind us. He screeched onto the road and drove like someone with nothing to lose. He laughed at my knuckles white against the dashboard, my lip mashed under my teeth. He'd take me to Sofie's, but he'd do it his way, and I'd let him. Somehow I'd lost the right to ask him to slow down.

We tore over the bridge into town. A dark shape smacked into the grill with a sound like a melon against pavement. He jammed on the brakes and pulled over.

We got out at the same time, slamming our doors. Plastered to the grillwork was a dark mass of feathers, a pigeon with neck and wings twisted into impossible positions.

"Shit." Danny picked up a stick and poked at the dead bird, scraping off as much as he could. "At least there's no dent." He kicked the broken body into the gutter.

I leaned against the front fender and threw up in the street.

Danny reached back and tossed the stick far over the bridge, into the river. We watched the stick bob and float between icy spots until it disappeared under the surface.

"Get in," he said. "I'll take you to the old lady's."

"I'll walk," I said. "It's okay."

"Just get in."

When I didn't move, he opened the door and nudged me into the car.

The silence and the stench of burning feathers made the ride to Sofie's longer than it was. Danny stopped in front of the house.

"Is this it?" I asked. "Or can we be friends somehow."

"I can't," he whispered, looking out his window. "I can't right now."

"I'm sorry," I said. I wanted to hold him, wanted to feel his kisses on my neck. The car was full of wanting—his and mine.

"Go on," Danny said roughly.

"It's hard," I said.

"Go." With both hands Danny wiped his cheeks and pushed his hair back in one smooth motion. "Go."

"I'm going," I whispered.

He peeled down the street the moment I slammed the door. I watched him drive away.

∗   ∗   ∗   ∗

Sofie leaned heavily on her cane and followed me to the kitchen. "What's wrong?" she demanded. "For a week now you are wearing that old sad face."

I ran water over the breakfast dishes wishing I didn't have two cakes to make. Sofie would keep at me until I told her everything. How Danny wouldn't answer his phone. How he'd given up his place in the lunch line to avoid me. How he was right about me having no friends.

"Turn off the water." Sofie whacked the floor with her cane. "What's going on? Your brother hasn't burned anything, has he?"

I rinsed a glass and set it in the drainer.

"Your mother? She is drinking?"

I gripped the edge of the sink, breathing deeply before turning to answer.

"No," I said, holding each word in my mouth before carefully pronouncing it. "I told you. Robbie's at the farm, you know, home for wayward boys. Mom hasn't drunk for thirty-three days." I wouldn't stop counting days until I could measure the time in years. "Everything's fine."

"Then it's that boyfriend of yours," Sofie said, shaking the cane at me as if it were a long finger.

"I don't want to talk about it." I pushed the cane out of my face and pretended to study an order slip. "This really is none of your business."

"About me and Martin you know plenty," she said. "You can talk to me. When will you learn it helps to talk?"

She shook her head at my hard silence. "Okay, suit yourself."

She paid no attention to the yellow sheet cake I set on the table. Silence—the itchy kind. Finally, with a small wave of her hand, Sofie indicated the cake. "So what do we do with this one?"

I showed her a black and white photo of a little, vine covered cottage, a house so perfect I could almost imagine marrying Danny and living happily ever after in it. "It's the house Pete Tomaski's mother lived in when she and her husband first came to this country. He wants it for her eightieth birthday. He said she never got over having to leave it."

"Leave it?" Sofie brought the picture up close to her glasses. "Those are wild roses growing up the walls. You can do those. You're the expert at roses. Why did his mother leave?"

"I think it was to move in with him. She's in a nursing home now."

"A nursing home." Sofie grabbed my arm and shook the picture at me. "First she is leaving her house to live with her son. Next is the home. She is eighty. How old was she when she left her house? Maybe younger than I am now."

"I bet she wasn't in as good shape," I said.

Sofie shook my arm as if she were an angry little girl and I were her rag doll. "You call what I am in, good shape?" she said, voice growing louder.

"Every day you're able to do more."

"If someday, I can't stay here in my house, please do me a favor and—"

"Stop it." I yanked my arm free and quickly filled a series of small bowls with mounds of white icing. "Don't worry. Here, mix some gray for the shingles and pink for roses. After this we have to make the Hawaiian Islands for Stan Pawlak's going away party."

Sofie didn't move.

"Do you think we can use the gray left over from the selkie skin?"

Sofie stared into space. She was not listening.

"Sofie?"

"I'm seventy years old." She stared at the photograph, running her fingers over the surface as if trying to feel the shingles, the rose petals, even the thorns.

"You've said yourself it's not your age in years that matters. Remember when I first started at Ida's you told me about your friends sitting around all the time. You've kept busy. And young."

"Since my fall, I am old." She leaned on her cane. She pressed her face close to mine, forcing me to stop moving, to look at her. "I feel old. I am wanting a promise from you. If I ever have to leave this house, make sure first I am dead."

Before I could say I couldn't make such a promise, Sofie went on. "But instead I will ask for something not so big. Swear you will never make for me a house cake."

Relieved, I asked, "You think this cake is a bad idea?"

"This Pete Tomaski is not thinking about his mother's feelings. Who knows? Maybe she'll like it, but I think he is having bad judgment. If you came with a cake like this to the nursing home, I'd throw it in your face."

I laughed, and then realized Sofie wasn't even smiling. "You liked the car cake, didn't you?"

"I hoped I'd drive again," said Sofie. "So, yes, I liked it. Now I'm not so sure."

"You'll drive," I said.

"A house, once you've left it for the nursing home or even your son's, there's no going back. I've seen it happen. I know what I am talking about." Her eyes dulled. She forgot the spatula in her hand, the cakes we had to make, me.

"Alright. Alright." I wanted her back. "I'll never make you a house cake." I wanted to say I wouldn't let her go to a nursing home, but I knew enough not to make any big promises, not even to Sofie. I'd been caring for too many people, too long.

Sofie adjusted her glasses, reached for a jar of pink coloring. "Don't be forgetting to start my car and let it run today for a few minutes."

"I never forget that." I cut the cake, building up layers, shaping a sloped roof.

Sofie stared into the bowl of rose colored icing she was mixing as if it could tell the future.

"And speaking of cars," I said, "my road test is Thursday. And Danny...I won't be able to use his."

"Ahh." Sofie held the bowl out for my approval. I nodded. "I knew it," she said, mixing a green. "Boyfriend problems.

"You can use my car," Sofie said. "But who will drive you? If only Martin were still here. Get me some water will you?"

I handed her a cup. Sofie thinned the icing, a drop at a time, thinking.

"Ivy Jane," she said. "She won't mind. When you come back, we'll make a celebration." Sofie grinned, nursing home forgotten.

When IJ bustled in for a two hour shift, freeing me to leave, Sofie asked about the driving test right off.

"With a license, you would be even more of a help around here," IJ said, tying an apron over her aqua pantsuit. "You could do the grocery shopping, take Sofie to her appointments."

"She can do more than that." Sofie smiled. "Now, go on, Ivy Jane and I will clean the kitchen." IJ big as she was, moved efficiently through the room with smooth, quick steps. She had already oohhed and ahhed over the cakes and cleared and wiped the table.

"I'll go start the car now." I retrieved my coat from a chair. I could never remember to hang it up without Martin there to take it from me.

"Open the garage door," Sofie said, as always. "I don't want to find you dead. Over the visor the keys are tucked."

"I know."

It was my time off. Without Danny, without the bakery, I had nowhere to go but home.

Sofie's car started right up. I imagined shifting into reverse, pushing the gas pedal to the floor. A faint smell of Ida's rose from the seat cushions. I wondered if Danny still smelled roasted pigeon when he drove the Bonneville. I hoped so. I hoped he'd smell it everywhere he went. I turned off the engine and slipped the keys into my pocket to see what they felt like before replacing them.

On the walk to my house I tried to calculate how many cakes I still had to bake before I made enough money for a car of my own, gas, and an apartment. Forty, maybe fifty, I figured. I considered a price increase—recalculated.

Traffic whizzed by on North Main Street, background noise, until a car slowed beside me. The Bonneville. A girl sat in my old seat, close to Danny. The numbers I'd been moving around in my head whirled away. I tried to see who she was. It didn't look like Antonia. Danny stared straight ahead. A bolt of electricity ran from my chest to the dark place deep inside that only he had touched. I wanted to shout at him. He sped up. The tail lights shrunk to red pinpricks in the winter dusk. A new girl I didn't recognize. I'd have to ask around. Danny hadn't wasted any time.

Saturday afternoon, almost evening. Maybe they were going skating. I imagined their linked hands.

I stood alone, with a pocket full of money, on a snowy sidewalk in front of Roy's package store, nothing to do on a Saturday night. Accident, free will, or destiny? I pressed my face against the window. The bottles on the shelves glowed as if they held molten jewels. Behind the counter, Roy watched a small black and white TV. Drunk, I might forget how bad I felt. I could try Southern Comfort. I could try whatever I wanted. Champagne!

I walked right up to the counter. Roy didn't care if you were under age but I'd heard he wanted you in and out fast. No wandering the aisles. "Champagne please," I said.

"What kind you want?" I didn't know what to say. I didn't know there was more than one kind. He looked me up and down. I was afraid he'd ask for an ID.

"Something cheap...inexpensive."

He nodded, dragged himself from behind the counter over to a rack of bottles, and handed me one. I read the label as though it meant something to me and nodded.

Next problem—where to drink it. Not the Rock or the Res with everyone else, where Danny and the girl might be. The only place I could think of was the playground, Avery Field, my own private drinking spot, sure to be empty on a cold, Saturday night. I felt in my front pocket for my money.

Crouched behind the locked rest rooms I tried to figure out how to open the bottle. I talked myself past the warnings about eye injuries and removed the wire cap. Holding the bottle at arm's length, squeezing my eyes shut, I twisted the cork. It flew high into the darkening sky with a sound like a gun shot. Champagne bubbled and gushed over my hands. I huddled against the building, sure the noise had brought neighbors to their windows. When no one came I lifted the bottle to my lips with sticky, wet fingers.

The warm champagne tickled my nose and tongue. Whether or not it tasted better than vodka, I couldn't say. I drank as much as I could as fast as I could, stumbled away from the building and flung the heavy, green bottle against the cinderblock wall. It shattered. Staring at the broken glass, I decided I must be turning into a juvenile delinquent. Some kid was going to get cut, and I didn't even care. Remembering I'd thrown up after swinging, I headed for the seesaw this time.

From where I sat on the splintered board, close to the ground, the empty end slanted way up toward the sky. I remembered a time from before I could talk— my mother's arms around me, looking up at my dad, a dark shape against all the bright, blue sky behind him, the feeling of catapulting up and looking down at his laughing face and always my mother's arm tight around my baby middle, Lucy's body warm and solid as the whole earth, against my back.

Champagne sloshing in my stomach, sour taste in the back of my mouth, I stood on wobbly legs, slid up to the middle of the seesaw, and sat, trying to keep it balanced. I played with leaning one way, then the other, until I felt sick again.

Had to get warm somewhere. People died, drunk, exposed to the elements. IJ put Sofie to bed on Saturday night. I couldn't show up there. IJ might report me to Martin; he'd fire me for being drunk on the job. I was cold. I wanted to see my mother, ask her if she remembered the seesaw.

I found my way to the house, knocked and opened the door at the same time. Either action by itself seemed wrong.

"You're home?" Lucy, wearing stockings and a slinky blue dress, looked surprised and disappointed. I was not the person she'd expected to see coming through the door. She set a dish of peanuts on the table near the couch. The smells of fresh coffee and perfume said company was coming. Except that Lucy never had company.

"It's Saturday night," she said, adjusting a glittery earring. "You always go out."

"Where's Kevin?" I asked, thinking I could at least take him bowling or out for pizza.

"He's staying with Bonnie. She's got kids close to his age. We're going to be doing some baby-sitting for each other."

"You could have asked me," I said, slurring my words. "Who is this Bonnie? Another drunk you met at meetings."

My mother approached me, frowning. "Drunk? Who's drunk? Wylie..."

I narrowed my eyes, daring her to say anything else.

Lucy squinted at the clock near the TV. "I'm having a few friends over." She smoothed her skirt and picked up a deck of cards. "I didn't expect you."

"A boyfriend?" I asked.

"People I met at a meeting. A friend." She blushed. "To play hearts."

"Oh, more drunks. One's a man, though, right? A special someone." My voice dripped sarcasm.

Lucy tilted her head and shoulders in a pretty little shrug. I wanted to be happy for her, but my head ached with champagne and meanness. Saturday night. My mother had friends and even a potential boyfriend, and I had a job nursing an old woman.

Lucy stopped in the middle of moving a bowl of chips and studied my face. "I don't want to fight with you now," she said.

I avoided her gaze. "We always eat chips right from the bag."

My mother put the bowl back down without noticing where. I stumbled, heading for a seat on the couch.

"So fancy all of a sudden." I crossed my legs and struck a pose. "Must be a special guy."

"You really have been drinking." Lucy's mouth hung open. I laughed.

"I can't believe it," she said. "I didn't quit so that you could start."

I laughed again. I couldn't stop. I was afraid I'd wet my pants. I tried to stand and move toward the bathroom, but I was laughing too hard. Tears streamed hot down my cheeks. My mother's face changed so fast from bewilderment to anger to concern to bewilderment again, it was as if we were playing a game of 'guess that emotion.'

"Takes one to know one," I gasped. "Sofie even has some German saying about it. Apples not falling far from their trees. I'm your daughter. Why shouldn't I be like you?"

"I didn't quit so you could start," she said again. "I won't let you ruin your life."

"Too late. My life is ruined." My laugh turned to a sob before it left my chest. I curled against the arm of the couch, burying my face in a pillow, pretending to disappear. I could hide my tears but the sobs racking my body shook the couch.

Lucy wrapped her arms around me from behind. "Don't," I said into the wet pillow. "You'll mess up your dress."

"You've got everything to look forward to," she said, resting her cheek against my back.

"Danny has a new girlfriend," I sobbed. "My brother's in jail."

"It's not jail." She hated it when I said that. "And Danny's a nice guy. Just not right for you. Be glad you had the sense to know it. And you did know it. You would've left him sooner or later. You just can't stand it that he left you."

She was right. Where did this mother come from? The mother who held me safe, high on the seesaw was back at least for the moment. A mother who was right. A mother who knew me. Or at least something about me. Inside, the dark emptiness shrunk. A car drove past outside. I remembered the guests. "Let me use the bathroom," I said. "Then I'll head back to Sofie's."

"You don't have to leave. You could meet them if you want," Lucy offered.

"No thanks."

"They say your brother's doing good." She followed me to the bathroom and stood outside the door. "He can have visitors next weekend."

"I'll have my license by then," I said, over the flushing of the toilet. "If I pass my test on Thursday. I'll drive us there. Sofie will let me use her car."

"Are you alright to make it to Sofie's?" Lucy asked at the front door.

My head throbbed. "I don't even feel drunk anymore. Just sick."

"Have a coke. Do you want something to eat? Toast? Or some coffee?"

I wanted my mother to feed me, to move around the kitchen popping bread in the toaster, while I sat at the table, but even drunk I noticed how, as car headlights swept across the wall, Lucy looked past me, through the window, eager for her evening to begin.

"No, thanks." I hadn't even unbuttoned my coat. I said good-bye and slipped through the door quickly, afraid of losing what my mother had given me, afraid she would somehow take it back.

*   *   *   *

The warm smell of apple cake greeted me when I got to Sofie's the afternoon of my driving test. There was nothing in the thin blue driving manual in my coat pocket that wasn't also in my head.

IJ put down her dust rag. "You're not nervous are you?" She took off her apron. "Because you know you can always take it over if you fail."

"She won't fail." Sofie approached me, moving easily with the help of her cane. It would be a matter of days until she no longer needed it. I smiled. It felt unnatural; it had been so long since my lips had turned up on their own.

Sofie patted my arm. "I made for us a cake. Nothing fancy."

"She did it all herself," IJ said. "Wouldn't let me do a thing."

"Dancing on tables," I teased. "Pretty soon."

"Ach!" Sofie waved a dismissive hand, but her eyes gleamed as though she were allowing herself to believe it.

"Don't tire yourself," IJ warned her. "We can help set the table and make coffee or anything else when we get back. You're apt to wear yourself out if you keep this up."

"Ach!" Sofie shook her head and rolled her eyes.

"Don't spoil her fun," I said. "This woman lives to work."

Sofie winked at me. "Go on," she said. "You show them you know how to drive."

The test was a snap. I held the pale, green, cardboard license to my nose and sniffed the ink. Wylie Steele, five feet, three inches. Deciding what to put for eye color took longer than the test itself. The woman behind the counter didn't know what to do, faced for the first time with one blue eye and one green. Finally, she typed in bl/grn, and it was finished. With that license in my wallet, I sat tall in the driver's seat. IJ complimented me every time I signaled a turn or stopped at a stop sign. All that time with Danny I thought I needed a boyfriend. What I really needed was a car.

The Volkswagen centered perfectly in Sofie's driveway, I put on the emergency brake and hopped out to lift the garage door. I jumped back into the car, and it sailed into its space.

"Nicely done." IJ heaved herself out of the seat and led the way through the basement.

I slipped the license from my wallet, ready to show Sofie, then sensed, halfway up the stairs, that something was wrong. The gas burned high under an empty tea kettle. "Sofie?"

We rushed to the dining room. Sofie lay still on her side, on the floor, eyes closed, skin papery gray, legs partly covered by a lace tablecloth she held in one hand. The bottom drawer of the sideboard hung open beside her.

I couldn't move or make a sound.

IJ squeezed part way under the table to kneel next to Sofie. "Call an ambulance, right away." Voice calm, she held Sofie's wrist, taking her pulse.

The tablecloth slipped through Sofie's limp fingers. I had been so happy. Something broke inside me.

"Call an ambulance," IJ repeated. "Now."

"Is she dead?" I asked.

Lips counting soundlessly, IJ pushed me to the phone with her eyes. I dialed the operator, telling myself that if there was something for IJ to count, Sofie had to be alive.

"Hurts," Sofie whispered.

"Shh." IJ stroked Sofie's forehead. "An ambulance is on its way."

"Hurts."

"I think you've dislocated your hip," IJ went on. "I know it hurts."

Sofie whimpered. "Wylie?"

"I'm here," I said. Sofie lay between IJ and the open drawer. I couldn't get close.

Sirens. Two young men I thought I remembered waiting on at Ida's tromped in. IJ said something about Sofie's surgery. They put her leg in a kind of a splint.

"It hurts. It hurts," Sofie whispered, face crumpled in pain. "Don't touch."

"Sorry," one of the men said as they slid a board under her, lifted her like a rolled carpet, and carried her out to the ambulance.

"I'll go with them," IJ said. "You lock up. Call Martin."

"What will happen?" I asked.

"This isn't unusual." IJ paused in the doorway. "Especially for someone like Sofie who does too much too soon. They'll fix the hip. Then, of course, there'll be another recovery period."

"How long?" I asked as the door slammed. The siren faded.

In the dining room, three of Sofie's best cups and saucers waited on the sideboard. Slices of apple cake fanned around a dish of whipped cream on a large plate. Sofie had managed it all, then bent to reach the tablecloth or push the drawer shut with her foot and ended up on the floor. For me. All for me.

I'd have to call Martin and tell him his mother was back in the hospital. He'd ask how it happened, and I'd have to say that IJ was at the motor vehicle department instead of taking care of his mother.

I still held the license in my hand, a sweaty scrap of cardboard with bent edges. I collapsed onto the nearest chair, the tablecloth a puddle of lace at my feet, and smoothed the license against the polished wood of the dining room table. I slipped it into a plastic pocket of my wallet, covering a picture of Danny.

Martin's numbers, work and home, hung on the wall near the phone along with mine, IJ's and Ida's. I dialed his home first, expecting, and getting no answer, then tried work. When I heard his voice, so unmistakably his, so far away, so full of concern, I could hardly speak.

"Something's wrong," he said. "Wylie, what is it? Sofie?"

"She fell." The words squeaked past the lump in my throat. "They took her back to the hospital. Just now. IJ thought she dislocated her hip."

"Is she there?"

"I told you they took her to the hospital." The kitchen faded in and out of focus. I gripped the phone.

"No, I mean IJ."

"She went with Sofie. I wanted to go with her, but she went. She just went right in the ambulance. Sofie asked for me. She wanted me."

Martin said, "It's okay. I'll call the hospital. I'll get a flight as soon as I can. If they fire me here, I can always help you with your cakes, right? I'll call you back. Will you be there?"

"No," I said. "I don't want to stay here by myself."

"I'll call you at your mother's house then."

My mother's house. I noticed a small, wrapped package with my name on it on the counter, almost hidden by the mixer. I picked it up.

"You take care," Martin was saying. I ripped the paper from the package. A key ring. A peacock feather, frozen in clear plastic.

"Oh," I said.

"What?" Martin asked. "Are you alright? Remember. We haven't heard from the doctor yet."

"You didn't see her." I clutched the key ring. "You didn't see her on the floor."

"Wylie, go home. I'll call you there."

But this is my home now, I wanted to say. I wanted to keep him on the line. "I have my license," I said.

"Great! You can pick me up at the airport. I'll arrange a flight and let you know when I arrive." He took a loud breath.

"I'll make some calls and get back to you," Martin said. "Everything's going to be okay."

Sofie would want me to cover the apple cake with waxed paper and put the whipped cream in Tupperware. She would want the lace cloth folded and smoothed into its drawer. I couldn't. The key to the Volkswagen was still in my pocket. I threaded my new key ring through the hole, turned off the lights, locked the door, and drove home, leaving the cream to sour and the cake to dry out. Sofie and Martin wouldn't have left a mess like that, but they weren't there. Without them I couldn't be there either, not even for a minute, certainly not for the time it would take to put everything away.

No one was home at five o'clock when I pulled up at the house. I fell, exhausted, onto the couch and slept without a flicker of a dream or a nightmare, the imprint of my mother's body in the battered cushions cradling me.

*   *   *   *

"Here she is!" Kevin leaped on me and patted my hair. Lucy switched on the lights. I sat up, squinting and blinking in the sudden brightness.

"We saw the car in front," Lucy said. "What are you doing here in the dark?"

"We went to McDonalds," chanted Kevin, "with Mommy's friend."

"Sofie's back in the hospital," I said.

"You have her car." Lucy lit a cigarette and inhaled. "Your test? You passed!"

"I did." It seemed like a long time ago. "But Sofie…"

"Robbie can have visitors this weekend. You sure it would be okay with Sofie to use her car?"

I couldn't answer. The phone rang. I leaped to pick it up. "Martin!"

He told me an orthopedic doctor had already popped Sofie's hip back in. She was back in traction. If all went well, she'd be out in a few days.

"They say she should progress faster this time," he said. "She knows the whole therapy routine. I'll be arriving at Bradley Field day after tomorrow. At four fifteen." He didn't sound worried at all.

"Okay, day after tomorrow, four fifteen," I repeated.

Lucy and Kevin had followed me into the kitchen. "What about four fifteen?" Lucy ran water over her cigarette butt and dropped it into the trash.

"I have to pick up Martin at Bradley Field."

"Two days after you get your license, you're borrowing someone else's car and driving on major highways?"

"Mom, you just asked me to drive to visit Robbie. That means taking the highway." I hadn't even asked Martin if I could use it, but I assumed he'd let me.

"Alright." She lit another cigarette. "Just be careful. You can get killed on those roads."

"You can get killed right at home too," I said. "People get electrocuted by hair dryers and drown in their own bathtubs."

"Can I visit Robbie too?" Kevin asked. "I want to see the jail."

"I told you, he's not in jail," Lucy said. She ruffled Kevin's hair. "He's told everyone at school that his brother is chained to a wall with only bread and water to eat."

"How could you drown in a bathtub?" he asked.

"Great," said Lucy. "Now he'll be afraid to take a bath. And no, you can't visit this time. Bonnie is going watch you. Maybe she'll take you sliding on the big hill at the end of her street."

"Will you bring Robbie a cake with a file in it? I want to see if he's wearing those striped clothes."

"With Sofie in the hospital, will you be staying here again?" Lucy asked, her tone neutral, impossible to read.

"Is that okay with you?" I asked. "You haven't gotten rid of my mattress or anything?"

"Of course not," she said. "This is your home. You can always stay here."

As I helped myself to a coke, I noticed that the refrigerator gleamed. Lucy cleaned to keep busy. The whole kitchen shone, cleaner than it had ever been when I was in charge. I drank without taking a breath until the glass was empty and set it in the sink. If doing dishes kept Lucy sober, I was willing to provide them. Seemed like I was leaving dirty dishes all over town.

*   *   *   *

"They call this a farm?" I said, pulling to a stop in the parking lot. I was glad I had a chance to practice driving before picking Martin up later that afternoon.

My mother and I surveyed the jumble of rectangular brick buildings. "Maybe they have some chickens or something," Lucy said, sucking hard on her cigarette before stubbing it out. Sofie's ashtray, never used before Lucy got in the car, over-flowed with lipstick smeared butts. "I think Robbie mentioned chickens."

I peered through the windshield trying to figure out where the entrance was or even the main building. "Are you sure it's visiting hours? It doesn't seem too crowded."

"Lots of the kids go home on weekends," Lucy angled the mirror and dragged a comb through her hair.

"This isn't a date." She wouldn't have fixed herself up to see me.

Lucy put on a hurt expression. "I want to look nice for my son. Come on." She stuffed her comb and cigarettes into her carpet bag.

"I still think we should've brought Kevin. He should see this place. Maybe he'll decide he doesn't want to end up here."

"Wylie?" my mother said, reaching to put a hand on my forehead. "Are you okay?"

"I'm fine." I jerked my head, shaking off Lucy's hand and opened the car door.

"Jennings says Robbie may start coming home weekends earlier than we thought if he continues to behave." Lucy followed me up the walk. "She says he's doing real good."

"Real good? Mom, this is a jail. Robbie is doing real good in jail. What the hell does that mean?"

"It's not a jail." Lucy was trying to remain calm, but her nostrils flared. "That's the whole point. It's not a jail." She flung open the heavy metal door as if it were cardboard.

The walls were plastered with signs warning not to bring in drugs or weapons. Lucy walked directly to a windowed booth where a bored guard drank coffee from a Styrofoam cup and studied a folded newspaper. Her anger at me had gotten her into the place. Standing before the guard, her determination leaked out of her. I moved up beside her and coughed. He marked the paper with a pencil stub, then looked up.

We gave him our names. He grunted. A younger, skinny guard with a giant ring of clanking keys on his belt beckoned for us to follow. We left our coats and Lucy's bag in a metal cubicle.

Long wooden tables, chairs on both sides, filled the square visiting room. If there had been any sign of food, it could have been a cafeteria. The guard pointed to two chairs. We sat. He climbed into a raised glass enclosure, like a projection room at the movies. Lucy pressed her fingers together. She wanted a cigarette.

The door across from us opened, and Robbie walked through. Lucy gasped.

"Got that haircut people used to nag me about," he said. "Didn't even have to pay for it." He didn't smile.

His neck looked thin and brittle. I thought of Sofie's wrists. People are stronger than they look, I told myself. Good thing, too.

"I see they let you walk around without handcuffs," I said.

"No chains either," Robbie said grimly.

"How are things going?" Lucy asked, tapping the table. Her knee jiggled against mine. What she was really asking was whether or not she'd done the right thing sending him there.

I held my breath, bracing for stories of cruelty, extortion, and bad food.

"They got school, just like on the outside, but no girls. Teach the same old boring shit." Robbie wouldn't have said 'shit' so casually before. With his friends, yes, but not in front of our mother. Lucy rested an elbow on the table and rubbed her forehead.

I tried another joke. "At least you don't have to make license plates or eat bread and water."

"Food's real bad," he said.

I wondered how time at the Farm was supposed to squelch his fire setting urges. Enough time inside these sickly green walls and I'd be tempted to start fires myself.

Lucy wasn't saying much. She was one mother to me and another to Robbie. Forced to sit in the same space with both of us, sober, no TV, cards, or Kevin to distract her, she didn't know who she was.

"Kevin thought Wylie should make you a cake with a file in it," she said with a tentative smile.

Robbie glared at me. "Why would she do that? She put me in here."

"I did not." My voice echoed in the empty room. The guard looked at us.

"Even your homo friend wasn't going to report it," he said. "You made Mom tell."

Bristling, I swallowed a childish, 'I did not.' Lucy had to say something. I chewed the insides of my cheeks, waiting. Robbie stared squinting at me, then Lucy.

Lucy squirmed. She looked around the room, the screened windows, the guard, Robbie's new blue work shirt and jeans, shorn head—everywhere but his face and mine. Robbie had given her the chance to go on being his buddy. He'd let her believe she wasn't a bad Mom. He'd go on as her good little boy, unlucky to be caught by the police. On the other hand, she'd stopped drinking, stopped pretending. When Lucy opened her mouth I had no idea what would come out.

"Nobody made anybody do anything," Lucy said. "The fires had to stop. I decided to tell your probation officer."

I gave Robbie a see-I-didn't-do-anything shrug. Under the table, where Robbie couldn't know, Lucy rested a hand on my thigh. I felt the shape and weight of every one of my mother's fingers through my jeans.

Robbie laid his head on his folded arms, his short, short hair inches from my hand. It looked prickly and soft. I wanted to touch it. But I kept my hands to myself and avoided looking at my mother. I didn't want to find her silently asking what to do next.

"So…" Lucy cleared her throat. "They treat you okay?"

Robbie was silent long enough to give the impression he wasn't going to answer. He lifted his head. "Nobody bothers me."

"They tell me you're behaving." Lucy laid her free hand on his arm. He softened long enough to meet her approving gaze with a flicker of a grin. Her other hand nervously rubbed at a groove in the tabletop. She couldn't touch both of us at once. "It won't be long until you're coming home weekends. We miss you. Your brother misses you."

Robbie tried to look bored, but his lip quivered.

"I miss you," I said.

"Yeah, right." He stared at me without blinking, wanting me to convince him.

"Time's up," said the guard.

Lucy shook her head. "So quick?"

"Time flies when you're having fun," said Robbie, his voice layered with feelings I had no names for. Yawning, he stood and raised both arms in an exaggerated stretch.

"We'll see you soon." Lucy rubbed her hands together, a helpless gesture. I wasn't coming again. The visits would be easier for everyone if I waited in the car.

We stood, looking at the walls, the floor, the table, avoiding each other's eyes, waiting for the guard to descend and show us to our respective doors.

"Hey," I said suddenly, deciding to take a chance. "Can I feel your hair?"

A screw-you look flashed in Robbie's eyes. The guard clanked closer. Just as I began to regret asking, just before I turned away, my brother leaned over the table and bowed his head.

CHAPTER 6

▼

MARTIN

Another jangling phone call. Years of punctuality and hard work made taking a second leave from my job in less than two months possible. Even when Erich was dying, I had always gone into work. The details, the dailiness, kept me functioning. I preferred to function. If Sofie lived nearby I would have fit hospital visits in after work and hired housekeepers and companions by phone during my lunch hour.

Saturday night Michael and Jean Paul bought me drinks at Poseidon's. Everything sparkled. The neon, the wood, even the imitation Tiffany fixtures seemed to glow as richly as real ones. Conversation bubbled around us. I'd worn one of Erich's elegant striped shirts and cufflinks. Every time a cufflink caught the light I felt Erich winking at me. After my second martini, I glimpsed an attractive older man in the window and realized it was me. What was different? The clothes, of course, but also the easy smile, the shoulders back, the chest open. If someone wanted to shoot me in the heart, he could. There it was, protected only by a Brooks Brothers shirt. It felt like enough. "Feel this fabric," Erich always said. "That's quality."

Jean Paul raised his cosmopolitan. "To life," he said. We clinked glasses. Early the next morning Michael drove me to the airport.

The woman behind the ticket counter offered a window seat. I was about to insist on an aisle as I usually did, then felt myself nod. I wandered toward the gate, clutching my boarding pass and suitcase. It was not a crowded flight. No one sat beside me. I could sit on the aisle should I decide it was best. I fastened my seatbelt and during take off, watched the ground drop away and San Francisco become a peninsula, a shape on a map. Somewhere down there stood my house, the Berkeley Marina where I'd tossed Erich's ashes from the end of that pier as the sun set behind the Golden Gate Bridge. Angel Island, where we'd picnicked and walked. Strange, how small it all was.

At the other end of the flight waited Rivertown. As the plane descended, I'd watch until the landscape of Connecticut filled my vision. But I would have seen, and would remember, that if I went high enough—San Francisco, Connecticut—I could see it all at once. My house, Erich's ashes dissolving in the bay, Robbie's fires, Johnny's pit bull, Wylie's cakes, Sofie in her hospital bed, could all be seen at the same time if one had strong enough vision and a long enough view.

Wylie met me at the gate, looking as tired as I'd expected to feel after sitting in a plane for hours.

"Martin," she called, car keys clinking in her waving hand.

"You made it, I see." Her wiry hair tickled my chin as I bent to hug her. I noticed the peacock feather key chain.

I remembered a hat my father had given Sofie on a birthday, a dark green felt hat trimmed with peacock feathers—very elegant—too elegant. She'd never worn it. Years later, I must have been about Robbie's age, I found it in a striped hatbox on a closet shelf and tried it on, posing in front of the mirror, tilting my head, smiling at myself over a shoulder. When I heard the downstairs door open, I panicked, jammed the hat in its box, stuffed it back on its shelf, and with my heart pounding so hard it hurt, pretended to be doing my homework. I'd never done anything like that again, until Erich coaxed me to dress up for Halloween and New Year's parties.

"You look good," Wylie said.

"I feel good." I swung my suitcase. "For an old man."

"Is that all your luggage?"

"I left things here the last time. Figured I'd be back in the spring to check on Sofie. And you. Didn't think it would be this soon. Which way to the car?"

Wylie paused, confusion crumpled her face. I waited. "I forget. I'm sorry. I was hurrying. I was so glad I made it…I mean driving was fun but…I forgot…"

"Wylie." I took her arm. "Calm down. It's here. We'll find it."

She nodded.

"Just think for a minute, remember where you entered the terminal. If you can't, we'll just walk through the parking lot. I could use the exercise after sitting so long."

"It was my fault Sofie fell again," Wylie said. "IJ would have been there, but she drove me to my driving test."

"That's ridiculous," I said. "It was Sofie's idea IJ take you. She insisted. At least that's what she told me the last time I talked to her."

"She was trying to make a little party for me," Wylie said.

"She tries to do too much," I said. "That's her, not you. I'm glad she had something she wanted to celebrate."

"But..."

I put down my suitcase. Right in front of the terminal where taxis and limousines unloaded and picked up passengers, skycaps rushed back and forth with carts piled with luggage, I held Wylie's shoulders, and bent my stiff knees to look her in the eye. "It is easy and entirely fruitless to blame oneself for things like this. When you say things like that I start thinking about how I shouldn't have gone home when I did. I shouldn't have left Rivertown to begin with. You say you should've walked her to the house the first time. Get started on that line of thinking and I should have been here shoveling her sidewalk. I should have been here to take you to your driving test. What happened, happened. We are who we are. We did the best we could. Okay?" She nodded and I released her, the ache in my fingers telling me I'd squeezed harder than I meant to.

"Sofie's a grown woman. A stubborn, grown woman. She does what she wants to. If she wanted to make a party for you, she would've done it no matter what you said."

"I bet she regrets it now," Wylie whispered. "I bet she regrets she ever saw me."

I fought the urge to scold her for stepping into the quicksand puddle of self-pity. I'd spent hours sinking in it myself. I vowed I'd keep out of it this time, offer her a hand, but if she didn't take it, or if she tried to pull me in with her, I'd stay on solid ground. I led the way into the parking lot, scanning the lines of cars.

"I see it," Wylie announced. She pointed. The VW waited, near the end of a long row, empty spaces on either side.

"I realized, on the plane," I said. "That you aren't covered by insurance."

"Here," Wylie held out the keys, body slumping.

"No, no, you go ahead. I'm more likely to have an accident than you are, after a day of traveling. First thing in the morning, I'll add you to Sofie's policy." Normally, I wouldn't take such a chance, but I was tired and the girl seemed to need a vote of confidence.

"How much will that cost?" she asked. "A lot I bet."

"Don't worry about it. Sofie needs you driving. I should've thought of it before and put you on right away."

"It is right away. I only got my license the day before yesterday." She laughed.

We got into the car, Wylie concentrating hard as we left the airport. "You drive like you've been doing it forever," I complimented.

"I've been waiting forever to drive," Wylie said, eyes on the road. "My mother says when I was little they'd stop me crying by putting me in the driver's seat of the car. I'd pretend to drive. My first words were engine sounds. I did drive to visit Robbie. I didn't think you'd mind. I forgot about the insurance." She looked in the rearview mirror. "Do you want to go right to the hospital?"

"We should." I decided not to ask about her brother. "Sofie sounded discouraged when I spoke with her."

"IJ said she'd heal fast, that all they had to do was pop it back in."

"Patience is not one of Sofie's virtues," I said, wincing as Wylie pressed the accelerator to the floor to pass a tractor trailer. "You know she was counting the days until she got rid of the cane. She looked forward to moving back into her upstairs bedroom." I cleaned my glasses.

"It'll take a little longer," Wylie said. "That's all."

"That's what we'll have to tell her," I said. "We'll have to be her cheerleaders."

"You're looking at the one girl in Rivertown who never wanted to be a cheerleader, who wouldn't be a cheerleader for a million dollars." Wylie swerved around a station wagon. "See what you made me do!"

"A million dollars. I think you would," I teased. Had I ever teased anyone before? "In fact, I bet deep down inside you always wanted to be one. Every girl wants to be a cheerleader if she's honest with herself."

"Does every boy want to be quarterback?"

I grinned. "Okay, okay, let's say coaches then. We'll be Sofie's coaches."

"What is it with the sports talk?"

I gave an exaggerated shrug, wiggling my eyebrows high above my glasses. "We'll be in Rivertown soon. I'm preparing myself."

"Don't forget you're from San Francisco," Wylie said gravely.

"I live in San Francisco," I said. "I'm from Rivertown. Like it or not, I was who I am long before I left this town."

"When you joined the navy."

"Saw more of the world than I ever thought I would. Saw for myself that most of it is water."

"Weren't you fighting Germany?" Wylie asked. "How could you fight your own relatives?"

"I might have had to. I spoke German. One might think there would have been a use for me in Europe. But fortunately for me, in the government's infinite wisdom, I was sent to the Pacific."

"Did you kill people?"

I tensed. I rarely talked about the war. Even with Erich who hadn't served. Few people had the tactlessness or the heart to ask that question. "That's what we were there for," I said. When Wylie swallowed hard, I added, "They were trying to kill us. You can't imagine the noise, the pounding ocean, the smoke, the bodies and blood on the deck. I didn't know what I was getting into. None of us did. I was a kid. Your age.

"Thanks to the government I went to college." I changed the subject. "I'm grateful for that. Don't know if I would have gone otherwise. It wasn't just the money. If I hadn't seen the world beyond Rivertown, Connecticut, I don't know if I could have imagined it."

"Didn't you ever read *National Geographic*?" Wylie wondered. "Didn't you ever look at maps?"

"The first time I saw San Francisco, I knew I'd live there someday. It was the fog. I loved the fog. Clouds you could walk through and touch without leaving the earth. People don't believe me, but I never tire of it. The exit's coming up. Can you get over?"

Wylie swung the VW into the right lane.

"How come you let Sofie boss you around?" Wylie asked, squealing to a stop at the bottom of the exit ramp.

I surprised us both by laughing. "Next I get to ask you a personal question," I said. "And you have to answer."

"Alright." She turned her blue and green gaze on me. "But answer that first."

"You'll see, when you leave home and come back, how easy it is to fall into old patterns of being. It was always easier for me and for my father too, for that matter, to do things Sofie's way, than to argue. She's a tough lady. But you know that. We learned to pick our battles. There are situations when you choose to be quiet."

"Yes, but are you really choosing, or are you so scared there really is no choice?"

A car behind us blared its horn. Wylie turned onto the River Road. We weren't far from the hospital.

"I think it's alright, as long as I knew who I was, who I am. As long as somewhere, someone else knows."

"I guess that's better than nothing," Wylie said. "Somewhere. Someone."

"Wylie," I said. "It's a lot better than nothing."

We drove up the hill to the hospital.

"What do you want to ask me?" she said, pulling into a parking place.

I thought for a moment. "Nothing comes to mind right away and I don't want to squander this opportunity." I pinched the creases in my trousers. "I'll take a rain check."

She looked disappointed. Was there a question she'd wanted to be asked? I couldn't imagine what it was. She led the way across the slushy parking lot, shoulders hunched against the wind, her back telling me nothing.

In the glare of the hospital room Sofie slept, her face shriveled and gray against the white pillowcase. Only a faint, damp snore indicated she still breathed. At the foot of the bed I hesitated, then slipped my arm around Wylie. She leaned close. Her hair smelled like the cold outside.

"She wouldn't like us watching her sleep," I whispered.

Wylie stiffened. "You're right." She moved along the side of the bed to Sofie's pillow. "Sofie," she said. "Martin and I are here. I brought him straight from the airport."

Sofie's eyelids flickered. We stood ready to respond to her request for glasses, teeth, water, anything. "I'm tired," she muttered.

"Alright," I said. Her hands lay, all knuckles and loose skin on the blanket. I took the one with the claw between my own and held it. Wylie hung back.

"Tired," Sofie mumbled again.

"We can come back tomorrow." Wylie's voice sounded too strong, too healthy, too eager. She lowered it. "Or later."

"Did you pass your driving test?" Sofie rasped.

"Yes!" Wylie stepped closer. "It wasn't hard. Thanks for letting me use your car. I'm so sorry—"

"I knew you would," Sofie interrupted.

"She drove to the airport and back," I added. "Very competently. No problems."

"The Volkswagen," Sofie said. "It's yours. I'll never be driving again."

Wylie's breath caught. She and I exchanged glances.

"Don't be so sure…" I began.

"I can't…" Wylie started.

"I want Wylie to have my car," Sofie insisted, voice louder. Eyes closed, she grimaced, exposing dark gums.

"You'll need it," Wylie said. "I'll borrow it until you're out of here. When you're back home, I'll drive you around. Just for a while until—"

"The car is yours!" Sofie hollered in her scratchy voice. "Yours. Did you find the key chain? Put the key on it. It is all one gift, the key chain, the key, the car. I am not any more going any place. You are."

Wylie fished the key ring from her pocket and showed Sofie. "I love it," she said.

"It's from a hat Oskar gave me. I thought since we have been talking about feathers…I wanted you to have something so beautiful from nature." She gestured for her glasses. I handed them to her. She peered at the plastic encased feather. "Nobody colored that. It grew like that from the bird, you know?"

"You never wore that hat," I said.

"Where would I be wearing it?" Sofie asked. "To the bakery? Here, in the hospital?"

Wylie laughed. "You could. We can bring it next time we come."

As suddenly as she had perked up, Sofie faded. "No hats. Martin, go home and find it on the shelf in my closet. Give it to the Salvation Army."

"No!" Wylie said.

"Alright, give it to Wylie."

"No, you can't be giving everything away," Wylie wailed. "You could wear that hat…to…my graduation."

Sofie shook her head, tore her glasses from her face, and flung them onto the bedside table where they clattered against a vase of carnations. "Why aren't you hearing me?" she said. "I am not going anywhere. I am tired. *Ich bin mude.* I have had enough. Enough pain. Enough sitting. Enough of my broken body. Enough. *Genug.*"

"It's late in the day," I said. "We'll visit again tomorrow. You'll feel better."

"Why is everyone telling me how I will feel?" Sofie whispered, eyes squeezed shut. "I am the one knowing that."

On the way out, a nurse stopped us to say Sofie's physical health was not so bad. Her emotional health was the concern, her complete unwillingness to cooperate in physical therapy, her refusal of medication.

"She's stubborn," was all I could say. "Stubborn and determined."

"Unless she decides to get well," the nurse said. "I don't know how much we can do."

"We'll have to help her decide," Wylie said. "We'll make her change her mind."

"No one makes Sofie change her mind," I said. "You know that."

"Well, this is a battle worth fighting. I won't take her car. And we won't give that hat away."

"You can talk with the doctor tomorrow," the nurse said, before hurrying off.

We stood in front of the elevator. "If she doesn't want to get well…" I stared straight ahead at the closed doors, hands dangling at my sides, a mounting sense of dread in my stomach.

Wylie pushed the button.

"I'm glad you're here," I said. "What if there's nothing we can do?"

"We'll think of something," she said. The light over the elevator showed it rising steadily. She kept pushing the button anyway, until the doors slid open.

*   *   *   *

"If we don't give her a bedpan, she'll have to get out of bed," Wylie said, a week later after Sofie had been home a day. In the hospital Sofie had spoken to the doctors and nurses only to refuse medication and insist on going home. They'd reluctantly decided that respecting her wishes might improve her attitude and hasten her recovery.

I sipped at a hot cup of tea, burning my tongue and the roof of my mouth.

"Why would a little setback like this make her stop living?" Wylie asked. "After working so hard to get back on her feet last time. Why would she give up now? Everyone says it's not so serious."

"I think that's just it." I drained my cup, sucking on my burned tongue. "She's tired."

I took more time and attention than necessary to fit my cup into the depression in the saucer.

"You're tired," Wylie said. "I'm tired." She began chanting, "I'm tired. You're tired. He, she, it is tired. We're tired…"

"Stop it, please," I said. "Please."

"How do you say it in German?" Wylie asked.

"Wylie, be quiet! Please!" She was beginning to irritate me.

Tears filled her eyes before her head sank to the table. Blisters were already forming on the roof of my mouth. Why hadn't I waited for my tea to cool? It wasn't as if I was late for work or anything. Our discouragement filled the kitchen. Sofie would wither away in bed, and we would fossilize, frozen for eternity at the table as it rusted.

"Let's fly one of your planes," Wylie said suddenly. "Please, it might be fun. Just for a change."

I shook my head. "The planes I have here are all from when I was young. Powered by rubber band essentially. Like the one I gave your brother. The models I have in San Francisco have engines and transmitters and really fly. These might make it halfway across a football field if you're lucky."

"That's okay," Wylie urged. "I want to watch. I'll make Sofie's lunch. Then we can go. We're suffocating in here. IJ could come over if you don't want to leave Sofie alone."

I thought about my boyhood room full of models untouched except by Sofie with her dust cloth.

"Come on," Wylie persisted. "We'd feel better if we left the house for a while. It would be a good example for Sofie. We could offer to take her."

I wavered. "She won't come," I said. "But alright."

I found a single propeller pusher model still in working order if the rubber hadn't disintegrated. As carefully built as it was, it wouldn't go far. I put it in the Volkswagen and went back to Sofie's room to tell Wylie I was ready.

"Here," Wylie was saying. "Put your glasses on."

"Nothing I want to see," Sofie whispered.

"Come on." Wylie tried a joking tone. "What about me? Don't you want to see me?"

"I'm tired," Sofie said.

"Sofie." Wylie's voice rose in a frustrated whine. She took a breath and started again. "You're discouraged. Unless you help yourself, you'll spend the rest of your life in bed. Eat something." She held a spoonful of soup in one hand, a cracker in the other. Sofie pressed her lips together, turned her head, like a willful child. I noticed that my own mouth hung open. I wanted to rush in and jam the spoon into my mother's stubborn face.

"Okay, you don't want me feeding you. I can understand that. Feed yourself then." Wylie pushed the spoon at Sofie's clenched fist. Soup spilled on the blanket. Tomato—it would leave a stain. I waited for Sofie's reaction. She didn't even blink.

"You're going to die!" Wylie said. "You're killing yourself. As long as you know that." She dropped the spoon into the bowl of soup with a splash.

"I do know," Sofie said. I moved into the room, close to the bed, took the napkin from the tray and wiped at the spot of soup. I couldn't look at Wylie. "This broken body," Sofie went on. "What good is it to me? Everybody saying it's not so bad. But you don't live in this body. Enough is enough. Oskar, Hanna, I want to be with them."

"What about me?" Wylie said the exact words flashing through my mind, and then added, "What about Martin?"

"You shouldn't be using all your time caring for an old lady," Sofie said to the ceiling. "Martin has a job to do. You have cakes to make. College."

"I can take time off," I said. "It's all arranged."

"Let me decide how I want to spend my life!" Wylie said. "Eat something!"

"Let me decide how I want to spend my life!" Sofie echoed. "Take that soup away. Let me rest."

Wylie left the tray and ran from the room. I followed her. "Come on, I've chosen the plane. Let's go."

"She's going to die!" Wylie threw herself on the couch.

I sat on the coffee table beside her. "She made changes in her will," I said. "She talks about my father all the time. Sitting still is too hard for her. Sofie misses the old country, her sisters, my father. As long as she's busy, full of purpose, she can bear the longing. When she stops, it hits her. I've kept busy myself since Erich's death, working constantly to keep from feeling bad. Only since the last visit have I started to go out with friends, fly my planes. It takes time."

Wylie curled tight in a ball, knees to her chest.

"What are you thinking?" I asked.

She wouldn't answer.

"Okay," I said. "Remember, you owe me an answer to a question. I'm asking you now. What are you thinking? This isn't a time for secrets." Her forehead wrinkled. "Come on, has Sofie said something I should know?"

She shook her head.

I stood, towering over her, feeling angry, without knowing why. "Well, then, what is it?"

"She wanted grandchildren," Wylie said. "If she had grandchildren, I bet she wouldn't be doing this. She'd have something to live for. She'd want to see them graduate and get married and all." The words exploded in the air.

"I know that," I said. "Nobody knows that better than I do."

"Maybe you shouldn't have said anything about…Maybe you should have let her think you might…" Wylie sat up. "Maybe if you hadn't…"

I trembled with the urge to slap her. How, after all the time we'd spent talking, getting to know one another, working together, could she think I shouldn't have come out to my own mother? How could she be blaming me for Sofie's current state? She put words to a fear I hadn't even voiced in my thoughts.

"You're saying I'm responsible for Sofie refusing to eat, to move?" I wrung my hands to keep from grabbing her. "Everyone has the right to be known. I waited a lifetime to tell my mother. I thought you understood what it means to be known by the people you love." I wouldn't accept this responsibility. "We are not responsible, ever, for our parents not getting what they want in life. Do you understand that? I didn't ask to be born. I am who I am. I'm a damn good son, partner, friend, electrical engineer and a multitude of other things." Steadied by the truth of what I'd said, I took a deep breath. "Sofie may not feel like she wants to live, but it has nothing to do with me. Do you think your mother's drinking is your fault?"

Wylie put her face in her hands. "Yes," she said.

"And do think that her inability to be a strong parent for you and your brothers is your fault?"

Wylie was crying too hard to answer or even nod.

"And your father, did he leave because of you?"

I paced the length of the living room carpet, waving my arms like a preacher. "You don't have that kind of power, honey. Face it."

"Wylie, Martin." Sofie's voice from the other room sounded as though it came from another dimension. She'd heard everything.

I felt cleansed, strong. I held out my hand to Wylie, clasped her fingers, and pulled her to her feet. "Are you okay? Do you believe me?"

She sighed.

"Thank you," I said, arm around her shoulders. "I feel twenty years younger. I needed that." Wylie squirmed. My arm stayed in place.

Sofie wriggled to a sitting position, resting against several pillows, her voice startling in its strength. "If I had a grandchild, Wylie, already she would be older than you are, all grown." She reached toward me, took my hand.

"Come here," she said. Wylie accepted Sofie's other hand. I slipped my arm from Wylie's shoulders and held her empty hand, making a complete circle.

"No one is to blame," Sofie said simply, eyes unfocused and full of silver light. "I'm so tired." She closed her eyes. Her breathing became soft and regular, her fingers limp. We brought her hands to rest on the bed and let go of them.

*   *   *   *

I stood in the middle of the snow covered football field and wound the propeller. "You can do the next flight," I said. "The trick is to wind it as much as you can without pulling the tail assembly to the front of the plane, tight but not too tight. Then you have to keep it wound until you let it go." With a swoop of my arm I released the plane. It rose and flew to the ten yard line. "Not bad," I said.

"Well made, you see. Tested, adjusted until it flew level and straight. I spent weeks on one of these things."

Wylie ran across the field to retrieve it.

"Go ahead," I hollered. "Wind it up. Send it this way."

Wylie cast the plane toward me. It sputtered and fell. "You need to wind it more," I shouted. We ran to the downed plane to check for damages.

"When you've got a transmitter, you're in control. You see it hit a thermal, rising air, you catch the plane in the middle, make it circle. With this old fashioned kind you just have to watch." I examined the wings. "Looks alright. Try again. The trick is in that winding."

She turned the propeller counterclockwise. I told her when to stop. She tossed it. It flew, sailing to a smooth landing on the snow. "This plane lands well. That's why it's still here. Most of my models survived less than ten flights before they barely flew. Then I'd set them on fire just before releasing them, pretending they were enemy planes shot down from the sky."

"Don't tell Robbie," Wylie laughed.

We took turns flying the plane until it hit a goal post and smashed to the ground. "Oh," Wylie wailed. "I'm sorry, Martin. You've had it for so long."

I patted my pockets. "I've got some matches here somewhere. Go get the plane. Hurry." The quiver of anticipation in my chest felt unfamiliar. It had been a long time since I'd played or made mischief.

Wylie crossed the field with the broken skeleton of the plane. "Will it fly at all?"

I examined it. "Should."

"You seem glad."

"Well going out in a blaze of glory was always a more than adequate consolation prize. You have to pay attention though. It's over in a flash. Wind it up."

She twirled the propeller. I struck the match. "Ready." I touched the flame to the fuselage. She cast it into the deep and darkening winter sky. I wished Robbie were there to see it burn so sudden and bright.

*   *   *   *

I let myself in with the secret key and went to check on Sofie. I'd dropped Wylie at her house. Full of satisfied exhaustion from an afternoon of exercise outside in the cold, I felt really hungry for the first time in weeks.

Sofie opened her eyes as I approached. "Martin," she said. "I want for you to write a letter to my sisters. I know what I want to say, but I am too tired to hold the pen."

"Of course," I said. "I'd like to eat first. I'll bring you something too. We'll eat together."

Sofie shook her head, with a close lipped smile. "Martin, Martin how many times am I having to tell you, I am not hungry? Please. The letter will not have many words. I have been waiting for you all this afternoon. Don't make an old lady wait longer. I am so tired."

I shrugged off my coat, found paper and pen, switched on the lamp, and pulled a chair up to the bed. Sofie stared past me, eyes on the line where the ceiling met the wall. "*Liebe* Amalia *und* Dora," she began. I copied the words onto the paper in my most careful handwriting. I had no trouble with the German though it had been years since I'd used it. It reminded me of my childhood, my mother and father and I around the oilcloth covered table, just the three of us, playing games, the rattling of the dice muted in the leather cup, the whispered counting, even my own, always in German.

"Dora? Not *Schwester* Gabriele?" I asked.

"Dora," Sofie said.

She began the letter with all the usual how is everybody, hope you're well, preliminaries. Then she said, "This is the last letter you will have from me." Sure I'd heard wrong, I had ask her to repeat it. In my head I had to translate it into English twice.

"But...Mother?"

Sofie held up her hand to stop me. "Please, I would be writing this myself if I could. Please, write what I say. We can afterward talk."

She went on dictating. "I am always thinking of you. We have always been the three Bauer sisters, Sofie, Amalia, and Dora, like three steps in a row. I am the oldest so it is right I go first to...wherever I am going. Dora, you say you pray for me every day. Maybe your prayers are enough to get me into heaven if there is such a place."

I lifted the pen from the paper. My throat filled. She had no right to use me like this. She couldn't be serious. "I can't write this."

"You must," Sofie said. "Please. For me to do myself it would be too much. They wouldn't be able to read my chicken scratchings. Please, go on. I would have asked Wylie but I can't be spelling all the German word by word. I'll call her if I have to." She paused, frowning. "While I'm thinking on Wylie, tell her that

VW is in top condition. It can drive a long way. Not just back and forth to Ida's Bakery. Are you going to write?"

I cleared my throat. "I'll do it. But Mother, the doctors say there's no reason you can't get well if you…"

"I am tired of hearing doctors saying this and that. Will you write?" My opposition withered under her fierce glare. I nodded, pen poised, chest aching.

"Amalia, we never talked about heaven or hell. I think that to you, the garden is heaven. Working in the garden you are happy. Imagine what it is like not to work anymore, to instead be making work for other people, and you will be happy for me that I have moved along. I have known for sometime I would not be making another trip to Germany. It is not so terrible because I know that in our hearts we are together. We will always be together in our hearts. On this earth or not. Always your sister, Sofie

She closed her eyes, depleted.

"IJ brought some soup I think," she said. "Get yourself something to eat."

My stomach felt tight as a fist. I tapped the pen against the pad of airmail paper, unable to get up. I watched her sleep. A tough lady. I never remembered her sleeping when I was a child. Always up before me in the morning and still awake when I went to bed at night. I never remembered her sick. Maybe that was the problem. She'd had no practice being a patient. Perhaps men, more used to being cared for and waited upon, made better patients than women. Telling myself that just because she wrote the letter didn't mean she was about to die, I dozed off in the chair to the rhythm of her breath into kaleidoscopic dreams of airplanes and cakes, birds and cars, and fire and gardens, images repeating, reflecting and fading into each other.

An irregular silence startled me awake. Just outside the circle of lamplight, Sofie lay still, mouth open, eyes closed. I knew without moving closer that she was dead. If anyone could decide it was time to die and then do it, Sofie could.

I wanted to shake her, willful, stubborn, controlling woman that she was. I looked at her bent finger. She'd never tease me with it again—Don't you look. Here comes the crooked hook. It won't do you any harm. Just go right under your arm. She'd tickle me until I fell limp from giggling, one of the few situations in which, as a child, I'd laugh. I'd been such a serious little boy. A serious boy, grown into an even more serious man.

My mother, my mother's body, lay dead, inches away from me, and I was thinking I should laugh more. Erich thought I should laugh more. Erich had taught me to laugh more, without even tickling me. I heard Wylie's laugh as the plane burned in the sky, saw the grin I'd felt on my own face. The airmail pad had slipped down into the chair beside me. I reread the letter. Tears slid down my face and fell onto Sofie's words, smearing the ink, soaking the delicate paper.

*   *   *   *

The sun rose, and I knew I'd have to tell Wylie. I didn't dare call for fear I'd spill it all on the phone. I had to see her in person. Without reentering the room where just a few hours ago they'd come to take my mother's useless body away, I shaved, dressed, added another paragraph to Sofie's letter to the aunts I barely knew and affixed the postage. IJ saw the ambulance and had come right over, sitting with me part of the night, helping with a list of things to do. Telling Wylie was the hardest thing, the one task IJ couldn't help with. My head felt full of sand. My father, my partner, my mother. All dead.

When nobody answered the door at Wylie's, I realized the doorbell was broken and knocked. Her mother answered in her bathrobe, questions in her eyes.

"My mother died last night," I said. "I wanted to let Wylie know."

"So sudden!" Lucy held the door open wide. "I'm so so so sorry. Please, come in, sit down. You look like you could use some coffee. Wylie's still asleep."

I followed her through the shadowy house to the kitchen. She gestured to the table, poured coffee from a pot on the stove, and set it before me.

"You must be so upset," she said, sitting beside me. "Wylie's going to take it hard. I can't even bear waking her up. I thought Sofie was getting better."

"When she reinjured her hip it was as if she decided to die. The actual cause of death was most likely a pulmonary embolism. Medication could have prevented it, but she wouldn't take it. 'Enough,' she said. 'I've had enough.' I keep hearing her say that. I should've tried harder to keep her from giving up."

Lucy slid her chair close enough to touch my shoulder. "I'm so sorry," she repeated. "I lost my mother when I was young. It's hard."

"What's hard?" Wylie emerged from her pantry, rumpled with sleep. "What are you doing here?" Panic showed in her face. "Sofie?"

"Dead," I said. "Last night."

"She couldn't die. She couldn't." Wylie punched the wall. "Where is she? I want to see her."

"They took the body." My voice sounded mechanical.

Wylie screamed, kicking the trash can. "Why? Why? Why? Why?"

I could hardly hear through the ringing in my ears. The room seemed small, like the kitchen of a dollhouse. Wylie raged and sobbed. I hadn't even thought of carrying on like that, and it was my mother who died. If Lucy hadn't grabbed her, the girl would be breaking up furniture.

"She wanted to die," I heard myself say. "You know that. If she had wanted to live she would have taken the medicine."

"We could have hidden it in her food!" Wylie smacked the table. "You didn't tell me she'd die if she didn't take it. I would have forced her."

"She didn't eat either," I said. "Remember."

"We let her die!" Wylie screamed. Her little brother stumbled into the kitchen. Lucy hurried to keep him out of the way leaving me to deal with her alone.

"It's complicated," I said. "I believe she knew what she wanted. She knew what she was doing. However you or I feel about it." I took her hands across the table. "Take a deep breath. Come on."

All those deaths, Oskar, Erich, Sofie, I'd never screamed, kicked, or punched. Maybe I should have. Wylie squeezed my hands so hard it hurt. Tears streamed down her face. Her nose ran. "I didn't even get to talk to her. What did she say? Were you there when she died? Why do people die? I need her!"

"I'd dozed off by the bed," I said. "She must have died peacefully and fast. I didn't hear anything. Except silence. The silence woke me."

"What were her last words?"

I struggled to remember. "She dictated a letter to her sisters, my aunts in Germany."

"The last thing she said to us before we went to fly the planes was about being tired." Wylie's voice softened. She let go of my hand to wipe her nose on her sleeve.

I tried harder to recreate the conversation Sofie and I'd had after the letter. Had there been any? "She told me to get myself something to eat," I said. Remembering filled me with surprised pleasure. "Good advice. Typical of Sofie, don't you think?"

Wylie smiled and cried harder at the same time. "So what if she wanted to die. That doesn't make us miss her any less. Selfish…" She paused. "She missed your father. And her baby girl.

"Now what?" Wylie asked. "Now what do we do? How could she leave us like that?"

"I'm going to the funeral parlor now," I said. "She wanted a simple graveside service. That's all. I'll call you later today." I'd kept my coat on the whole time. Wylie followed me to the door and out onto the porch. I saw her in the rearview mirror and realized I'd forgotten to tell her what Sofie had said about the car being in top condition and able to drive a long way.

CHAPTER 7

▼

WYLIE

Back in bed, I hid under my covers, wondering how I'd spend the day and the next day and the next. No Danny. No Sofie. What did I have left to lose? In the kitchen, my mother sat at the table, coffee within easy reach, dealing game after game of solitaire. Kevin watched cartoons. The beeping of that irritating roadrunner filled the house. I'd seen a picture of a real one in Sofie's biggest bird book, and it looked nothing like that ridiculous cartoon. Nothing. And that poor coyote, chasing it all the time. Why didn't he know enough to give up? Sometimes it made sense. Enough is enough. Sofie. Understanding nibbled at the edges of my anger. I wiped my eyes and got dressed.

"Want to play some gin rummy?" Lucy asked, her eyes sympathetic.

"No, I'm going over to Sofie's." When I heard myself say the words I knew I had an appointment, a mission.

"Why?" Lucy asked. "Martin said he'll be out doing errands. Stay here."

"No." Sofie's empty house pulled at me. I ran the whole way and let myself in with the secret key.

"Martin?" I called. No answer.

Sofie's cane leaned against her chair. I sat in her carved rocker. Sofie couldn't leave me without a good-bye. She wouldn't. I gripped the arms of the chair, closed my eyes, and listened with my whole body. I waited for a word, a breath, a moan. The furnace clanked. The refrigerator hummed. From far away a car honked. I opened my eyes.

I forced myself to enter Sofie's room, to look at the empty bed. The covers lay pushed back and rumpled. The pillow held the barest impression of her head. I ran my hands over the sheets where her body would have been, feeling for warmth that wasn't there. I considered stripping the mattress, washing the sheets, then made the bed instead, smoothing the last wrinkles from the spread by working them under the pillow. I felt a whispery breeze at my neck, a flutter of air next to my ear. Sofie's voice said, You know vat to do, don't you? And I did know.

I went to the kitchen, took off my coat. You'll find vat you need in the freezer, said the voice. Seven loaf cakes waited for me. I took them out to thaw. I covered a board with foil and prepared to mix an industrial sized batch of icing. Don't you be using shortening in that!

In the refrigerator, I found pounds and pounds of butter. As I unwrapped each one, it softened in my hands, soft enough to mix with sugar.

Shaping the cakes, gluing them together, listening to the voice in my head as I mixed colors I never knew existed and would never be able to recreate, I lost track of time. The butter cream, usually next to impossible to work with, held its shape better than any shortening. I lost myself in the cake, the last cake Sofie and I would make together.

The door to the garage slammed. Martin's footsteps sounded on the stairs.

I squeezed out the last wing feather and slumped into a chair.

Martin flipped a switch and the fluorescent light swallowed the shadows hiding me and the cake. "Wylie! You startled me! What are you doing sitting here in the dark?"

He stared at the cake.

"I made it for the funeral," I said, breaking a long silence.

We stared at the tremendous bird I'd carved and decorated. Part parrot, part eagle with feathers of every imaginable color, golden talons and curved beak, and large eyes, the dark, colorless gray of water reflecting a cloudy sky. Sofie's eyes. One seemed to wink. Surprised and not surprised at all, we both saw it but said nothing. Our arms touched.

The bowls I'd used to mix colors covered the counter. Crumbs littered the table and floor and stuck to the bottoms of my boots. "I'd better clean up," I said.

"I'll help. Would you like some supper?"

I wanted the bird to pick me up and take me away.

"Tea?"

"Alright."

We left the bird in the center of the table while we drank.

"Martin," I said. "I've been meaning to ask you. Did you ever see Janis Joplin in concert?"

Smiling, he shook his head. "I prefer classical music. You know that."

"Do you know any hippies?"

"No." He grinned.

"But...Haight-Ashbury..."

"I never go there." He wrinkled his nose. "Dirty, desperate kids. Selling their blood at the plasma center to buy drugs. What would I want with that?"

I wanted to smack him, had to remind myself he didn't know he was talking about my friends. "But they can't all be on drugs? And some drugs aren't so bad.

"They look so happy." I sounded ridiculous but couldn't stop myself. "They believe in everything good like love and peace and music." Janis believed in all that and she wasn't happy. I wasn't a fool. Why couldn't I shut up?

"A friend of a friend of mine...actually, a friend of Erich's, well, he's a friend of mine too I suppose, works with street kids, has for a long time, even back in the Haight-Ashbury heyday. A lot of them ran away from tough family situations. Some are homosexual and their families threw them out. Some had parents who abused them. Those kids are no more free than you are. Sitting on the sidewalks wrapped in dirty blankets begging for spare change. So they have some flowers in their matted hair or rings on their filthy toes. That doesn't mean they're happy."

I began cleaning the kitchen, not knowing what else to do. Martin hovered beside me. We were both upset and didn't know how to fix it so we did the dishes. He washed. I dried.

"Guess I'll head home," I said, dish drainer empty.

"Take the car." Martin draped the dishcloth over the faucet, both sides even. Neither of us would ever be able to do it any other way.

"Don't you need it? I have school tomorrow so I won't be able to bring it by."

"I can walk downtown. Besides, it's your car now."

"My car." Sofie had succeeded in giving it to me.

"It's right that you should have it. Sometime this week we'll go to the DMV and put the registration in your name."

"Thank you," I said. "Thanks a lot." All the money in my cigar box. I could use it to rent an apartment. I could go somewhere and have rings on my toes and flowers in my hair and a bathtub too.

"Don't thank me," Martin said. "Sofie left it to you. She said it would take you places. And not just back and forth to Ida's."

My car. I'd fill it with gas, change the oil, wash and wax it until it reflected light like a ruby. Even Danny, who hated foreign cars, admitted a Volkswagen was easy to maintain. A tough, little car, like Sofie. I'd buy a book and learn how to keep it running. I'd be able to go anywhere without breaking down.

*   *   *   *

Under gray skies, a small group clustered around the fresh hole in the earth. A low headstone with Oskar's name on one side and Sofie's on the other rose from the grass near the minister's leg. I stood between my mother and Martin on one side of the grave. On the other side stood IJ and Johnny, a few ladies from the German Hall, and Tony, unfamiliar in a dark suit and polished shoes.

I was surprised Lucy wanted to come, surprised I'd let her. Because Lucy had been there when Martin delivered the news, she seemed a part of things. She stood, steady as a door frame, and reached for my hand. Our fingers knit together.

Sofie wouldn't have liked the minister's religious ramblings, or maybe she would have. A list of questions I wished I'd asked her tumbled around in my head. What did she believe in besides butter? Was Oskar her first love? How did she feel when the boat pulled away from the dock? Were her sisters there to wave good-bye? I could ask Martin, but he seemed to think I knew Sofie better than he did.

"Amen," said the minister with finality. Two men in overalls, holding shovels, leaned against a tree, waiting for everyone to leave so they could fill in the hole and eat lunch. Martin threw a rose onto the polished coffin and motioned for me to do the same. A waste, burying perfectly good flowers. Sofie would have agreed. The funeral director invited everyone back to Sofie's house.

The bird cake presided over the food table. "Lord," IJ said. "While I was setting up the food I had the feeling that bird was watching to be sure I arranged everything the right way. I swear I redid the meat tray because it gave me a dirty look. I can tell you for sure, I'm not going to be the one to stick a knife in it."

I suppressed a laugh and though the bird didn't wink, there did seem to be a silvery twinkle in its eye. "I'll cut it," I said. "I made it to be eaten."

Knife in hand, I leaned over the cake. People oohed and ahhed. No one heard me whisper, "Shortening would keep longer, but since I used butter…" A dollop of icing fell from the knife. I popped it into my mouth with a quick finger and let it melt on my tongue as I served slices to everyone.

Martin and I kept running past each other between the kitchen and dining room, keeping ourselves a lot busier than we needed to, refilling the tea and coffee pots. Lucy helped IJ in the kitchen, one of Sofie's aprons tied over her navy blue dress. The ladies from the German Hall passed along the compliments Sofie had given me over pinochle during the past few months. "A lot on the ball, she'll make something of herself, a head for business, hard worker, talented, a good girl." The lump in my throat thickened each time one of them quoted her, like a snowball growing as it's rolled across a field. Soon, I'd have to cry or choke.

I avoided conversation until Tony stood right in my way. "I've got to get back to work," he said.

I nodded, trying to step past him with my tray of dirty dishes.

"She was right about you." He folded his arms, stepping to one side or the other as I did, blocking my path. "Ida's isn't the same."

"You're not trying to hire me back, are you?" I maneuvered the tray around him and set it on the counter. Lucy began washing the cups.

"You wouldn't come, would you?" He gestured toward the remains of the bird cake. "Aren't you making a lot of those? No one in Rivertown wants a regular cake anymore. Lucky for Ida's they still eat donuts."

"Business is booming," I said. Sofie's line.

"Actually, your mother asked about a job."

"Mom?" Lucy concentrated on rinsing a saucer. "You asked for a job? At Ida's?"

"Is she any good?" Tony asked, grinning. "Does she take after you?"

I was used to Tony in a dirty white tee shirt, white pants, red bandanna, flour covered shoes. I was used to my mother at the kitchen table with her cards, on the couch watching TV. What were these strangers in dark clothes doing in Sofie's kitchen? What was Sofie doing dead and buried?

"If your mother wants the job, it's hers," Tony said. He slid his arm into a coat sleeve.

Lucy turned off the water and rearranged her hair with damp hands. "Really?"

Tony patted my back. "You come by and see how she's making out. Give her some tips."

"I've got to go home," Lucy said noticing the time. "Kevin will be there in twenty minutes."

"I'll give you lift," Tony said.

Lucy gave me a stiff hug. She meant well, but we both needed practice. She followed Tony out the door.

"Do you know who's the richest man in the world?" he was asking her.

I sat down in the empty kitchen with what was left of the bird cake.

"They're gone." Martin swung open the door. "Wylie…" He knew not to ask what was wrong, or tell me everything was okay. He sat beside me while I cried. I missed Danny. Every time I saw him he was with a different girl. He'd find the right one eventually. I missed Sofie. Soon, I'd be missing Martin.

"What now?" he asked, when I finally dried my eyes.

I poked at the crumbs of the bird cake. "It might be hard for you to believe," I said. "But when I was a kid I never cried. It was a matter of pride with me. I'd scream and yell and crash around the house sometimes, but tears…no way. The past few months I've made up for it. All I do is cry."

He could have said something about how crying was good for me or that maybe I was making up for lost time, but he didn't. He held me with his silence for exactly the right amount of time and then said, "Sofie left you a substantial amount of money, the one stipulation being that you use it for college."

"What?" He might as well have been speaking German.

"Sofie left money for you to go to college," he said.

"That's nice," I answered. "But I'm not going to college. I didn't apply or take SATs or anything. I'll be lucky if I graduate from high school."

"You'll graduate. Nothing says you have to go to college right away. Take some time. Figure out what you want to study, what you want to do with your life."

"My life." How did anyone figure out what to do?

"No one says you have to use the money. I'm just telling you it's there if you need it."

All I wanted was sleep. "I'm tired. Can I take the car home?"

"Don't ask. It's yours." He followed me to the door, reluctant to let me leave. "Tomorrow I'll start sorting through her things. Come by. See if there's anything you'd like to keep. I'd like your company."

"I'll be here."

"The cake was perfect," he said.

*   *   *   *

I sat on Sofie's kitchen floor, surrounded by boxes, glamorous in the peacock feather hat Martin had placed on my head like a crown. He wrapped plates in newspaper. "I thought you'd like her baking things," he said. "Even though you have your own. When you start a business and have people working for you, you'll need spatulas for everyone."

"That'll be the day," I said. I filled a carton with the cake pans and pastry tubes.

"A man's coming from Hartford tomorrow. What I want to keep I'll put in storage. He's buying the rest for a flat price." Martin tucked sheets of newspaper around a glass mixing bowl and put it in my box. "Take anything you can use. Is there any furniture you want? You're welcome to it."

I understood Martin's hurry to get home to San Francisco, but everything was happening too fast. The plastic covered couch, rugs, the gleaming coffee table? My family could have used it all, but I'd agonize over every inevitable ring on the polished wood, every cigarette burn on the upholstery. Sofie's furniture didn't belong in our house.

"No, thanks. Her car and all this," I pointed to the box I'd filled, "are plenty." I wanted the rocking chair but didn't say so. Martin, Sofie's son, should keep the chair his father had made.

"I've almost finished in here," Martin said. "Would you mind emptying the dresser in the den?"

The room Sofie died in.

"Strange, isn't it? That all her things should be here and she's gone." He pushed a box out of the way with his foot. Sun lit the golden wood of Sofie's chair. I wanted to sit and rock for awhile, think. Instead, I shoved empty boxes through the door of the den.

The bottom dresser drawer was packed with neatly stacked photo albums, packets of letters, things Martin should sort through. I eased a heavy red album from the top of the pile. The black and white pictures were carefully mounted with black paper corners, photos of people in dark clothes with serious expressions, sitting in or standing behind straight backed chairs.

I flipped through the book until I came to a girl with daring gray eyes. Two girls with hesitant half smiles stood behind her. Sofie and her sisters. Dark haired and smooth skinned, she looked about seventeen.

I rested the open album on the dresser and examined my reflection in the large, round mirror. Tangled hair, strange eyes that matched the blue and green of the peacock feathers in Sofie's hat. My hat. Determined chin, like Sofie's. The chin and mouth of a girl strong enough to leave everything familiar in search of something she needed. A girl who would leave her family, cross an ocean or a continent. Sofie had done it. And I would too.

Martin's reflection appeared in the mirror beside me. "My favorite picture of my mother," he said, studying the photograph. "That's Tante Amalia and Tante

Dora behind her. No mistaking Sofie. The face of a practical romantic if I ever saw one."

He stood with his hands on my shoulders. Our glances met in the mirror. "She was about your age then."

"I could tell." He gave my shoulders a squeeze before crouching to pick up a packet of letters.

"Look." He removed a brittle greeting card from the bottom of the pile. It was black and cut in the shape of a fluffy cloud. In the corner beamed an unnaturally red cheeked baby with a halo and wings. Printed white letters said, "Every dark cloud…" Martin opened to an inside lined with foil where the sentence ended with, "has a silver lining." "*Ich liebe dich.* Oskar" was printed in the corner in tight letters.

"He gave her this when my sister died," Martin said, opening and closing the card. "She showed it to me once. I didn't understand. I liked the silver foil. I could see myself in it."

It seemed strange to give your wife a sympathy card at the death of your own child. No wonder Sofie had felt so alone.

"My father was a quiet man," Martin said. "He couldn't find words." He turned the card over and over as if looking for some writing he'd missed.

"It's sad. We so rarely talked about anything that mattered. Even when my father died."

He slipped the card back into the packet of letters and played with the ribbon that held them all together. "You know, I think I'll just pack all these papers and pictures and take them back with me. It could take months to go through them all.

"Mother told you things," he said, suddenly. "For years, since my father's death, I'd planned to tell her about Erich. I'm not sure I could've done it if you hadn't made the opening, if you hadn't been there. We were able to talk around you."

He leafed through the album before closing it. "My father was a kind and decent man," he said.

"I would hate it if people used those words about me after I died," I said.

"You'd hate being called kind and decent?" Martin asked.

"I don't know." I couldn't explain it. "It's boring."

"What would you want people to say about you?"

"Nothing. I don't know."

"Well I wouldn't mind being known as kind and decent," Martin said. "And caring." He stacked photo albums in a box.

"You are all those things." I thought of the plane he'd given Robbie, the warm silences he'd wrapped me in while I cried, his reluctance to call the police when Robbie set the fire, the way his fingers smoothed Sofie's blankets, and the tremor in his voice when he talked about Erich losing his hair. "People would say that about you."

"So I'm boring." He smiled. "Thank you." He folded closed the flaps of the carton and gave it a pat. "Now, come on. It's your turn."

"I don't know." All the phrases Sofie had used to describe me to her pinochle partners clattered in my head. "Something about not wasting what I've been given. That I made the most of what I had."

Martin just nodded. "Tell me if there's any of this you want," he said again, indicating the front room furniture with a wave of his arm. "Besides your gorgeous hat. Anything."

I stared at the empty rocker.

He followed my gaze. "Ah. The chair." He stepped close to it and ran his fingers over the carved wood.

"Never mind. You should have it. Your father made it."

He sat down and began rocking. He looked awkward with his long legs stretched way out in front of him.

He smiled. "I don't even fit in this chair," he said. "It's yours. Mother would want you to have it. Father too, if he'd known you."

He sounded certain he was doing the right thing. Confident I'd appreciate it and care for it as well as Martin would or Sofie herself, I said, "I'll bring it with me wherever I go."

He laughed at my fierce tone. "And when you're settled in San Francisco or New York or Boston or wherever, I'll visit you and sit in it. Or maybe I'll just watch you sit in it."

A room built itself around the chair, lace curtains the sun shone through making patterns like giant snowflakes on the wood of the chair and the floors, windowsills crowded with healthy green plants, and a couch that unfolded for Martin to sleep on.

✳   ✳   ✳   ✳

"Flight 237 to San Francisco, now boarding at gate 5."

Martin adjusted his glasses and the strap of his leather shoulder bag. "That's it."

He opened his arms, and I threw myself against him.

"I wish I could go with you," I said. What would I do for the next four months until graduation, without Sofie, Danny, or Martin?

"We'll be in touch." He stroked the back of my head. "I'll call you."

"Everybody's leaving me."

"It won't be long until you're leaving yourself." He'd been stuck in Rivertown, even though it was years ago. Why couldn't he remember how long four months were when you were seventeen?

The loud speaker blared, calling passengers in rows one to fifteen. "Go on." I hardly recognized my own voice. "You'll miss your plane." I clung to the back of his belt.

"Wylie." My name sounded solid coming from deep in Martin's chest, something I could hold. "Work on your cakes. Keep busy. In June, you'll leave. If you can't decide where to go, start with a visit to me. I've got plenty of room. San Francisco might suit you."

Still hanging onto him, I leaned back to see his face. His eyes looked misty. "I love you," I said, quickly so it ran together like one word.

"And I love you," Martin said matter of factly. "You'll be alright."

One last hug and we were waving good-bye. He disappeared through the gate. I fell into the nearest chair. Strangers with full suitcases rushed past. I didn't cry. I wept. I wept, and it was good. I wept until I had no tears left, washed my face in the restroom and walked to Sofie's car. I considered driving to Rivertown, stopping only long enough to pack some clothes, my hat, my decorating kit, and Sofie's chair, and starting cross country, Martin's plane a dot in the sky over my head. I eyed the back seat, imagining how I'd tip the chair to fit it inside, knowing exactly how it would feel to push the gas pedal to the floor and speed down Main Street, past the mall, driving, driving, never stopping until I found the right spot to set that chair down. I'd find that spot if I went far enough, looked long enough. I'd sit and rock, the sun warm on my shoulders, my feet on the ground.

*   *   *   *

At home the smell of chocolate filled the kitchen. Egg shells, bowls sticky with batter, cake tins with pieces of cake stuck to the sides, dripping spoons, and three almost empty cans of ready made icing covered the counter. At the table Lucy was smearing white icing from a fourth can on a huge and messy cake.

"How do you keep the crumbs from mixing with the frosting?" she asked. "If I'd known it would be so hard, I wouldn't have used white. She stepped back, pushed her hair out of her face with a sticky hand, and waved a knife coated with icing at me. "Remember, I told you we're going to visit Robbie for his birthday, even Kevin. You can drive, right?"

"I would've made the cake," I said. "It's my job." I began rinsing the bowls.

"I'll clean up later," said Lucy. She studied her creation. "It doesn't look as good as yours, but I wanted to make my boy his birthday cake. I can't even remember the last one I made for any of you. Pathetic. Some mother."

"You bought them," I said. "They were okay."

Lucy rotated the cake, stepped back, rotated it again. "I tried using icing to even it out, where it baked crooked. Didn't work too great, I guess. That's alright, it'll taste good anyway. How do you get them to come out of the pans without breaking?"

"They have to cool—not too long or they stick, not too short or they crumble." I hadn't gone to visit Robbie since the first time. I didn't want to go now.

"Oh, so that's the secret."

"When are we supposed to be there?" I asked. "Do you want me to decorate it? Write something on it at least?"

"You can if you want." Lucy smiled at the collapsed mound of cake and frosting. "But it might work better just to throw on some colored sprinkles. That's what I was going to do." She looked at the clock. "We have to go soon anyway. Hand me that bag, over there, will you?"

My decorating equipment was all in boxes. I liked to take my time designing a cake for a person, especially someone I knew as well as Robbie. This cake was Lucy's idea. Lucy should be the one to finish it. I handed her a bag holding a box of candles and three plastic containers of sprinkles, enough to coat the cake an inch deep all over. I went to find Kevin.

We drove to the Farm, Lucy with the sprinkle encrusted cake in her lap, Kevin bouncing in the back seat. Robbie smiled when he saw us. A different guard from the last time brought plates and forks and sang along with us on "Happy Birthday."

Robbie admired the cake. When he cut it an avalanche of sprinkles fell onto the scarred table. Kevin licked them up before Lucy could stop him. Some stuck in the carved initials, curses and declarations of everlasting love. Kevin wet a finger and poked at them.

"Your hair's longer," I said.

"How come you didn't make my cake?" he asked. "You could have made one of the woods on fire."

Or Sofie's house, I thought.

"I wanted to make it," Lucy said.

"I told her to put a file in it," Kevin said. "Oops." He looked over the guard and covered his mouth.

"Wylie certainly could have made a prettier one," Lucy said. "But I hadn't made a cake in so long, I wanted to see if I could still do it."

"It's great, Mom." Robbie cut himself another piece with the plastic knife and scooped some crumbs into his mouth. "Thanks."

We were the only family in the visiting room. Kevin, finished eating, began fidgeting, tilting his chair back.

"It's great, Mom," Robbie said again. "Isn't it, Wylie?"

I looked at the mess of cake and icing and rainbow sprinkles left on the plate, the scattered crumbs, Kevin flicking escaped specks across the table and laughing, mouth dyed from all the artificial coloring, Robbie and our mother waiting for my answer.

"Next time I'll know to let the cake cool before dumping it out," Lucy said. "There must be some other tricks Wylie can tell me before she leaves. We have some time left before June."

"You're still going, huh?" Robbie asked. I knew him well enough to read the other big question he was asking with his eyes. What if Mom starts drinking again?

I wished I could tell him it would be okay. I hoped it would be okay. "Yeah, I'm going," I said. I had a friend in San Francisco and a good car.

"Where?" He studied the table, tracing the outline of a carved heart with his little finger.

"Not sure. California, probably."

"Maybe I'll visit you," he said. "Better than you visiting me here."

"You can all visit," I said. California was far away. It would take them a long while to save the money. I'd have time to settle, find a place to park my car, a place for the rocking chair, a place to work.

"The cake tasted good, Mom," Robbie said. "Didn't it, Wylie? She did a good job."

"Maybe the next one I make won't look like someone sat on it," Lucy said. "Now that I've had a little practice."

Practice. I heard Sofie's voice in my ear. In California, in jail, in the old country, in Rivertown, at home, we are all of us looking for crumbs. Find what you need. Give what you can. Finally Vylie you are understanding, this business of life, scattering and searching. And making roses. Practice. Practice. Practice.

"It wasn't bad." I held out my plate for another piece.

978-0-595-38501-0
0-595-38501-X

Printed in the United States
49358LVS00005B/202-219

9 780595 385010